Adolphe Belot

The Drama of the Rue de la Paix

Adolphe Belot

The Drama of the Rue de la Paix

ISBN/EAN: 9783337376918

Printed in Europe, USA, Canada, Australia, Japan

Cover: Foto ©Andreas Hilbeck / pixelio.de

More available books at **www.hansebooks.com**

POPULAR FRENCH NOVELS.

THE DRAMA

OF THE

RUE DE LA PAIX.

By ADOLPHE BELOT.

TWENTY-FIFTH THOUSAND.

LONDON:

VIZETELLY & CO., 42 CATHERINE STREET, STRAND.

1886.

THE DRAMA OF THE RUE DE LA PAIX.

PROLOGUE

POLITICAL affairs so completely absorbed the public mind of Paris in the early part of the year 1848, that but little notice was taken of the numerous private tragedies which occurred during that troublous period, and gave no inconsiderable occupation to the judicial tribunals. Revolution and its attendant perils completely cast in the shade what, in more peaceful times, would have sufficed to glut Parisian curiosity. How, indeed, could any drama enacted within the walls of a private dwelling-house, or the doors of an assize-court, rival in interest that which was being unfolded in the public streets, which revelled in excitement, and in which, seeing that it touched the dearest interests of all, every individual was immediately concerned? The roll of the drum, the rattle of musketry, and the cannon's roar, deadened every other sound, and rendered the world deaf to all but popular cries.

Thus it happened that in the beginning of March, 1848, a trial took place almost unnoticed, yet so dramatic and extraordinary as to surpass in interest well-nigh all that stand recorded in the annals of justice.

In the following pages will be narrated the history of this case in all its details, based partly on those which appeared in the public prints at the time, and on personal experience, and partly on private information subsequently communicated.

PART I.

CHAPTER I.

AT seven o'clock on the morning of the 20th October, 1847, the diligence, which at that date still furnished the means of communication between Marseilles and Paris, deposited at its halting place in a court of the Rue Notre-Dame-des-Victoires, two females eminently calculated to attract attention. Both young and remarkably handsome, their carriage and personal appearance generally betra ed at a glance an origin undoubtedly foreign ; one of them, moreover, was of a type full of startling contrasts. Her brow was of a purity almost angelic, her eyes were large, blue, and exquisitely sweet, but on her full and pouting lips passion stood confessed, whilst her clearly defined eye-brows, nearly meeting in the centre, revealed an indomitable will. Her complexion approached that of a brunette, enriched with the rosy tints of youth, and masses of blue-black hair surrounded a face whose perfect oval might have been envied by the virgins of Perugino. It was evident that the warm rays of an Italian sun had left their impress on both her countenance and her mind.

Julia was, indeed, a Genoese, as was also her companion, a tall and handsome brunette of shapely figure.

Further than this they were only remarkable from each carrying, besides various parcels, one of those large orange-branches laden with fruit, still green, which are brought from the South as curiosities, and one of the palms used at

Rome in certain religious ceremonies, and principally culti-
vated at Bordighera, one of the loveliest towns in the Mount
Como district.

These two Italians were at the same time Parisian in their
knowledge of the customs of the place, and the court where
the *diligence* stopped appeared perfectly familiar to them.
She, whom we have called Julia, nevertheless hesitated to
leave the conveyance, and seemed to await a friendly arm,
but suddenly overcoming her hesitation, she made her way
to the room where the arrival of the passengers was awaited
by their friends, or others actuated merely by curiosity.
She evidently did not find the person whom she expected to
see there, for after a rapid survey of the room she hurried
into the street. There, also, her scrutiny was futile, and
Julia, with an air of thorough disappointment, rejoined her
companion, who by this time had descended from the diligence, and was occupied in paying the fares.

" He is not there ! What can be the meaning of it ?" cried
she on approaching her.

" Patience, signora, he is sure to come."

" Patience ! Patience ! When I have not seen him for
two months, when I ought already to have embraced him a
hundred times !"

" Here, before all the world ?"

" Is he not my husband ?"

" Doubtless, doubtless, madame has a right—"

" Madame ? You style me madame now ?"

" We are in Paris."

" And is that to change the terms on which we are ? I
have already told you, Marietta, that I expect you to continue on the same footing here with me as at Genoa. You
are my foster-sister, and my country-woman, and I will
not allow you for a moment to consider yourself a dependant.
When did you ever see such a thing ? Even in France it

would scarcely be permitted. Ah! if my husband were here, he would read you a lesson. But I hear a carriage ; it must be he."

With petulant haste, in itself charming, she rushed towards a carriage then entering the court, but returned almost at once.

" No," she said in a tone of vexation, " it is a gentleman, but oh! so ugly. It is not my husband."

" Are you quite sure that he has received your letter ?" asked Marietta.

" Why not? I put it in the post myself at Marseilles two days before we left, and the post is always several hours in advance of the diligence."

" Then M. Vidal must have overslept himself. Did he not say in one of his last letters that he had been obliged to discharge his servant, and was living *en garçon ?*"

" Yes, but do you think he could sleep while he was expecting me? You don't know how he loves me," added she, with a bewitching smile which exposed to view her pearly teeth.

All this was said with rapid haste, half in Italian, half in French, for Julia, with true southern vivacity, seized haphazard on any word in either of the languages which the other did not furnish quickly enough.

A servant of the diligence company now interrupted them for the purpose of examining their luggage. This was but a short process, and then the perplexed pair stood looking at one another.

" What are we to do now?" said Julia at last.

" Call a cab, and make our way to your husband's apartments."

" And suppose he crosses us ?"

" We shall see him, or at all events they will tell him here that we have gone, and he will come after us."

"Come, then," said Julia, looking round the court again in vain.

The vehicle which had brought the ugly individual was on the point of leaving, and Marietta hailed it.

"What is the matter with you, cara mia?" she cried, as Julia sighed deeply on taking her seat.

"I am—I had pictured to myself so much joy in once more entering with him under that roof where I have experienced such happiness since my marriage."

"But, my dear mistress, you are going to rejoin him there."

"I do not know, I am afraid."

"What an idea! Do you think he is ill? He never is. Besides, have you not had news of him within the last two days in the letter which was forwarded after you to the diligence office at Lyons?"

"It is of no use, I am uneasy," Julia could not help saying, "this cab is so slow; we shall never get there. What need has the driver to choose the boulevards to reach the Rue de la Paix? it is far too long."

"He takes us for strangers," replied Marietta, "and he is artful enough to present Paris to us under its most seductive aspect. He is right. Look, I have never seen the boulevards so gay; they glisten in the sun to such an extent that we might fancy ourselves in Italy."

Paris was, in fact, rejoicing in one of those delicious days which summer, when just about to wing its flight, gives now and then as if to make the world regret it the more. The air was so fresh, and the sun so bright and warm that one might almost imagine spring to have returned by mistake. On a day such as this we forget that the leaves are putting on their autumnal tints, and that the swallows are gone, or that yesterday, in order to be warm, it was necessary to warm ourselves, to which state we shall probably return to-morrow. What matter? We are astonished, but delighted; we cannot keep quiet, we must be out and moving, and we are much tempted to go back to Baden or Trouville. The streets and the boulevards are soon crowded, the early rising habits of summer reassert themselves, there is a general desire to make the most of the last fine days, everybody says, "how d'ye do?" cordially, shakes hands heartily, and smiles on everything; in a word, there is a new birth and a new life. To change Paris thus, from one day to another, a sense of warmth and a glimpse of blue sky have sufficed.

Our two travellers, like true daughters of the sun, felt, perforce, all these impressions; they could not but be amenable to the charming influences of that lovely day. Gazing from the windows of their cab they saw with all their eyes, and appreciated with all their heart.

Julia forgot her ill-humour, and not a trace of uneasiness remained on her lovely countenance. But a short space separated her from him she so longed to see once more, but a few minutes could elapse before she would take him by surprise at home. She even rejoiced that he had not met her.

"He never received my letter, and he does not expect me," said she. "How happy he will be!" The blush of joy overspread her cheeks, her eyes sparkled, and she smiled on the passers-by, who stopped in admiration of her beauty.

Suddenly, the cab quitted the boulevards, and, entering the Rue de la Paix, stopped at the door of No. 6. Julia's first movement was to look up at the windows of the *entresol.* "It is not open," she cried, "the lazy fellow, he is still asleep."

And, without paying any attention to her companion, but leaving her to settle with the driver and arrange about the luggage and all the miscellaneous articles with which the vehicle was laden, she burst open the door, leaped out, rushed past the porter without a word, ran up a flight of stairs, and pulled the bell with an eager hand.

Some seconds elapsed, and the bell remained unanswered. She gave a second peal, and listened. Not a sound came from the room.

" I was right," she said to herself, " he has gone to meet me, and we have passed each other on the road." Descending the stairs precipitately, she asked the porter if her husband had gone out ?

" Ah ! madame, it is you," was the reply. " And have you had a pleasant journey ? "

" Oh, yes, exceedingly so—but my husband ? "

" I have not seen him this morning."

" And he said nothing to you when he went out ? "

" He cannot be out at all."

" Well, then, why does he not open the door ? "

" Perhaps madame has not rung loudly enough—shall we go up again ?"

" Yes—come."

Julia went upstairs with the porter, and rang with all her might. There was the same silence.

" It is very extraordinary," said the porter. " The gentleman has been expecting madame for the last—"

" Ah, then he received my letter ?"

" Two days ago."

" He is evidently at the diligence office," said Marietta. " If you wish, I will return there at once.

" Oh, do," said Julia.

A cab was passing, and Marietta got into it. She had chanced on a remarkable one, for the horses broke at once into a gallop.

Julia resigned herself to wait, but she could not rest in the porter's room. She walked feverishly to and fro in the street, casting unceasing glances on the still darkened windows. As she looked intently at them she thought she could perceive that the blinds were down, so that complete darkness must reign in the room. Her husband, then, was not yet up. She hurried again to the porter and requested that the door might be burst open.

The porter went in search of a locksmith, and five minutes afterwards returned with one, just as a vehicle turned the corner of the street. It was Marietta, who was leaning out of the window.

" Well ?" cried Julia to her.

Marietta replied by shaking her head.

Julia once more ascended the stairs, and with her the locksmith.

"You will have a troublesome job," said the porter. " There is an extra bolt, which holds to some purpose."

To the great astonishment of the locksmith, the extra bolt was not shot; the lock was only turned once, and the door opened at the first attempt.

Julia sprang into the room. She crossed the outer room, the dining-room, the drawing-room ; everything was in its wonted state. She entered the bedroom, the door of which was wide open.

All at once Marietta heard a scream—a terrible scream. She ran towards the sound. In the middle of the room lay Julia insensible. Close to the bed, half on the floor and half resting against the mattress, was stretched a corpse, covered with blood—the body of a man assassinated—and on an open memorandum-book, such as is used by men on the Bourse, were these words, written in blood—

" *Julia, avenge me—the assassin's name—*"

Death had laid his icy grasp on the hand of the victim at the moment when he was about to write the name of his murderer. On the law now developed the task of completing the unfinished sentence.

CHAPTER II.

ONE of the first questions which would occur to the mind of a magistrate would be as to the motive for the assassination —was it theft?

The reply would appear simple if it were ascertained that the victim, at the moment of his death, had either on or about him effects which had disappeared. Nevertheless, the circumstance that such effects were not forthcoming would not suffice as a starting point in a criminal inquiry. Justice would not overlook the fact that theft is oftentimes an expedient towards disguising some act of revenge, or diverting suspicion.

Justice would also devote herself at once to a most minute investigation into the antecedents, mode of life, and habits of the victim. We will accompany her in these inquiries.

Maurice Vidal, born at Nantes, in a house in the Rue de Sully, in the month of March, 1815, was at the time of his death a little more than thirty-two years of age. He had resided in Paris about twelve years, and had achieved a remarkably rapid fortune owing to a keen insight into the money market, and, above all, to an untiring activity.

After a stay of a few months only in a broker's office, and having there been initiated into the practical details of financial operations, he was not slow in setting up on his own account, and, as a stock-broker, quickly made for himself one of the foremost connections in Paris. To attain to this end, so vainly sought by so many young men of the present generation, what trouble, what care, what incessant

labour had fallen to his lot! But he was known to have
solved the problem of being at once a man of the world, a
man of pleasure, and at the same time an indefatigable
worker.

For ten years he might have been seen at every *fête*, ball,
or supper. He had led a cotillon at the residence of a
banker in the Chaussée d'Antin up to two o'clock in the
morning, and had afterwards figured in the last frantic galop
of an evening with one of our most celebrated *hetairai*.

Many a time, at six o'clock in the morning, had his friends
left him at his door, somewhat elevated, half-dead with fatigue, and overpowered by sleep. Nothwithstanding all
this, at least a dozen persons could bear witness to having
found him by ten o'clock thoroughly fresh, alert, clean
shaven, and occupied in his rooms, at an hotel in the Rue
Lafitte, in receiving orders for the day's Bourse.

This Nantais, now become a Parisian, understood perfectly
the age in which he lived—an epoch eager for contrasts and
prone to extreme frivolity under an exterior guise of gravity.
He knew that the most formal man of business never neglected an opportunity of interspersing jokes amongst his
figures ; that an attorney would willingly break off in the
study of a bundle of papers to ask for news of the latest
ballet ; that a presiding judge was on the alert for the last
good story, and that a Minister, though denied to the impor-
tunate, was easily accessible to those who could amuse him.

He knew also—none better—that business is not a forbidden topic even at a masked ball or in the boudoir of an
actress ; that it is easy for a man of intelligence to secure,
between a couple of glasses of champagne, a commission at
the Bourse ; and, in short, that a client will avoid people
who are tiresome, unfashionably got up, and belonging to
another world than his own, whilst he will, on the contrary,
run after those who can both join in his amusements and

hand him a profit on his account. To this may be traced not a few of the catastrophes of our time.

It is hard for the breath of suspicion to touch the honour of such a man, and, without the shadow of hesitation, you trust him with your all. You see him every hour of the day—in the morning he breakfasts with you at Bignon's; from noon until three in the afternoon you are walking together under the columns of the Bourse; at five o'clock you find him "at home" with some fair dame in the world of fashion, with whom you are both, possibly, smitten; at seven you discover him at an adjoining table in the Café Anglais—and you wind up the evening with him at your club, or the opera, or a first night at some theatre.

And throughout the day, having lived the same life with him, you have never found his good temper wanting, or his gaiety forced; but he has provided a fund of entertainment for you in his own successes, or yours, or your latest speculations. He has advised you to sell your four-and-a-half per cents.; he has been delighted to retail the latest scandal for your benefit, but at the same time has given you excellent advice about some doubtful stock.

You are very far, indeed, from imagining that this companion, so spruce, so obliging, so sportive, and yet so calm, who is thinking, he tells you, of building out of his brokerage a house in the Champs Elysées, has during the day realised all your scrip, and will, when, he leaves you, be off to the Antipodes. Maurice Vidal deserved the full confidence of his rich connection. He was one of a numerous cluster of men on the Bourse whose ways might appear eccentric to those of a decidedly serious turn, whose life, out of working hours, is often stigmatised as irregular, but who in business have the reputation of being regular to a degree and scrupulous to a nicety.

If, by way of furthering his own interests, he had felt

himself bound to mix in the pleasures of others, he had not forgotten, whilst so doing, to make numbers of useful and well-connected friends. It had only depended on himself on several occasions to be admitted to the "parquet," and every time that the appointment of *agent du change* had fallen vacant, such capital as he might require had been placed at his disposal. But he had always energetically refused such offers, under the pretext that he wished still to enjoy some years of youth and liberty.

This liberty, however, to which he seemed so to cling, he one day surrendered. It was suddenly buzzed about that he had married a young lady whom he had known at Genoa during a visit paid to that town in 1846. And when some surprise was expressed at his having married a foreigner, when he could have made an advantageous match in Paris, he treated his friends to the following little speech—

"Gentlemen," said he to them, "in the eyes of you Parisians marriage is merely the means to an end; with me, a Breton only, it is the end itself. You marry a woman who is almost an object of indifference to you, in order that her dowry or her friends may help to build up your fortune; in my case I have chosen a woman who pleases me, so that she may help me to spend as agreeably as we can an income laboriously acquired by ten years' hard work. But in these luxurious times your wife, instead of enriching you, would eat up both her own dowry and your small savings, whilst mine, who has not breathed the lively air of Paris since her infancy, will be blessed, I think, with a smaller appetite. *Au reste*, if she learns to eat I shall not complain—she has such pretty teeth."

By way of peroration to this speech Maurice Vidal presented his wife to several of his intimate friends. To them he said simply, without elaborate phraseology this time— "There she is—I adore her, and she loves me."

And his friends decided in his favour.

In fact, never was a marriage contracted under happier auspices. Maurice was over head and ears in love with Julia, and she loved him with that Italian *furia* of which we in Paris have but a slight idea.

For three days nothing was talked of on the Bourse but their marriage, their love, and the brilliant beauty of Madame Vidal. Afterwards, as nothing happened to foster this enthusiasm (for Maurice, not seeing any advantage in making a show of his wife, loved her at home), the new Benedict was forgotten. The stock-broker, who resumed his customary business, was alone remembered.

Occasionally, it is true, a client, after having charged him with some commission, would say to Maurice—"Well, is the honeymoon to last for ever?"

The reply was, invariably—"My friend, I am the happiest man in the world."

This happiness lasted for a whole year, and probably would have lasted for ever had not Julia received a letter summoning her to Genoa, where her mother, attacked by an illness thought to be mortal, wished to see her. Maurice let her set out alone with Marietta, a servant, but almost a friend, whom she had educated, and whom she had wished to bring with her from Genoa after marriage.

Why, it may be asked, did he not accompany her himself? The hurried departure was one reason, and the absence was to be but for a week—though in the end it reached nearly two months. Last of all, perhaps, fate had decreed that Maurice Vidal should remain alone in Paris at the mercy of an assassin !

Informed of these details of his life, the magistrates could not long dwell on the idea that Julia's husband had fallen a victim to revenge. What enemies could this young man, whose life for ten years had been devoted to open pleasure

and honourable work, have made? He had wounded no
susceptibility—compromised no interest. His frank and
open manner had conciliated the sympathy of all, and though
he was somewhat hasty, and occasionally, in money matters,
a little brusque, he had always been so completely master of
himself that nobody could remember having been involved
in a quarrel, or even a discussion, with him.

Could his marriage, then, have roused any jealousy or
envious feelings? On this point the Law, careful of every
detail, desired some information. But during the whole of
his career as a man about town Maurice was never known
to have had a serious love-affair.

As for Julia, no one knew her except the two or three
intimate friends to whom Maurice had presented her. In
marrying her he had had no rival to engage or get rid of.
She had quitted Genoa tranquilly enough, and was regretted
only by her family.

All things considered, theft must be held to have been one
of the motives of the assassin. But had a theft been committed? We shall easily answer that question by publish-
ing the various reports on the affair, which we owe to the
kindness of one of the chief *employés* in the office of the
public prosecutor.

We shall, however, take care to substitute as often as
possible for the official *procés-verbaux*, which, from their dry
and prolix character, might fatigue our readers, certain
confidential notes, such as are often exchanged between
magistrates in France during the progress of a criminal inquiry, and which were found in the portfolio containing the
records of the case.

CHAPTER III.

Confidential Notes attached to the Official Report of the Commissary of Police of the First Arrondissement, Tuileries Section.

"ACTING on information received at 9 a.m. on the 20th October, 1847, to the effect that a crime had been committed in the Rue de la Paix, I hastened to the spot, after having called to my assistance my secretary, M. Vibert, and M. Godin, police officer, who happened to be in my office at the time when the news reached me.

" On our arrival at No. 6, we perceived that a crowd had assembled, large enough to frustrate the efforts made towards its dispersion by several *sergents de ville.* It was extremely difficult for us to reach the street door of the house.

"Opinions of all kinds, but for the most part contradictory, were held by the various groups through which we made our way. But on one point they were all apparently agreed— that the name of the victim was Maurice Vidal, and that he was on the Bourse.

" One said that his wife, an Italian of great beauty, had arrived in the morning from a journey, and had given way to the most violent despair ; a second declared that the assassin had been arrested, whilst a third maintained that nobody knew who had committed the crime.

" On going up the stairs we heard the following colloquy—

" ' It was his wife, perhaps—those Italian women are capable of anything.'

"'Didn't you hear that she adored her husband?'

"'Oh, they often seem to adore their husbands, but hate them all the time.'

"'Well, then, she was not there at all; she has only been back an hour.'

"'Bah! couldn't she have had an accomplice who did the business? That's simple.'

"When we reached the *entresol* the *sergents de ville* recognised us and let us into the room where the crime had been committed.

"Orders were at once given to clear the staircase, shut the street door, and to allow no one to enter the house except the lodgers or the authorities. Special messengers were at the same time despatched to the office of the public prosecutor, to the Prefecture of Police, and the chief of the detective force.

"After having passed through the outer room and the dining and drawing-rooms, where we did not remark anything unusual, and where the furniture appeared to occupy its usual place, we entered an elegant study.

"Here were two women who, overwhelmed with grief, did not appear to notice our entrance. One of them seemed to be the attendant or maid of the other. She was kneeling at the feet of her mistress, and held her hands as she murmured:—'Courage! courage! my dear Julia. You need your courage to avenge him.'

"Suddenly, she who had been called Julia sprang to her feet, and cried—'Yes, yes! I will avenge him! I swear it!'

"And she drew herself up and stretched out her hands, whilst her eyes sparkled with excitement.

"The police officer, M. Godin, leaned towards me and whispered in my ear—'This woman's grief seems sincere enough! I don't think anything of what we heard on the staircase.'

"Such was also my opinion. My secretary, who has on several occasions given me proofs of great acuteness, did not appear to share our impression. He thought this grief rather theatrical, and he was tempted to accuse Madame Julia of acting a part.

"We pointed out to him that according to our information the lady in question was an Italian; that in her country a little exaggeration is admissible, and that it was difficult to judge her as he would a Parisian. Moreover, the blow which she just received was so terrible and so unexpected that her grief was perfectly legitimate.

"M. Vibert did not give in entirely to our reasoning, and continued to observe Madame Vidal with attention.

"During this time we were making a minute examination of the study in which we were.

"The girl Marietta, the attendant or companion of Madame Vidal, assured us that nothing had been disturbed there by her or by her mistress. All the furniture was exactly as it was when they two had entered the room about half an hour previously.

"The result of our examination is as follows :—

"1st. The two doors which communicate from the study to the drawing-room and bed-chamber were open, and were so found. In the whole room the entrance door alone was shut, but not fastened from within. It may, therefore, be assumed that the assassin passed through this room on leaving the premises, and contented himself with shutting the door on the top of the stairs.

"2nd. A lounge and a chair overturned in the centre of the study, various objects scattered on the writing-table, and a candlestick on the ground, were a sufficient indication that this study had been the scene of the first struggle. But had the assassin here struck his victim, and had the latter managed afterwards to reach the bedroom to die? or had

Maurice Vidal, after in the first instance defending himself in the study, taken refuge in his bedroom, whither the murderer pursued him and where the fatal blow was struck? This latter supposition would gain credence with any one who remarked, as we did, that after the strictest search we could not discover any sign of blood in the study.

" Pre-occupied with the important duty of ascertaining whether theft had followed in the wake of assassination, we searched one after the other all the drawers of the writing-table. One drawer only, the centre one, was half-open ; the key was in the lock, and a sum of twenty-five louis in gold lay before our eyes. There were also papers in the drawer, the key of which we took possession of in order to restore it to the rightful owner.

" In the rest of the room there was neither box nor receptacle of any description for money or securities.

" As we were about to cross the threshold of the bedroom door, Madame Vidal, who up to this time had been kept passive by the girl Marietta, escaped from her arms and wanted to follow us. We begged of her, with every possible delicacy, to observe that her presence might impede us in our investigation, and that in her own interest she was bound to leave us entire freedom of action. She heard what we had to say with more calmness and *sang-froid* than we had expected, and without replying, reseated herself on the sofa which she had just quitted. This woman appears to be endued with wonderful energy, and, so far from being a hindrance to justice, may prove of great assistance. M. Vibert continued his scrutiny of her without intermission, but he seemed to have altered his opinion with regard to her.

" Subjoined is an account of the state in which we found the bedroom—

" To the left, on entering the room, a small piece of rosewood furniture, presenting no point of interest. At two paces from it, a large padded easy-chair stained throughout with blood; stains of blood were also noticeable on the carpet in front of this chair. Here, no doubt, the victim was struck but not killed immediately, as he had had strength enough to drag himself along for a short space in order to call for help. The blood stains were continued to the side of the window looking out into the court-yard, and indicated in an unmistakeable manner the route taken by Maurice Vidal.

" Having succeeded in gaining the window, stains of blood show that he had clung with one hand to the curtains, no doubt to raise himself up to reach the fastening, but in vain. Apparently he had then tried to break one of the squares of glass, which bears the marks of his closed fist, but here his strength failed him. At this moment he had in all probability felt himself lost beyond recall, and he had but one thought, vengeance on his murderer.

" Maurice Vidal must then have looked about for the means of writing, and seeing his memorandum book on a table near his bed, must have crawled to it. It was but a couple of yards, and it is easy to trace his course.

" His hand at first rested on the foot of the table, then reaching up bit by bit, leaving a trace of blood on a glass of water which by chance came in his way, he succeeded at last in grasping the memorandum book of which he was in search.

" Then he commenced to write by the light of a candle which was on the table, but his eyes were dim. It seemed to him, no doubt, that the pencil would not mark, and after having dipped it in the blood that was welling from his wound, he wrote these words—

" ' *Julia, avenge me—the assassin's name——* '

" He can do no more—the blood rushes to his heart, he is

suffocating. His hand lets fall the pencil and the book—he makes a supreme effort—he feels himself becoming power-less; he tries to fight against death. But all is over. His body, half raised, falls on the bed, and in this position we found him.

" Such, sir, are the private notes which I have been able to make, and I have the honour to transmit them to you in accordance with your instructions. I forwarded yesterday to the judicial authorities, my official report."

(*Signed*)   ——

Report of the Doctor, ordered by the Public Administration to examine the Body of the Victim.

" 1. Maurice Vidal was struck with a sharp instrument.

" 2. One of those instruments, called a dagger paper-knife, found on one of the pieces of furniture in the study, where the murderer must have thrown it when his crime was accomplished, answers perfectly to the form of the wound.

" 3. The blow was mortal, having caused deep lesions in the upper clavicular region. Nevertheless, owing to the narrowness of the wound, the victim lived for some moments, and succumbed only in consequence of internal hemorrhage.

" 4. No other wound is to be found on the body of Maurice Vidal. One blow alone sufficed, but it must have been struck by a very powerful arm, or by a person to whom anger lent tenfold strength, as the knife, which is in a very bad state, would not have penetrated into the body except it had been impelled with great violence.

" 5. The death, to judge from the rigidity of the corpse, must have occurred about eleven or twelve hours before the fact was ascertained, which was at 9.35. a.m.

" 6. The supposition that Maurice Vidal committed

suicide, and endeavoured to disguise it by the device of certain words written in his memorandum book, cannot be seriously entertained for a moment, seeing that the blow was struck downwards, either by a person of taller stature than the victim, or at a moment when the latter was stooping. If he had killed himself, Maurice Vidal must have struck the blow either horizontally, or upwards; a vertical blow would have caused a greater laceration of the flesh, and would have been of more considerable extent."

(*Signed*) ——

CHAPTER IV

Extract of Examination of the Porter of No. 6, Rue de la Paix, by the Examining Magistrate, in the Room where the Crime was committed.

" Q.—When did you become aware of the assassination into which we are inquiring?

" A.—An hour ago.

" Q.—Did you notice anything extraordinary last evening, or during the night?

" A.—No, sir.

" Q.—As the window of Maurice Vidal's room looks on to the courtyard, and you live opposite, it appears strange that the cries of the victim did not reach you.

" A.—I had visitors, my brother-in-law, who is an attendant in the office of the Minister of Finance, the porter of No. 41, Boulevard des Capucins, and a cousin of my wife, who were in my lodge the whole evening. We were taking our coffee with a dash of brandy in it up to eleven o'clock, and we heard nothing.

" Q.—At what hour did Maurice Vidal come home yester-day ?

" A.—At half-past seven ; as soon as possible after his dinner.

" Q.—Did you speak to him ?

" A.—Yes, sir, to ask him if he wanted me. He said that he did not, adding that he was going to write two or three letters, and that he should retire to bed early, in order to be up in time for the arrival of the diligence from Marseilles on the following day. I asked him if I should call him, but he said that it would be useless as he was sure to awake of his own accord, if indeed he succeeded in sleeping at all.

" Q.—You had attended on M. Vidal, then, for some days?

" A.—Yes, sir, I went up to him for orders at ten o'clock every morning, and saw him no more until his return in the evening.

" Q.—Had he any visitors ?

" A.—Two or three friends, but always the same. They invariably appeared to be in a hurry, conversed for a moment on business matters, and then left immediately.

" Q.—You have not lately noticed any stranger with M. Vidal ?

" A.—I forgot, sir. The day before yesterday, about five o'clock, a person called whom I had never seen. He was a tall, fair, young man, very elegant and very good-looking, but with a used-up manner. On hearing that M. Vidal had gone out and would probably not return, he appeared very much annoyed, and said that he would call again on the following morning.

" Q.—And did he ?

" A.—No, sir.

" Q.—You are quite sure of that ?

" A.—Yes, sir, I even remarked upon the circumstance to M. Vidal, who replied, ' Oh, his visit is of no importance.'

" Q.—To receive such an answer, you must have known his name and mentioned it to M. Vidal?

"A.—No, sir, but I described him to M. Vidal, and he recognised him at once.

"Q.—Are you positive that this person did not return last night?

"A.—I did not see him.

"Q.—You would easily recognise him again if you were to see him?

"A.—Very easily.

"Q.—Have you examined the dagger paper-knife found in the room, with which the crime was evidently committed?

"A.—Yes, sir. It was I who first saw it, and I at once called the commissary of police.

"Q.—This knife probably did not belong to M. Vidal?

"A.—On the contrary, sir, it was always on the table where he worked, and he has made use of it on several occasions as a paper-knife.

"Q.—Think well of what you are saying, as this is a detail of great importance.

"A.—I am quite certain I am right. Besides, Madame Vidal, Mademoiselle Marietta, and all his friends know the dagger."

Confidential Memoranda furnished by the Commissary of Police.

" At the time of his death Maurice Vidal could not have had any considerable effects in his house. On the previous evening he had lodged thirty thousand francs, the produce of his savings and his latest earnings, with M. R—, a broker, whom he had commissioned to buy government stock to that amount in the name of his wife. As regards any scrip entrusted to him by his clients, whether for sale or transfer, it is a well-known fact that M. Vidal was in habit of depositing them in the bank or with M. R——, who has at this time in his possession some railway shares.

"M. Vidal had only a small number of clients of long standing, and he rarely made new ones. This reserve was generally attributed to a heavy loss which he had sustained in the year 1845, at the hands of a certain Blondeau, who absconded to America when liable for considerable differences.

"Another person, known on the Bourse as Albert Savari Montbrisé, was also thought to have been for three years in debt to M. Vidal to the extent of about fifty thousand francs. This debt gave rise last year to an unpleasant scene. M. Vidal, suddenly catching sight of his creditor, went straight up to him in the Bourse, and said, in a loud angry tone— 'When a man neglects to pay his differences and disappears on settling day, he ought, at all events, to have sufficient sense of shame to prevent him showing himself here.'

" 'Sir,' replied Savari, with considerable assurance, 'I do not require any lessons from you.'

" 'You'll receive one to-day, at any rate, for I'll show you the door and shut the Bourse against you henceforward.'

"It would probably have been a case of a 'word and a blow,' although M. Vidal's adversary was a big man, if several persons had not hastened to interfere. The result of the affair was, that M. Savari, in order to appear again on the Bourse, had to give bills to the amount of fifty thousand francs, which would become due some time in the present month. It appears, moreover, that these bills have never been put in circulation, M. Vidal having kept them in his own house. He remarked lately to M. de Rostain, one of his friends, who lives at No. 14, Rue Taitbout, and from whom we have this information direct, that he knew the bills would not be met at maturity. He knew, he added,

that he would have to pay for his whistle, seeing that the
law does not recognise debts arising from Bourse speculations, but that he should, nevertheless, take proceedings for
his own satisfaction against M. Savari, whose cool effrontery
and bad faith had disgusted him. He added, in a very
bitter tone, that he had often obliged people who owed him
money when they had found themselves involved in unfortunate circumstances beyond their own control, but this
was not the case with M. Savari. As regarded him, he
awaited with impatience the moment when he could tell him
what he thought of him.

"Such is the information gathered up to-day. Anything further that may come to my knowledge shall be communicated in due course.

"On the Bourse, where Maurice Vidal was much liked
and esteemed, his death has caused a great sensation.
Every moment I see groups forming, whose sole topic of
conversation is the tragedy in the Rue de la Paix."

Whilst these preliminary reports, which form the basis of
every criminal information, were being sent in from different
quarters to the office of the *Procureur du Roi* (all this
happened, be it remembered, in 1847) Julia Vidal was a
prey to the most profound grief. She had been precipitated
in an instant from the height of happiness to the depth of
an irremediable misfortune. She had arrived, after a long
absence, almost beside herself at the idea of return, intoxicated, as it were, with the thought of again seeing him she
loved so well, quivering with happiness and feverish with
impatience, when suddenly, without any preparation, without
even the slightest clue towards a suspicion of misfortune, she
found Death holding full sway in her home, with crime at her
bedside. The arms which she fondly hoped to see stretched
out to clasp her in their fond embrace lay powerless and

cold ; the heart wont to beat in unison with her own was still, and the lips, which would have sought hers, were pale and chill as ice.

When one we love falls a prey to serious illness we rush to his assistance, we lavish on him all our care, we surround him with every tenderness, we love him so much the more that he has not long to be with us, all our affection is bestowed on him. The disease increases in intensity, and we cling more and more closely as he seems to be slipping from our hold, we hang upon his words, we seek to divine his latest wish, we long to do something for him, however small. His last thought is for us, for us his latest word, his parting smile. And when he is no more we live in his short past, and the mementoes he has left, all cruel though they be, aid us, perhaps, to suffer with greater courage and more complete resignation.

But to sustain a blow such as that which befel Julia Vidal so unexpectedly, and not to have had the supreme consolation of dwelling on a word, a kiss, a look—to have left a man in the pride of his strength, his health, and his love, and to return to a corpse—it was horrible ! And near her was no mother, no relative, not even a friend but Marietta, and she alone. For Julia was a stranger in Paris, and giving herself up to her passionate love, she had never, in the egotism of that feeling, thought of making friends or surrounding herself with acquaintances.

If only she could pray and weep at will near that dead form which she felt to be her all—but no, even that did not belong to her, but to Justice. To Justice belonged the right of watching it, of caring for it, of ordering a *post mortem* examination, should there be one. Justice was father, mother, widow, relatives, all in one, seeing that it represented more than a family—it stood in the place of society outraged by a crime.

And this crime, notwithstanding the mystery which en-
veloped it, and which we have not yet penetrated, could not
remain unpunished. How will Justice set about her task ?

CHAPTER V

Two important letters, for they make us acquainted with
one of our principal characters, came to light in the midst of
the mass of papers bearing on this tragedy. They are a
little yellowed with age. The first is written on ordinary
and very cheap note paper, and is indeed scribbled rather
than written. The hand that traced the characters had
evidently no time to spare ; it might have been indited by a
bailiff in the scant interval between two writs.

The second letter in no way resembles the first, it being
as aristocratic as the other is plebeian. The paper is cream-
laid, thick, and stamped with a crest. No economising
space here—there are not fifty words on a page. The writing is large and pointed, having a self-satisfied air quite
pleasant to look at. It is not after the English style, nor is
it round-hand ; it is not too formal, nor too careless—it is
simply the writing of a man for whom correspondence has a
certain charm and serves as a distraction, a man who dresses
himself before he writes, and most probably puts on ruffles
after the manner of M. de Buffon.

But it is high time to acquaint our readers with the contents of these letters—

M. VIBERT, SECRETARY OF THE COMMISSARY OF POLICE, OF THE
FIRST ARRONDISSEMENT, TUILERIES SECTION, TO THE MARQUIS
DE X——, PEER OF FRANCE.

"M. le Marquis—It is to you that I owe everything. You

it is who, in remembrance of some services rendered in former days to your family by my father, took care of my childhood, and gave me an education such as is to be found in our best Jesuit boarding-schools. I ought, out of gratitude for all your kindness, to have followed a career according to your wishes, and to have adopted whatever walk of life you might have been pleased to point out. In that case I should, thanks to your protection and unalterable favour, to-day find myself curate in some pleasant town parish, or vicar of some quiet village. But I had a vocation, one that was irresistible and strongly opposed by you out·of regard for me, but in vain, to my shame be it said.

"Whence comes this vocation? I have often asked myself that question, but without obtaining any reply. That a young man should feel himself drawn towards painting, writing, or oratory, is intelligible; he might become a distinguished speaker, or author, or artist, and at once attain to fame and fortune. But to desire, as I did, but one thing in the world, to have but one aim, and that to devote myself to the police as a profession, is, I admit, peculiar.

"Such, however, has been the solitary dream of my life, and now that this dream has become a reality I am still constrained to confess that I do not regret any one of those vocations which I might have followed. I cast my eyes round about and. I recognise no career more enviable than my own. May not this inclination be the result of a physical peculiarity and not of a moral one, as might be imagined? Just as we continually see a great, big, broad-shouldered, jovial fellow turn soldier, may not I have been unwittingly drawn towards the police because I am short and slightly out of the perpendicular, because my temperament is bilious, and my eyes so weak that I am obliged to wear blue spectacles.

"Do not imagine, M. le Marquis, that the vocation springs

from an honourable source, such as the desire of being useful to my country. To you, who are making a species of collection of moral depravities, who take a pleasure in stumbling across them and in ridiculing the age in which we live—to you I may say that when I am engaged in police business neither the interest of individuals, nor of the government, nor of my country, has any weight with me. I work for the sake of art and my own personal gratification. How many there are who would eagerly throw themselves into my career, if they could appreciate the pleasure of entering, as I do, into the lives of others !

"Reflect, M. le Marquis, that my physical defects have ever stood in the way of my living on my own account, and have left me a thousand longings unassuaged, a horde of small passions self-contained. Ah, well ! I indemnify myself for my forced inaction and my unavoidable want of power, by seeing others live and living their life. I join in their pursuits, I share their feelings and their passions, I rejoice with them, and with them I suffer—in a word, I put myself in their place.

"Such, M. le Marquis, are the principal reasons which make me one of the oddest of government servants—a servant who loves his place, who is content with his lot contentus suâ sorte and who does not pick holes in his chiefs or the State. That is a real phenomenon, and I have every right to expect that, after my death, a special corner will be reserved for me in one of our museums, with the following inscription, 'A contented civil servant' (extinct species).

" ' But, Vibert,' you will say, ' to what end this long rigmarole ? I will do you the justice to confess that you have never written to me unless you wanted something. What can you want now that you are so contented ?'

"Ah ! M. le Marquis, now we come to the point, but round the corner, as becomes the police. Yes, all-satisfied

B

though I be, you have divined rightly, my dear protector, that I want something, but it is neither a question of advancement in the service, nor of increase of salary. The Fates forbid ! It is simply a matter of change. I wish, for some time at least, to pass from the sedentary (if I may make use of a term hitherto applied to the magistracy only) to the active police. Instead of hearing the reports of men in uniform or those in plain clothes, of those who carry a sword, or those who have merely a card—in a word, recognised policemen, or secret agents—I wish, in my turn, to be empowered, as they are, to make reports.

"Fancy me, M. le Marquis, emerging one day from my house completely transformed ; my goggles have given way to spectacles on nose ; I wear an imperial, and heels to my boots which make me two inches taller ; in my right hand is a sword-cane, and in my pockets are a warrant or two, and a pair of handcuffs. A foreign order decorates my button hole—blue, green, yellow, or red, as my fancy or my taste may dictate, for you are aware, M. le Marquis, that the members of the detective force, the better to disguise their individuality, bestow an infinite number of such honorary distinctions upon themselves. Then, so disguised, I go in search of the malefactors, who have been described to me ; I run, I climb, I tumble down, I ride in carriages, or behind them, I go ten leagues in every direction, or I stop for twelve hours in the same place with my eyes riveted on a front door. Ah, what incomparable happiness !

"Up to this time, I have but spoken of ordinary pleasures, of everyday nourishment, such as swindlers, thieves, old offenders, escaped convicts,—vulgar criminals in fact. But sometimes I may be bidden to wage war against some terrible enemy of society. Then one has to arm for the fray, to rush upon the foe, to expose one's life, to pay for it with one's blood, to beat or be beaten ; or else you dodge about,

manœuvre, lay plots, and so in the end come off victorious.
Yes, M. le Marquis, it ought to be a grand satisfaction to be
able to say, thanks to me, this miserable assassin has been
discovered; I have avenged an outraged society which but
for me would be still at the mercy of his blows ! The gendarmes and *sergents de ville* lent me physical help, I admit;
the examining magistrate was the most able of his class ; the
crown advocate spoke with greater force and eloquence than
the counsel for the defence ; the presiding judge, not content
with summing up in a few words, made another speech for
the prosecution ; the jury did not hesitate, but found the
prisoner guilty without retiring ; the Court of Cassation maintained the conviction ; the recommendation to mercy was
disregarded ; the executioner sternly performed his awful
task ; every one, in short, did his duty. But I it was who
made this duty plain. I both framed the indictment and
constructed the scaffold !

" If I grow thus warm, whilst dealing with an imaginary
assassin, a fictitious criminal, an ideal case, you may judge,
M. le Marquis, what my zeal would be in a real occurrence,
with an actual offender. The very thought of it makes my
spectacles radiant with the glances from my eyes, my heart
beats faster, and my trembling right hand drives home the
sharp penknife into the leathern arm-chair of the commissary.

"The fact is, I know of an affair, a superb affair which at
this moment engages the attention of Paris, of France, of
Europe. I allude to the tragedy in the Rue de la Paix.

" What ! you know the murderer ? I think I hear you say,
M. le Marquis,—no, I do not know him, but this tragedy
interests me, and something tells me that I alone can put
Justice on the track of this mysterious assassin.

" And with two words from you, two words written to the
Prefect of Police, I emerge from the police office in the Rue

St. Honoré, I have all the necessary resources placed at my disposal, I enter on the campaign, and I come out of it victorious.

" Will you, my dear protector ? Will you ? Think, not only is there the punishment of a great criminal, but the avenging of a woman. A woman, did I say ? If you only knew her, the most charming, the most virtuous, the most beautiful of women ! And I dared to suspect her—her ! Never shall I forgive myself such a thought until I can say to her—' Here is the murderer of your husband, I give him up to you !'

" I pray you to excuse the length of this letter, M. le Marquis, and to continue my kind patron."

REPLY OF THE MARQUIS OF X—, PEER OF FRANCE, TO VIBERT.

PARIS, 22nd October, 1847.

" On my honour, young man, your letter does not annoy me in the least. On the contrary, it amuses me. You are in the full swing of that moral decay which I have foreseen. The immortal principles of '89, the rights of man, and the over-throw of monarchies, could not bring about any other results. Like all people of your generation, who are stayed upon nothing, who have no solid faith, you are corrupt to the very marrow of your bones. I cause you to be brought up after the most honourable fashion, I fill you to the brim with excellent principles, I destine you to be a notary or a priest, and one fine day your sole ambition proves to be to turn police-agent !

" But a truce to sentiment, Mr. Sub-Commissary, I am about to tell you the truth with regard to yourself. What seduces you in the new duties which you wish to undertake is to live on the outskirts of society, to be brought in contact with every vice and every corruption, to assume without acknowledgment the airs and graces of the rascals you are told off to watch, to share their pleasures, and to become little by little familiar with their libertine manners.

" In my time, sir, those who had a taste for libertinism went in for it openly before all the world. Then you could at once restrict them to a corner of society, circumscribe them to the Galeries de Bois at the Palais Royal, or send them to the Bastille, as happened to the Marquis de Sade. But your generation has not even the courage of its vices : in place of letting itself be caged it wishes to cage us ; it decks itself with the mask of virtue, or else tries, as you wish to try, to play corrupter under cloak of the law. It has succeeded even in no longer calling persons and things by their proper names.

" But here am I talking as though I were out of temper ! I am giving a moral lesson to a police-agent ! What pretension have I to correct you ? Had I the power, I should not have the will. All's well that ends well ; and you of the police, I hope, will end by falling from drop to drop, from degradation to degradation, and by being punished for your revolutionary vileness. 'Tis all the good I wish you.

" As regards yourself personally, my good Vibert, I wish nothing of the kind ; you belong to your age, and, in saying that, I have said all. It is not your fault if your ancestors overturned kings, and if in your plebeian veins there runs some of the old Jacobin blood. I know you, in spite of your frankness ; you are less of a hypocrite than the rest, you do not attempt to conceal your defects. Consequently, I have lost no time in acting according to your wishes. I have seen the Prefect of Police, I have spoken highly to him of your zeal ; he awaits you to-morrow, when he will give you the neces- sary permission to vacate your post in the sedentary police, as you call it.

" Above all, do not thank me. I do not like it. I believe neither in public nor in private gratitude. But if, in your own proper interest, you wish to please me, keep me fully informed of this mysterious affair; and see that I, before all the world, am told of all the vicissitudes of the case. Great crimes have always preceded revolution, and if we could in 1848—

"Whilst on this subject, did you not tell me that a lovely woman is mixed up in the Rue de la Paix affair? The more reason that I should know all that goes on. Notwithstanding my sixty-six years, I hold still that woman is the better part of man.

"Adieu, dweller in the Rue de Jerusalem! Put yourself on the scent, hasten to discover the trail. I await your report."

CHAPTER VI.

FROM the earliest rumour of the tragedy in the Rue de la Paix every newspaper alluded to it constantly, and, under pretence of superior information, gave news to-day which some rival sheet was sure to contradict, to-morrow. In this way Julia Vidal committed suicide one morning, and was brought to life again the same evening. On the following day the murderer was discovered, had confessed on the spot, and would be brought up for trial at the next assizes; they even went so far as to publish his portrait. Within a week a dozen people were arrested by these journalists, to suit their respective versions of the matter. Several of these protested, and were graciously released; others were killed, for the simple reason that they had never been alive, and their inventors continued to lay an infinity of offences at their doors, in order to provide sustenance for Parisian curiosity.

The journals, however, did not fail very soon to discover,

from information received, that Justice was decidedly embarrassed. For a long time no case had been surrounded with so much mystery. That a crime had taken place was indisputable, and all idea of suicide had been perforce cast aside. But the assassin, beyond the terrible wound inflicted by him, had disappeared, and left no trace. The weapon he had made use of belonged to his victim; and, after the most careful research, no discovery had been made in the room in the Rue de la Paix such as, in ordinary cases, suffices to enlighten a magistrate, and very often to convince a jury. In a recent case in England a hat, forgotten by the murderer, brought about the sentence of death. A pen-knife, dropped by Latour near the bed of his two victims, led to the terrible ending of that trial, which took place last year in the Department of Ariége; even the accidental dropping of a shirt stud has caused the fall of more than one head. Here nothing of the kind had occurred, nor was there a single indication to justify an arrest, or even a summons. It was necessary to fall back upon moral probability, and to enter the vast region of hypothesis and supposition.

Who would have had any interest in killing Maurice Vidal? That was the point of departure, and to that every one returned. Whoever it might be, he had still to be found. Was it his wife? No one who thought seriously of the question could entertain the notion for a moment. Julia was worthy of all sympathy. The blow which had killed her husband had well-nigh caused her death too. So far from suspecting her, the first thought should be to avenge her.

Was it a common robber—a thief by profession? His presence would have been noticed in a house in the Rue de la Paix; he could not have resisted the gold found in the table drawer; he would have abstracted some of the costly articles which were scattered about the room; and, last of all, Maurice Vidal would not, in his dying moments, have thought of writing a name which he could not have known.

Was it a lodger in the house? That would tally with the statement of the porter that he had not, on the evening of the 19th October, answered the door to any stranger. But all information collected with regard to the lodgers at No. 6 —who, by-the-way, were very few—tended to show that they were quiet people, who had never had any dealings with a court of justice; and who could not, with any show of reason, be suspected of a crime. On one only of them there rested a momentary suspicion. This was an American, of about forty years of age, who for two months had been the sub-tenant of a room on the fourth floor. A search was ordered in his domicile, but nothing particular was discovered. He was subjected to an examination, and came out of it with flying colours.

Was it one of those persons whom Maurice Vidal was in the habit of receiving? They appeared as witnesses, and, from their clear and precise depositions, as well as from universal testimony in their favour as regarded their characters, it was clear that not a shadow of proof could be brought to bear against them.

Last of all, was it the individual mentioned by the porter, as having called on M. Vidal on the 18th October, and of whom the commissary of police of the Bourse quarter had given so detailed an account in his report? Did he gain admission into the house in the Rue de la Paix without observation ?

Albert Savari, for such was the name of this personage, was not entirely unknown in the office of the public prosecutor. Without ever having suffered a conviction, he had been on several occasions brought in contact with the law ; his antecedents were by no means all that could be desired, and there was more than one obscure corner in his life. He was, moreover, a debtor to Maurice Vidal for a large amount, and the bills he had given were nowhere to be found. Here was sufficient to attract the attention of the law, and a summons for his appearance, closely followed by a warrant for his arrest, was issued against him.

These energetic measures were also due to the great publicity given to this affair. It was in everybody's mouth, and it was certainly well calculated to excite the public mind in no ordinary degree. As is often the case in Paris, where the most serious matters are somewhat flippantly treated, bets were made as to whether or no the culprit would be discovered. Several of the opposition journals also profited by the occasion to reflect on the police, and professed their astonishment that assassination in a much frequented street should be so easy, and the discovery of the assassin so difficult. One of the most advanced of these publications gave its readers to understand that a person in high quarters was mixed up in the whole of the business, and that the police had therefore received an order to hold their hands. The arrest of Albert Savari was the first reply to these attacks. With this man we will now enter the office of the examining magistrate, M. Gourbet, to whom the preliminary investigation was entrusted.

The office in question was much as others devoted to judicial purposes. A door opened on to a long corridor lined with benches, which served as a waiting-room for the office attendants, bailiffs, witnesses, and persons cited to appear. A smaller door, less open to observation, led to the prison, and through this the accused were brought. The magistrate's writing-table was so placed that the person seated at it had his back to the light, the person under examination being exposed to its full glare. This facility for observing the slightest change of countenance on the part of a prisoner was, indeed, of great use. A man may betray himself as easily by a gesture, a movement, a look, or a sudden blush, as by his words ; and very often an unexpected question put point-blank to a criminal, up to then impenetrable in his reserve, has sufficed to open a magistrate's eyes. A small table close to the other was devoted to the use of the registrar, on whom fell the duty of taking down the *vivâ-voce* examination. A leathern arm-chair, with two or three ordinary ones for the witnesses and the accused, according to their social position or the degree of interest which they excited, completed the furniture of the room.

M. Gourbet ceased to exercise the functions of an examining magistrate in 1850, and he died some years ago, so that a word may be said in his praise without the danger of wounding any susceptibilities. As a magistrate he has left behind him in the Palais de Justice an unimpeachable reputation. If those who knew him are to be believed, he possessed, in an eminent degree, those peculiar qualifications so indispensable to his profession. He had the art of uniting to firmness, and an often very necessary severity, a great amount of benevolence and, in certain cases, delicacy, thorough common sense, and a manner of reassuring the timid, encouraging the weak, and comforting the guilty, which won for him their entire sympathy. In a word, he had solved the problem of doing good even to those whom his conscience told him must be dealt with severely. One of his registrars once said of him that half his time was passed in search of proofs to send people to prison, and the other half in finding reasons for letting them out again or mitigating the hardships of their confinement.

At the moment of our entry into his office about 11 o'clock in the morning of the 2nd November, M. Gourbet, standing with his elbow resting on the mantel-piece, was conversing with a young lady in deep mourning, who was seated in an arm-chair. It was Julia Vidal, with whom he had had

several interviews, and who was now present in obedience to
his order.

"Then," said he to her, "you have nothing new to report
since yesterday?"

"No, sir."

"Do not be afraid to tell me even things which may
appear insignificant to you. In a criminal investigation it
sometimes happens that a ray of light flashes out from a
circumstance to which no importance seems to attach. You
have been courageous enough, I am told, to remain in your
domicile in the Rue de la Paix, and you continue to live in
the room where the murder was committed."

"Yes, sir," cried Julia, interrupting M. Gourbet, "I will
never, except at the last extremity, quit the house where we
loved so well." And, as she spoke, heavy tears, long restrained, welled from her eyes.

Since the day when we saw her alighting so gaily from the
Marseilles diligence Julia had greatly changed. Her face
had grown longer, there were dark rings round her eyes, and
a dull pallor had replaced the warm colour in her cheeks.
Grief was ingrained, as it were, into her whole appearance.
But she was so young, her features possessed so perfect a regularity, beneath her paleness there was still so much health
and life, that she had lost nothing of her beauty, but, on the
contrary, had gained one charm the more.

The magistrate could not help contemplating her with
interest for a moment ; then, as he saw her grow calmer, he
said—"I must crave your forgiveness for thus reviving your
grief, but you can be of immense assistance to me in arriving at an end, to the attainment of which both my duty and
my inclination impel me."

"Ah! yes," said Julia, quickly raising her head, "you
will attain that end, will you not? You will avenge my
husband—we will avenge him together."

"I hope so," was the reply, "but I must tell you that in my career, already a lengthy one, I have rarely met with a case so surrounded with mystery as this. All the threads which I think I have succeeded in joining break in my hands. I can only feel my way, and that with the greatest caution, for if it is annoying to the self-love of a magistrate, whose power is so wide, and whose resources are so great, to be compelled to give up the quest of a culprit, it is still more trying to his conscience to arrest an innocent man, even though he has to release him."

"But, then," cried Julia, with animation, "the culprit will not be discovered. My husband commanded me to avenge him, and I would obey him!"

"And, I repeat, I wish to assist you. But we have yet to find the murderer, and I much fear we are not yet on his track."

"Nevertheless, I read last evening in a newspaper that the assassin had been arrested."

"The papers are misled, madame, or they mislead their readers for the purpose of appearing well informed. A man was, indeed, arrested yesterday by my orders, and he will presently be brought before me. There is certain evidence against him which justifies his arrest, but this evidence is quite insufficient to bring about an absolute conviction in my mind. The proofs against him are, as yet, rather moral than material. I will go farther, and confess that nearly all material proofs are wanting. Here," added M. Gourbet, taking several papers from his desk, "is a minute of proceedings drawn up by the commissary of police ordered to arrest this person. From it his attitude does not seem to be that of a guilty man; he appeared excessively astonished and surprised when the warrant for his arrest was made known to him, and, if he is playing a part, it must be confessed that he is a good actor, seeing that he has succeeded in deceiving one of our sharpest officers. His lodging has, according to custom, been most carefully searched ; but the result, without being entirely negative, has not furnished us with any conclusive proofs. I have now only to rely upon the examination for which I am preparing myself, and which," said M. Gourbet, looking at a clock on the mantel-piece, " will take place at once."

Julia understood that he wished her to go, and rose to take her leave ; but, before retiring, she ventured to ask the name of the accused.

" Albert Savari de Montbrisé," replied M. Gourbet ; " I have already mentioned him to you by name, madame, and you have said that he is unknown to you. The information which you might have been able to give me in connection with him would have been very valuable."

" No," replied Madame Vidal, after a momentary silence, devoted to a last appeal to her memory, " I do not think I have ever heard my husband mention this person, and yet, as his name left your lips, I suddenly experienced again the same sensation which came over me on a previous occasion."

" What sensation ? What do you mean ? Explain yourself, pray."

" That is just what I cannot do ; I do not understand the peculiar feeling myself. The day when I heard, for the first time, the words, 'Albert Savari de Montbrisé,' it seemed to me that I turned pale, that my heart beat faster, and I wanted to see whether I was mistaken, or whether the same phenomenon would be reproduced, and so I asked you, in this instance, to say the name again, although I knew it, and it has been in my thoughts without intermission."

" That is in no way extraordinary," observed M. Gourbet, " on very slight reflection. This Savari is the only person who is seriously compromised in this affair—of that you are aware, and his name naturally causes you some emotion."

"Possibly so, sir. You requested me to impart all my impressions, and I have obeyed you."

"I thank you for it, madame," replied the magistrate, as he escorted Julia to the door of his office, and, just as he was taking leave of her, he added, "Did you not tell me, in our last interview, that you had been assailed by a perfect crowd of persons, who come to your residence with offers of service?"

"Alas! yes, and their countenances are by no means re-assuring as a rule. The majority pretend to belong to the police and to be directed to search my house."

"In future, madame, you will only receive those who bear a written order from me. That will, at all events, secure respect for your grief, and will preclude your being a victim of either the inquisitive or the intriguing."

"This very morning" said Julia, with her hand on the handle of the door, "an individual called who was persistent in his efforts to see me. But Marietta, knowing that I was preparing for my visit here, refused to admit him. He left his name, and said he would call again."

"And his name?"

"Vibert, I think."

"Vibert," said M. Gourbet, as if trying to recollect something.

"Ah! I have it. If you take my advice you will see him. He is to all appearances an intelligent man, both active and zealous. He might, on occasion, be of great use to us, and he was yesterday recommended to my notice by the Prefect of Police after a very pressing fashion."

"I will see him," said Julia.

After having bowed to the magistrate she was preparing to turn the handle of the door, when she perceived that some one was endeavouring to open it from the outside. She drew back, and the door opened to admit a little man of about fifty years of age. After having whispered a few words in the ear of M. Gourbet, he proceeded to take his seat at the registrar's table in the office.

"The arrival of the prisoner is announced," said M. Gourbet.

"Ah!" replied Julia, "I will go then." But coming to a sudden stop as she was going out, she again approached the magistrate with a determined air, and said, shortly, "I should like to see him."

The dried-up little man, occupied at his table in mending a pen, raised his head quickly, as if he thought her speech a peculiar one. As for M. Gourbet, less astonished than his registrar, by reason of the conversation he had just had with Madame Vidal, he looked attentively at Julia, and, doubtless satisfied with his examination, said—"Your request is not unreasonable, madame."

The little man, more and more surprised, made so brusque a movement with his pen-knife that, instead of mending his pen, he marred his finger.

During this episode M. Gourbet, addressing Madame Vidal, resumed—"Have you courage, during the whole of this examination, to be silent and not betray, even by a gesture, your presence in my office?"

"Yes, sir; I shall have courage enough."

"Even if it should happen that Savari acknowledges himself the assassin of your husband?"

"Yes; I may, perhaps, expire from indignation, but I will die in silence," said Julia, with an Italian enthusiasm perfectly natural in her.

M. Gourbet made a sign to the little man, who glided towards him. We use the word "glided" advisedly, in speaking of the registrar. He had a way of walking entirely his own; his feet did not leave the floor, his legs did not lift themselves, his knees did not bend—he seemed to make no use whatever of his joints. He advanced all together, just as a railway carriage glides over the rails.   An excellent man, too, was this registrar on springs, who is still remembered at the Palace of Justice.

How often has he been seen to bestow on the wretched prisoners, as they left the examination room, small packets of tobacco purchased out of his savings.   " Poor devil," he used to whisper to them, " you have let yourself be nicely entangled.   1 have just read over your examination ; your little affair is pretty clear and you may make up your mind to ten years at least—take this to console you."   When the prisoner was an old acquaintance, an escaped convict from the galleys, a *cheval de retour* in prison slang, the little man would sometimes add to this packet of tobacco a penny clay pipe.

" It is all arranged, Cordier, is it not ?" said the magistrate, after an aside with the registrar.

" It shall be done as you wish," was the solemn reply.

Cordier called an attendant and directed him to arrange in one of the corners of the office a screen which had been put away in a closet.   He then took Madame Vidal by the hand with the utmost gallantry, and, without speaking a word or looking at her, still gliding over the floor, he led her behind the screen, seated her in an arm-chair, carefully closed the screen round her, and returned to plant himself in his accustomed spot before his desk.

These preparations were scarcely completed when the prisoner was ushered into the office.

CHAPTER VII.

ALBERT SAVARI, as he had been described by the porter of No. 6, Rue de la Paix, in his examination, was a fair man, of commanding stature and exceptionally good address. At first sight he might have been taken for forty, but attentive scrutiny would show that he was but thirty-four or thirty-five, at most, and that wakeful nights, and fatigue of every description had aged him beyond his years. It must be confessed, moreover, that these signs of premature age, his somewhat lazy movements, his hair turning grey on the temples, and his used-up look, far from taking away from his physical appearance, lent an air of distinction and a peculiar charm to his features.

His dress, when he presented himself before M. Gourbet, was simple, but elegant. No one was with him, orders having been given to the gendarmes who brought him up for examination to wait for him at the very office door.

He bowed to the magistrate without any affectation, seated himself in accordance with an invitation conveyed to him, and, before any question could be put to him, commenced the proceedings by saying in a rather harsh, though calm tone of voice—"May I ask, sir, why I was so unceremoniously arrested yesterday, and for what reason I now find myself in your presence ?"

"Sir," replied M. Gourbet at once, "you are here to reply to such questions as I shall have to put to you, and not to interrogate me, as is apparently your intention."

"It is but natural and right, nevertheless, that I should

wish to ascertain of what offence or crime I stand accused.
I have inquired in vain of the officers charged to arrest me—
they refused to reply."

"They but did their duty," replied the magistrate firmly.
"But what they were forbidden to disclose I am about to
tell you, and, indeed, I should already have done so, had
you not spoken first, in defiance of all the rules in force in
this office."

"I am ignorant of those rules, sir, and I am not accustomed to find myself here."

"I congratulate you on that, and I hope you will not
again have to appear before me. You are not accused of a
mere delinquency," continued M. Gourbet after a pause,
and looking fixedly at the prisoner, "you are accused of a
crime."

"Ah ! really. What crime ?"

"Of having assassinated a young man called Maurice
Vidal."

Albert Savari did not move a muscle on hearing this curt
and precise charge, and as he addressed the magistrate his
countenance betrayed no sign of emotion.

"I must say," he remarked, "that I was far from expecting to be compromised in this affair, which, for several days
past, has been talked about in my presence. Would it be
indiscreet to ask," he continued, with perfect courtesy, and
as if he were in a drawing-room, "what has led to my being
suspected of this crime ?"

"You will soon know that; but now that your first
curiosity is satisfied, let us proceed in order. Will you have
the goodness to state your Christian name and surname ?"
And, turning to the registrar, he added, "You can commence to write, Cordier."

"I am called Albert Savari," replied the accused, turning
towards the little man, at whom he looked with interest.

"Have you not been in the habit of bearing another name?" observed the magistrate.

"Certainly, sir; I have sometimes been called de Mont-brisé."

"According to my information, you have no right to the appellation. Whence does it come to you?"

"From some land which formerly belonged to my family."

"That does not constitute a right. But let it pass. What is your age?"

"Thirty-six."

"And your profession?"

"I have none."

"How, then, do you live?"

"Pretty well, thank you."

"Excuse me," said M. Gourbet with severity, "I cannot for a moment permit you to make use of that jocular tone in replying to me. If you are not yet as serious as befits your position as an accused person, I shall not hesitate to send you back to the Conciergerie, and to postpone the examination till some future day."

Savari listened to this reprimand without movement or reply.

"I ask you again," continued the magistrate, "what are your means of subsistence?"

"Sir," replied the prisoner, in a tone more serious and, indeed, quite free from levity, "if by means of subsistence you imply money in the funds, title-deeds of property, or private annuity, I must confess that I have none of them. Like many young men of the present age, I live from hand to mouth; sometimes rich, by accident—more often poor, from force of habit. Occasionally I do a good stroke of business on the Bourse, and occasionally the cards favour me. I have had fifty thousand francs at my disposal on the 10th of a month, and on the 15th have been without the means of paying my rent. All this is out-of-the-way and irregular, I know, but it is true, and, since you appear desirous of the truth, I have told you it."

" A sad truth, which will not tell in.your favour with a jury."

" A jury!" said Albert Savari, without being in the least moved by the word, which the magistrate had purposely used. "I trust I shall not have to appear before a jury. You cannot be long in recognising my entire innocence."

"We will deal with that question by-and-by. At present I am going on with your examination. Had you not on one previous occasion, when barely twenty-five years of age, to appear in a court of justice ? "

" Yes, in connection with a duel."

" In which you killed your adversary ? "

" That is true ; I had that misfortune, but I was acquitted."

" The proceedings in that matter stamped you already as a profligate ? "

" Ah, sir ! I was neither more nor less profligate than the young men with whom I lived, and who have since become men of honour, and steady withal. Some are physicians, others notaries, others magistrates. Ask them to tell you after what manner they lived between eighteen and twenty-five years of age, where they passed their evenings, what society they frequented, and if they will speak out they will be as open to the reproach of profligacy as I am."

" But you also had the reputation of being extremely violent ? "

" In that no mistake was made. Unfortunately for myself, I have ever been very violent."

" And you are not afraid of confessing it ? Such an admission is of great importance in connection with the matter now in hand."

"How that can be I am at a loss to understand, seeing that I have nothing to do with the present case."

M. Gourbet stopped, astonished by the coolness and natural demeanour of the man before him. In his extended career he had sometimes had to struggle with really great actors—some culprits had defended their liberty and their lives step by step, boldly for days together, pitting stratagem against stratagem, their shrewdness against his. But now he had to contend against novel tactics—the accused appeared to have called candour to his aid, and to be using it as a weapon of defence. Far from attempting to palliate his faults or his errors, he avowed them all without any bragging, but at the same time without whining; instead of attempting to put his questioner on a false scent as to his mode of life, he frankly admitted its irregularity.

"This man is either innocent, or he is endued with great energy and rare intelligence," mentally observed M. Gourbet, before resuming his examination.

"It was not only," he continued at length, "on the occasion of the duel that you came into collision with the law. There is another affair—"

"I was waiting for you to mention it, sir; I am here only to reply to your questions; you impressed that upon me, and I have not forgotten it."

"You are right. Be good enough, then, to tell me if you were ever mixed up in a gambling affair?"

"I was. The affair was, briefly, as follows. A young man lost sixty thousand francs at play, and, not being able to pay his creditors on the following day, accused them of having tampered with the cards; in other words, of having robbed him. Not a very uncommon occurrence—unlucky players, instead of blaming fortune and, sometimes, their own stupid system of playing, prefer to bring charges against their adversaries and make themselves out the dupes of roguery. This species of accusation spares them the neces-sity of paying their gaming debts, and they have therefore every advantage in appearing in the character of victims. In the case you mention, a complaint was lodged against a dozen individuals, of whom I happened to be one. We were taken before the public prosecutor, and examined ; the cards supposed to have been tampered with were produced, and the result of the uproar was that our calumniator paid his debts in full to us after a lapse of six months instead of on the day following his loss. It is but right to add that we requested him to send along with his bank notes a written apology for his conduct—a request with which he deemed it prudent to comply."

Albert Savari gave these details with such ease and in-difference, in a tone so genial, and he appeared so thoroughly comfortable in his chair that the registrar himself, for a mo-ment, forgot where he was, and, imagining himself in a drawing-room face to face with an agreeable talker, was surprised to find himself listening, instead of writing, as his duty was.

Behind the screen nothing betrayed the presence of Madame Vidal. She maintained, as she had promised, the strictest silence.

After some little reflection, M. Gourbet, not having any more preliminary questions to put to the accused, plunged into the heart of the matter with that abruptness which magistrates sometimes use, and which is calculated both to intimidate and confuse a prisoner.

"How did you pass the evening of the 19th October last?" was the sudden question put by him to Savari.

"How did you ?" was the reply.

This very unexpected answer was of a sort to irritate a magistrate, however long-suffering he might be. M. Gourbet rose, and, addressing the prisoner, said—"You forget, sir,

the respect due to the Law, which I at this moment repre-
sent. I shall at once give orders for your—"

"Sir," interrupted Savari in a firm voice, but with a tone
of perfect politeness intended to calm the legitimate irritation of his judge, "you have misunderstood the meaning of
my words, I assure you. I had not the slightest intention
of wounding a magistrate, who, though severe in manner and
language, I am bound to say has never for an instant been
wanting in courtesy and politeness. I merely wished, by
means of the question I asked in reply to yours, to make
you understand how difficult it was to answer you. You ask
me point-blank what I did with myself on the 19th
October, and I reply—'And you?' I am quite convinced
that, with the very best intentions, no one, suddenly thrust
into a corner, with an abrupt request to give an account of
his actions, would be able to comply with it."

"That depends very much on a man's mode of life,
whether more or less eventful," said M. Gourbet, reseating
himself. "The question you allude to, though embarrassing
to some, would not be so to all. But this conversation has
given you time to reflect; can you now reply?"

"I hope so, at all events. To the best of my belief, I
dined at the Café Anglais."

"Are you known there?"

"Perfectly, for several years past."

"At what hour do you think you left?"

"About eight o'clock, I should say."

"Be as precise as possible, I beg. Your replies are of
great importance, seeing that the crime under consideration
must have taken place between eight and nine o'clock," added
M. Gourbet, whose tactics for the moment were to appear
outspoken.

"If I had committed the crime," replied Savari, "I should
know at what hour I had committed it, and then I should have

told you that I had remained at the Café Anglais up to nine o'clock, and so have established an *alibi*."

"But your statement might have been very easily controverted."

"With very great difficulty, I imagine. The frequenters of the Café Anglais dine late ; it is by no means unusual to see people at the dinner-table towards nine o'clock, and out of half-a-dozen waiters at least half would in all good faith maintain that I was one of the last to leave. If, therefore, I say that I left the café about eight o'clock, I show my desire to approach as nearly as possible to the truth."

"Be it so. You left the Café Anglais at eight o'clock ; what did you do then ?"

"According to my custom, I must have strolled for an hour along the Boulevard des Italiens."

"Whom did you see there ? Did you stop to speak to any of your friends ? "

Albert Savari reflected for a moment in the most natural manner, and then replied—"No; I am under the impression that I walked by myself and did not meet anybody."

"That sounds strange," remarked the magistrate. "The weather was extremely fine on the 19th October, and there must have been, at nine o'clock in the evening, plenty of your acquaintances on the Boulevard des Italiens."

"Possibly so ; but fortune ordained that I should not see them. Besides, permit me to observe, that at nine o'clock in the evening the Boulevard des Italiens is less frequented than at any other moment ; people by that time have gone to the theatre, or their club, or some friend's house."

"After your hour's walk, where did you go, may I ask ?"

"I went home for a moment."

"According to you, that was at nine o'clock ?"

"About nine."

"Your porter, who has been examined since your arrest, asserts that he did not see you until towards ten o'clock."

"Nine, half-past, or ten, would be pretty much the same to a porter, who is asleep half his time in his lodge."

"And why did you go home, contrary to your usual habit, at that hour on that particular evening?"

"For a very simple reason, I had on a light overcoat and, as the evening had become chilly, I went to get a heavier one."

"Did you not put aside your light overcoat because it had on it certain stains which might compromise you?"

"Stains!" said Savari, with great unconcern. "What stains?"

"Two or three stains of blood. How do you account for them?"

"I do not account for them. I am positive they do not exist," replied Savari, firmly.

M. Gourbet had hoped that the prisoner, if he were guilty, would betray himself in face of this attack, and that he would attempt to give some sort of explanation with regard to these blood stains, accounting for them by his nose having been bleeding, or his hand cut, as murderers generally do under similar circumstances. Any such explanation would have damaged Albert Savari, and possibly have implicated him, seeing that, in spite of every effort, not a single trace of blood, such as M. Gourbet hinted at, could be discovered on the overcoat in question. So he had to put up with the failure of this new stratagem, either from the fact that Savari was innocent, as he maintained he was, or by reason of the subtlety and coolness which he possessed in no small degree. But, fearing that his ruse might be seen through, M. Gourbet was unwilling to abandon with too great haste the line of questioning he had adopted, so he told Savari that the coat would be submitted to the analysis of able chemists. This had no effect, either, on the prisoner, who simply turned towards the magistrate, as an intimation that he awaited the further progress of the examination.

M. Gourbet rose and paced to and fro, whilst Savari, who had also risen, leaned with his back against the mantel-piece, attentively studying the always impassable registrar. Suddonly M. Gourbet, remembering the presence of Julia Vidal, was anxious to know how she fared, and approached the screen. A look, unseen by all, sufficed to satisfy his curiosity. Julia, motionless as a statue, awaited in silence the conclusion of the examination. Her death-like pallor struck the magistrate, and recalled him to gravity.

M. Gourbet returned to his place at the desk, and, entering on a new train of thought, said—"You knew Maurice Vidal?"

"I did."

"For how long?"

"About three years."

"Under what circumstances did you know him?"

"One of our mutual friends, M. de Montoux, to whom I one day expressed my wish to speculate on the Bourse, suggested an introduction to M. Vidal. The latter gave me a very kind reception, and consented to execute my commissions."

"Without asking for any guarantee or security?"

"My word was sufficient, more especially as my commissions were on a very small scale, my differences on settling-day not exceeding one or two thousand francs."

"Such was not always the case, for it was not long before you lost a considerable sum."

"That is so. A political rumour which came to my cars induced me one day to depart from my customary caution. I sent M. Vidal, during business hours, an order which, unfortunately for me, he executed immediately. The rumour was false, and all my calculations were upset."

" How much did you lose over the transaction ? "

" Twenty thousand francs."

" My information says fifty thousand."

" Excuse me ; the first transaction which I have had the honour of explaining to you cost me twenty thousand francs. Subsequently I engaged in a second, and then a third, to recoup my loss, instead of which I increased my liabilities to the amount you have named."

" And M. Vidal made no attempt to stay this downward course, disastrous alike for you and himself, since the broker whom he employed would hold him responsible for your losses ?"

" M. Vidal had seen me discharge without delay certain other differences, not indeed equal in amount to these last, but still considerable, and he had no reason to doubt my solvency."

" And what was the result of all these losses ?"

" My account was handed to me in detail, and I was compelled to confess that I needed time to settle it."

" What was the reply of M. Vidal to that ?"

" I am bound to say that he took it in bad part."

" In reality, a lamentable scene took place on the Bourse between you and your creditor ?"

" Yes, sir."

" M. Cordier," said the magistrate to his registrar, " have the goodness to read over to the accused the report of the commissary of police of the Bourse section on this scene.

The little man took up a packet of papers from the table, and slowly read the report of which we have already given extracts. The reading over, M. Gourbet asked Savari if the report was correct.

" Entirely so," replied the prisoner.

" Then you admit that in consequence of your altercation

with M. Vidal, you gave him bills to the amount of fifty thousand francs ?"

"I did."

"What has become of those bills?" quickly asked the magistrate.

"They should have been found at my lodgings, since, I understand, they have been searched."

"Yes, they were so found, but how came they there ?"

"In a very simple way. I met them, and they were handed over to me."

"By whom?"

"By Maurice Vidal himself."

"When ?"

"The afternoon before his death, which was the morrow of the date when my bills became due."

"That is impossible ; you went to the Rue de la Paix, and nobody was at home."

"Yes, I was told that M. Vidal had gone out, and would not be home again until evening. But I was anxious to discharge my obligations to him. I knew that he regarded me with but little favour after our quarrel, and I feared the expense which might result, so I went in search of him, and found him."

"Where ?"

"In the Rue Vivienne, along which he was in the daily habit of walking when he left the Bourse. It must have been about half-past three."

"And it was there, in the street, that you paid him ? That is scarcely probable."

"Why? Securities of importance change hands every moment amongst men on the Bourse, on the staircase perhaps, or in the neighbouring streets. Fifty thousand francs don't take up much space."

"And I suppose you will say too that M. Vidal had about him your bills ?"

" I do.   He must have had them about him, seeing that he gave them up to me on the spot."

" That is hardly credible."

" Allow me to observe that my creditor, when I handed him the bills, warned me that he should proceed against me at once if they were not met on the day they became due. The day following that date had arrived without his having heard a word from me, and he had no doubt gone out with the bills in his pocket for the purpose of carrying out his threat."

M. Gourbet, evidently rendered impatient by these replies of Savari, reflected for a moment, and then resumed.

" This account, which, I admit, has been cleverly concocted by you, fails in one essential particular.   M. Vidal told several persons that he had no expectation of being repaid by you.   If that had happened, as you say it did, surely he would have lost no time in informing his friends of the pleasant intelligence."

" He would not have paid them a visit for that express purpose, and accident no doubt prevented his meeting them."

" There you are wrong.   He dined with one of them on the 19th October."

" Well," replied Savari, without being in the least disconcerted, " he must have been preoccupied with some other matter, or possibly he had his reasons for not publicly stating what had happened.   It is sometimes prudent to avoid mentioning to a friend that you have just received an unexpected sum of money.   That friend might attempt to borrow from you, and so put you to inconvenience or embarrassment."

" The latter feeling will never trouble you—you have always a reply, more or less happy, at command," replied M. Gourbet, this time visibly put out.   " What answer will you make to this question? How did you come by the fifty thousand francs which you pretend you repaid?"

The accused, who so far had replied without hesitation, was silent.

"Did you hear me?" asked M. Gourbet, "or are you under the necessity of arranging your reply?"

"Oh! sir," said Savari, with a smile, "if I needed to prepare my reply, I should have had, you must allow, time enough since the commencement of this long examination to do so. The question you have put is one of great importance, and I certainly anticipated it. My hesitation, however, proceeded from the fear that my reply may not satisfy you."

"It will not, then, be entirely satisfactory?"

"No, not to you, a practical man leading a regular life, and not disposed to allow of certain eccentric methods of raising money."

"Let us hear about these methods."

After having thus skilfully prepared the magistrate for what he was about to say, Savari proceeded—"I was for two months very much worried with respect to discharging my debt to M. Vidal. I knew that he was sufficiently ill-disposed towards me and I dreaded proceedings, the least result of which would have been the loss of my credit. I had then recourse to one of those methods, neither novel nor unusual with young Parisians in desperate cases, but which, as a rule, fail of success. At the beginning of October I sold some articles of jewellery and art treasures which I had contrived to save from the wreck of my effects at various times. I borrowed five-and-twenty louis from one friend and thirty from another, and thus managed to scrape together three thousand five hundred francs, with which I betook myself to Spa, where "roulette" and "trente et quarante" flourish. I hazarded a thousand francs there, and, thanks to a new system on which I had long been bent, I succeeded in winning nearly ten thousand francs in a couple of days."

The magistrate looked as if he did not believe a word of all this, but Savari did not appear to notice the effect which his tale had produced, and went on —

" From Spa I proceeded to Germany, stopping at Baden, Homburg, and Wiesbaden, playing at all these places with unbroken success. In short, after an absence of a few days, I returned to Paris on the 15th of October with a sum of fifty-five thousand francs, which I devoted to paying off my creditor in full. Such is my story—a very simple one in reality, but, unluckily for me, like anything truly simple, it appears at first sight exceedingly complicated."

" Undoubtedly so," replied the magistrate. " It has no weight with me, and since the facts you have adduced are incapable of being proved, they will not assist you in establishing your innocence."

" I beg your pardon—it can easily be proved that I left Paris at the beginning of October, that I stayed at Spa at an hotel near the ' Conversation ' Rooms, the Hotel d'Orange, I believe, where my name in full and other particulars are recorded. At Baden I occupied an apartment in the Hotel Victoria, and at Homburg, in the Hotel de Bellevue. Finally, if you wish, I can easily prove that I returned to Paris on the 15th."

" And how will you prove that you won fifty thousand francs ? "

" That is more difficult, I admit. Nevertheless, several people saw me both play and win."

" Germans, were they not, or Belgians, strangers or people unknown ; where will you find them again ? "

" Good heavens ! sir," cried Savari, with a certain amount of excitement as if he were annoyed at his word being so persistently doubted, " when I was seated at the gambling tables in Germany, I could not foresee that on my return to France I should be charged with murder, and that, in defence of my life and liberty, I should have to account for my luck in play. If I had foreseen any such thing, I should have taken care to forward every evening a declaration in form signed by those who held the bank and the croupiers."

Without replying to this outburst of sarcasm, during which the prisoner, for the first time since the commencement of the lengthy interview, lost some of his habitual calm, M. Gourbet rose, and, turning towards Savari, said to him—"My registrar will read over to you your examination, and will then ask you to sign it."

" Very well, sir, I am at your orders."

He brought his chair close to the desk of M. Cordier, and appeared to listen with unremitting attention.

Whilst this reading, which occupied more than half an hour and was not interrupted by a single remark from Savari, was going on, M. Gourbet, seated at his desk, was plunged in a deep reverie. He could not conceal from himself that, in spite of his efforts, he had utterly failed in penetrating the darkness surrounding the tragedy in the Rue de la Paix. Nay more, this darkness grew more and more dense. It was on Albert Savari that his suspicions had fallen ; of all the persons connected with this affair he was the only one on whom any possibility of guilt could be fixed, and he was escaping him. Yes, he was escaping him, or would very shortly do so, as it was evident that nothing, so to speak, but negative suspicions had been brought to bear against him. To the questions put to him he had not always replied in a thoroughly satisfactory manner, but none of his answers condemned him. If he had not given any certain proof of his innocence, neither could any serious evidence of his guilt be discovered.

M. Gourbet, without going beyond the bounds of legality, and without laying himself open to any reproaches of conscience, could still make use of rigorous measures with regard to Savari and could prolong his arrest, but he was fully conscious that no evidence had been brought against him sufficient to allow of his being actually committed for trial to an assize court.

All these reflections, with a magistrate as conscientious as M. Gourbet, signified much.

" Sir," said Savari to the registrar, when the reading of the examination was over, " the replies which I have had the honour of making to the magistrate have been transcribed by you with the most perfect exactness. I have nothing to say against these minutes of the proceedings, and I would sign them with both hands, if that were necessary."

He then rose, took the hat which he had put on the mantel-piece, and turned to M. Gourbet as if awaiting his orders.

" M. Savari," said the magistrate, evidently ill at ease and slightly put out by the polite manners of the accused, " I foresee that I shall have to put some further questions to you, and, pending that, I shall be obliged to keep you in arrest."

Albert Savari did not reply, contenting himself with a silent bow.

" But," added M. Gourbet, " I may in some degree render your position less unpleasant ; for instance, you will not be in solitary confinement."

" Oh ! solitary confinement does not frighten me. When one arrives at my age and has lived the life I have, isolation and the opportunity of recalling and reflecting on the past ought to be a matter for rejoicing. There is not much leisure in a Parisian existence—it is an incessant whirlpool of business or pleasure with time only to act, not to muse.

My captivity will be of advantage in that it will give my mind an interval of repose, and I shall emerge from prison, I hope, less excited, less feverish, and having gained in strength. So, whilst thanking you for your good intentions towards me, I beg of you most earnestly not to give them effect. Besides, I can assure you that I expect no visits; I have not a single intimate friend, and none of the companions of my pleasures will put themselves out, I know, to come and see me. If I could gain access for them to my prison, they might be tempted by curiosity, but an interview in a waiting room with which they doubtless would have to content themselves, would not be sufficiently attractive."

"As you please," replied the magistrate, bowing in his turn to Savari in token of their interview being at an end. Then turning to the registrar, he said, "Tell the persons who are in waiting outside that this prisoner is about to withdraw."

Savari comprehended the courtesy extended to him. He was to be allowed to leave the magistrate's office in the same way that he entered it, as a visitor and a man at large, not as a prisoner; he would only find his escort in the corridor. Bowing once more in acknowledgment of this piece of politeness, he opened the door himself and disappeared.

Then Julia Vidal, who had loyally kept her promise and had not interrupted the proceedings, so deeply interesting to her, by a word or a gesture, got up from her seat, pushed aside the screen which had concealed her, and advanced, looking pale and stern, towards M. Gourbet. When she was within two paces of him she stopped, and, stretching out her arm in the direction of the door through which Savari had passed, said with fierce energy: "The man who has just gone out through that door, the man you have just had under examination, is my husband's murderer!"

CHAPTER VIII.

WHEN he had recovered from his surprise on hearing this decided accusation hurled against a man whom he, a magistrate, was almost disposed to consider innocent, M. Gourbet endeavoured to persuade Julia that her grief had possibly rendered her unjust, and that her ardent desire to avenge her husband caused her to look upon everybody as guilty. To all the arguments brought to bear upon her she replied by these words : " I am not mistaken ; I am sure I am not."

" Did you notice," said the magistrate, " in the prisoner's attitude, or in his look, or his words, anything which escaped me ?"

" Nothing particular."

" Well, then, on what do you base your conviction, for it is more than a suspicion with you ?"

" On nothing, and on everything. From the moment that man entered the room I had within me an extraordinary sensation ; when he spoke my whole being thrilled. Why, if he were innocent, had he such an effect on me ? You have already confronted me with two accused persons, and I was calm enough then, but this man, Savari, is no stranger to me ; he is bound up intimately with my life—I have suffered through him, and I am certain, nay, I swear, I am destined to suffer again."

" You are an Italian, madame, and, therefore, somewhat of a fatalist."

" Possibly so, but at this moment I am logical. Whence comes the deep uneasiness which I felt in the presence of this man, whom I never saw and do not know? He is guilty—I tell you he is guilty !"

And her gestures, her attitude, the sound of her voice, the lightning glances flashing from her eyes, all served to strengthen this strange accusation. She was magnificent so; she might have been a priestess of ancient Italy, denouncing to the people a profaner of some sacred shrine.

Whilst M. Gourbet, rather dazzled, was looking at her and considering how best he could calm this excitement, an usher entered and handed him a paper.

" Is he there ?" asked the magistrate, after glancing at the paper.

" Yes, sir."

" Show him in."

A moment afterwards the door opened, and Vibert appeared. In his letter to the Marquis de X—— he has painted his own portrait, so we will not describe him afresh.

" You wished to speak to me," asked the magistrate, as the police agent made his respectful salutation.

" Yes, sir, I came to place myself at your orders in connection with the Rue de la Paix murder."

" It was you, then, who called at this lady's house," said the magistrate, pointing to Julia.

" Certainly, but I was not admitted," replied Vibert, looking over his blue spectacles in the same direction.

" Are you acquainted with this affair in all its details ?"

" Nearly so, sir. I was one of the first to enter the room in the Rue de la Paix, a few moments after the crime was discovered."

" I remember now, the commissary of police of the Tuileries section mentioned you in his report, did he not ?"

" Possibly."

" And he also mentioned, it appears to me, certain suspicions, entertained by you in the first instance ?"

"Suspicions both absurd and very much regretted by me," quickly replied Vibert, interrupting the magistrate, and casting a look full of repentance on Madame Vidal. "I can only say, in my excuse, that I entertained them but for an instant. They are fixed now in another direction."

"Ah, where?"

"On the same individual as your own are, sir, since you caused him to be arrested yesterday."

"You mean Albert Savari?"

"Yes, sir."

"Here are the minutes of his examination, just concluded, read them attentively."

Vibert seated himself in the chair of the registrar, who had gone out, adjusted his spectacles on his nose, leaned his elbows on the table with his head between his hands, and was soon absorbed in his reading. Meanwhile M. Gourbet, seated before the fire, conversed with Julia.

"Well, what do you think of it?" asked the magistrate, when Vibert got up from his chair after the lapse of a quarter of an hour.

"Am I allowed to speak plainly?"

"Certainly."

"Then, I think that it would be impossible to hope for a conviction, or even to commit the prisoner to the Assizes upon what appears on the face of these minutes."

"I agree with you. The proper order to make is that there is no ground for further proceedings."

"But if to these points others are linked?" added Vibert.

"Have you any?" asked the magistrate with interest.

"No, sir, but I will both seek and find some."

"If only you are on the right scent," said M. Gourbet, "if this Savari is guilty—"

"He is!" cried Madame Vidal suddenly. She had not lost a word of this conversation, which indeed was carried on aloud.

"Ah!" said the police agent, turning quickly to Julia, " Madame is convinced of the guilt of the accused ? "

" Yes, convinced ! "

" Bravo !" exclaimed Vibert, forgetting the magistrate's presence and giving rather loud vent to his joy. " Bravo ! Savari is lost, I am sure now of finding proofs against him."

M. Gourbet could not help looking curiously at this peculiar police agent, who brought candour and enthusiasm into the exercise of a profession ordinarily marked by dissimulation and reserve.

But he had not yet come to the end of his surprises. Vibert, who, after his boisterous outburst of joy, set to work to reflect, all at once put his hand to his forehead as if he had found an idea, and said—" The learned magistrate probably observed, during his examination of the prisoner, that the latter was a match for him ? "

" Undoubtedly," replied M. Gourbet, "innocent or guilty, Savari is a man of great intelligence."

" Then," replied Vibert, " we shall make no headway so long as he is in prison."

" Why ? "

" Because a man of his metal will not be beaten by a few days, or even a few weeks' imprisonment on suspicion. As for expecting him to make a confidant of a fellow prisoner, he is not the man to do that. It does sometimes happen that an ordinary criminal or an old offender falls in, whilst in the cells, with an old comrade, and confides in him, and that this old comrade is what is called a *mouton*, a man who will tell the police everything. By this means important information is occasionally obtained, but nothing of the kind can be anticipated in the present case. Savari is not likely to meet, either in the Conciergerie or in any other prison, with anybody he knows, and therefore he will maintain absolute silence."

" Well, what conclusion do you draw from that ? "

" If you will allow me, sir, to offer you advice, I should say that the prisoner should be set at liberty without delay."

" And what then do you anticipate ? Do you think that he will commit himself any the more because he is free ? "

" There will be a better chance of his doing so when he is free."

" And if terrified by what has already happened to him, and fearing a second arrest, he absconds—what then ? "

" That is not likely, sir ; if he had wished to escape, he would have attempted it after having committed the crime, always supposing, of course, that he did commit it. He must have relied upon his shrewdness and self-possession to counteract all your efforts, and he will have far more confidence in himself now that, after having been once in the hands of justice, he has escaped out of them. Besides all this, Savari is one of those genuine Parisians to whom the air of Paris is indispensable, who do not know how to live anywhere else, and who will face any danger rather than fly into exile. This is not the case amongst men of his class only—how many criminals there are who would be perfectly safe abroad, or even in any of the Departments of France, but who risk their liberty and lives to breathe once more the air of Paris, so necessary, apparently, for their lungs. I am still still supposing Savari to be guilty, and I imagine he would say to himself—' I have committed a crime which may send me to the scaffold. What line of conduct shall I adopt ? Shall I fly ? That would be an avowal of guilt. If I were captured en route, which is quite possible, it would be all over with me. If I succeed in escaping, I shall have to vegetate abroad without means of existence. Better stay where I am, and run the risk of arrest. I am too clever not to get out of the scrape somehow.' That is just what he has done. Of course," continued Vibert, after taking breath, for warming with his subject, he had spoken with a certain amount of volubility, "I propose, whilst liberating the prisoner, to subject him to close supervision. I will take charge of that, and he shall never know it."

"Be it so," said the magistrate, "I grant for the sake of argument that the prisoner is set at liberty and that you are appointed to watch him. What then do you propose, what is your plan of action?"

"My plan? That has to be carefully thought out at leisure. But I feel here," striking his forehead, "I feel here that it will succeed."

M. Gourbet looked at Vibert. His complexion, as a rule wan, had brightened; his eyes sparkled through his spectacles, his figure was drawn up, and he appeared convinced of what he said, and sure of his business. The magistrate, with his vast experience of men, saw at once that he had to deal with one of those police agents who treat their profession as an art which they love, and who are capable, when employed with tact, of rendering inestimable services to society. At once he resolved to secure the assistance of so valuable an ally, and though it is not customary for magistrates of his class to deal directly with police agents, or to entrust special duties to them, he resolved, under the peculiar circumstances of the case in hand, to depart from the beaten track.

"So you consider yourself sure of success?" said he, turning to the *protégé* of the Marquis de X—.

"If Savari is guilty," replied Vibert without any hesitation, "I hold myself responsible for bringing to you the proofs of his guilt. But I must stipulate certain conditions."

"Let us hear them," said the magistrate, who was becoming accustomed to Vibert's original manner of dealing with him.

"First of all, it is understood that he will be set at liberty to-morrow."

"That step may possibly be taken, but I must think over it."

"It would also be advisable to send a paragraph from the public prosecutor's office to the various legal newspapers, announcing his release from custody. These paragraphs should contain an expression of regret on the score of any charge having been brought against Savari, and an apparent conviction of his innocence after his one examination. That will prevent his suspecting a trap ; he will think himself perfectly free, and will be less careful of his sayings and doings."

"I approve of your idea," said M. Gourbet, compelled to admire the foresight of the agent.

"And what then ?"

"Then ? Ah, sir," said Vibert, "there comes the difficult part of the affair. I wish to have my hands entirely free in this matter, to be, for some time, free from all control, not to be interfered with by orders either from the public prosecutor's office, or the Prefecture of Police, and to have at my disposal such funds as may be necessary in case I should be compelled, in order not to lose sight of the accused, to adopt certain habits of luxury and dissipation."

"I will talk over your requests with the proper authorities, and I hope they will be acceded to."

"Then, sir, I have nothing to do but withdraw, and await your decision; if it is in my favour, I will at once arrange my plan of action, and take the field."

He said these words with the decided air of a general setting out for some great expedition, and taking leave of the Minister of War. Then, turning to Julia, who had been a silent listener during the whole of the interview, and in whose eyes Vibert, by his assurance and his promises, had assumed magnificent proportions, he said to her—

"Madame, I shall need an interview with you, shortly,

perhaps. Will you kindly give orders that I may be admitted ?"

"Certainly," said Madame Vidal, "I shall be at home whenever you present yourself."

Vibert bowed and disappeared noiselessly while Julia was taking leave of the magistrate.

CHAPTER IX.

THE various requests put forward by Vibert must have been acceded to, for, on the following day, this paragraph appeared in the *Gazette des Tribunaux* :—

"M. Albert S——, who was yesterday reported in our columns as being implicated in the murder in the Rue de la Paix, and against whom a warrant was issued, was almost immediately released, after an examination which disposed of every charge brought against him. From private information which we have received, it would, moreover, appear that the law has made up its mind on this subject, and the real culprit, who is known to have absconded to a foreign country, will not be long before he is discovered, and delivered up, extradition being an easy matter in cases of murder. Our readers may rest assured that we shall keep them informed of all the intelligence which may reach us so long as it is not of a nature to hamper the action of justice."

The good faith of this paragraph was entirely believed in, and the opposition journals (we are on the eve of the Revolution of February, be it remembered), did not neglect such a golden opportunity of reading the government a lesson. They expressed an immense amount of pity for the lot of M. Savari, and held him up as the wretched victim of another judicial mistake.

In Paris the most trivial occurrences sometimes assume gigantic proportions. An event is exaggerated to-day, because to-morrow it may no longer be food for gossip. For a week, therefore, Savari became a political personage, a martyr; his forty-eight hours' confinement was deplored as if he had been twenty years in a convict prison, and he was within an ace of being compared to Lesurques.

The *National* newspaper profited by the circumstance to fulminate a sensational article, which created quite a stir. Amongst our mass of documents relating to this case we came across this article, and we reproduce it entire—

" So, a citizen is spending his evening quietly at home, his feet on the fender, thinking of what has happened to-day or will happen to-morrow, when all of a sudden there is a loud knocking at his door, his domicile is invaded, his desk forced open, his most private papers read, and his inner life broken into. A gentleman in a scarf, aided by certain sinister satellites, is the presiding genius of this execution. And if the citizen, whose dwelling is thus violated, inquires the reason of all this harshness, he is told that it is no concern of his, that there is no account to be rendered to him, and that he can talk later on to the proper authorities. If he exclaims against this, if his blood gets up, and if, strong in his innocence, he dares to resist the gentleman in the scarf, the others throw themselves upon him, hurry him into a cab, and, if necessary, handcuff him. ' To the Conciergerie ' or ' to La Force,' they say to the driver, and very soon the prisoner finds himself mad with rage and grief, in a hideous room.

"There he is searched, his pockets emptied, his surname and Christian name taken down, not a word of explanation is vouchsafed to him, and at last he is led to a dungeon, and

the door closes upon him. He is in solitary confinement !
Solitary confinement ! a terrible word, and yet more terrible
thing, which means a leaden coffin for the living ! An instrument of torture to enfeeble the brain and crush the soul, as
the thumbscrew and the iron boot were wont to crush the
body !

"There he remains for a whole day, perhaps two, without
a word. Forty-eight hours—a century ! A century, during
which he has not seen a living person—he asks himself if it
is all a dream, or if, in a raving fever, he has been sent to
Bicêtre.

"At length he hears a step—some one approaches—gendarmes escort him—he traverses gloomy passages, ascends
winding staircases, and finds himself at last before the magistrate.

"'You are accused,' somebody says to him, 'of having
assassinated M. X——.'

"'M. X——? I? When?'

"'Eight days ago.'

"'Where?'

"'In the Rue Dauphine, in Paris.'

"'But eight days ago I was at Marseilles with my family.
All the world can vouch for it. I had only just returned
when I was arrested by your order.'

"'How is this? An *alibi?* Can you prove it? Why did
you not say so before?'

"'Before? To whom? Who has asked me a single
question? I have been imprisoned, and that is all.'

"'If, sir, you are speaking the truth, there will be no
delay in restoring to you your liberty.'

"'In doing that you will be merely giving me my due.
But what else will you give me?'

"'I do not understand you.'

"'Yes, who is to compensate me for the tortures I have

just undergone, for the discredit which will cling to me, for the bargains I was about to make which I have now lost? And my children, who have seen their father dragged to prison; and my aged mother, whom the least excitement might kill, and who no doubt is dead by this time? What do you think of all that? Do you imagine you have cried quits with me by saying—'We were mistaken, you can go home?'

"'You were thought guilty, sir; there were proofs against you, and the authorities have done their duty.'

"'No, sir, instead of issuing a warrant, you should have confined yourself to a summons.'

"'And if, being guilty, and afraid of the consequences of your guilt, you had attempted to fly?'

"'Then you could have arrested me, and you would have had justice on your side. It is too often forgotten in France that an accused person is not necessarily guilty, that some consideration is due to him, and that, instead of dragging him before the magistrate, the magistrate should question him at his own house, and not arrest him until after the examination, and then only if just grounds for such a course are shown.'

"'That is often done.'

"'And it should always be done.'"

All these articles were nuts to Vibert. "Savari," said he to himself, "cannot imagine that he is still an object of suspicion, and under supervision. He will forget his reserve, he will make a mistake, and I shall have him in my clutches." And the new agent of police smiled, smacked his lips and rubbed his hands.

CHAPTER X.

Three days after the examination of Albert Savari, a man of about thirty years of age, with free-and-easy air, blue glasses on his nose, wearing several foreign orders, and with a decent sort of stick in his hand, knocked at the door of the widow, Madame Vidal. Marietta answered the door.

"I wish to speak to your mistress," said the unknown.

"It is only nine o'clock, and Madame Vidal is not visible yet," said Marietta.

"I am come on important business."

"Who are you?"

"Your mistress would not know my name; tell her merely that I am the person she met in the magistrate's office."

"Oh! that makes all the difference. My mistress has spoken of you, and told me to admit you whenever you called."

She now threw the door, which she had up to that time prudently held just ajar, wide open, and showed the unknown in. But, as they were entering the drawing-room, she stopped and said—"You, probably, do not wish to be seen by any one but my mistress."

"Quite so, as far as possible."

"There are some people in this room, for ever since my master's death there has been no getting rid of the lawyers and notaries—"

"I will wait in the dining-room."

"No, everybody will see you as he passes out. Have the goodness to follow me."

She crossed a small passage, opened a door, and said—" I
will inform my mistress that you are here, and she will see
you as soon as she is disengaged."

Vibert (whom the reader has by this time recognised), as
soon as he was alone, looked about him. He found himself in
an elegant dressing-room, one of those charming nooks, thoroughly private, luxuriously furnished, redolent of a thousand
sweet scents, where only a subdued light can penetrate. The
upholsterers of Paris have a speciality, peculiar to themselves, for this species of oasis, not to be found either in the
provinces or abroad. As a rule, the life of a Parisian gentleman is entirely away from home; he is the visitor rather
than the visited; he is never to be found in his drawing-
room, except on special occasions; he gets up, dresses
himself, and rushes to his business; he comes home, dresses
afresh, and betakes himself to his pleasures. Of all the
rooms in his dwelling, his dressing-room is the most used,
and, consequently, he takes great pleasure in adorning it.

On a long table of white marble shine magnificent ewers
in porcelain and silver, bottles of all kinds, elegant caskets,
ivory-backed brushes of all sizes, and for all purposes. On
the mantel-piece is a clock of exquisite workmanship. Vene-
tian mirrors are on the walls, here is a statuette by Clodion,
and, scattered about are a travelling bag from Aucoc's, a
glove-box, a fan, a riding whip, opera glasses, a Russian
leather cigar case, and a half-open book. It is a pleasure to
be amidst this pell-mell of elegant disorder; there we can
lay our hands at once on the various articles to which we
are accustomed; here we feel at home, at our ease, and
realise what laziness is, and the luxury of the *far niente*, and
the delight of lying at full length in a dressing-gown, and
toasting our feet.

Maurice Vidal, when he was young, had, probably, tasted
the enjoyment to be derived from a well-ordered dressing-

room, and on his marriage had wished his wife to taste it also. He took a delight in furnishing this portion of his suite of rooms, and in adorning it with all the thousand and one nothings which he could collect. It was perhaps a boudoir and a museum together, rather than a dressing-room, but it was charming.

Seated in a large, roomy chair, with his hat and cane between his knees, Vibert, whilst waiting for Madame Vidal, was gazing with all his eyes. This sober individual, almost austere, simply both by reason of his temperament and his pocket, had never found himself in such a scene. Whilst performing his duties as secretary to a commissary of police, he had frequently had to present himself in luxurious abodes; he had found himself in a drawing-room glittering with rich gilding, and had walked upon elaborate carpets, but he had never before been brought in contact with the inner life of a woman of the world, and that woman a pretty one. So this was a perfect revelation for him; he experienced all the astonishment, the surprise, the delight of a child with a new toy, of a school boy in love for the first time, of a respectable woman drawn by curiosity to a masked ball, or of a shop-keeper clandestinely introduced behind the scenes of a theatre.

Sometimes he did not content himself with looking, but got up and handled one of the wonders spread around him, examining it, weighing it, and, as it were, inhaling it. He might well have been taken for a lover waiting for his mistress, and becoming intoxicated with his recollections of the past and his hopes in the future. And whilst he gave himself up to this mental inventory a myriad odours mounted to his brain; a *sachet d'iris*, a bottle with the stopper out, a dressing-case of Russian leather, and a sandal-wood fan yielded up to him their scents. By degrees he lost his head entirely, and remembered no longer that he was there on business.

The door of the dressing-room opened, and Vibert was recalled once more to a sense of his duty. It was Marietta, who came in search of him to conduct him to the presence of Madame Vidal.

"I regret having kept you waiting so long," said Julia to him, as soon as she saw him; "but I wished to be perfectly free before seeing you, and now I am at your service."

"You have seen last evening's papers?" said Vibert, without further preamble, after having taken a seat.

"Yes," she replied, "and from them I have gathered that Albert Savari is at liberty."

"In fact the magistrate decided to listen to me, and an order has been made that there is no ground for further proceedings."

"And, now, what hope have you?"

"Much, if you will help me."

"I?"

"Yes you, madame."

"Oh! sir," said Julia, with energy, "my duty, the sole end and aim of my life—are they not all devoted to the fulfilment of the last wishes of my husband—to avenge him? I have been told to trust to you; I do so, and I am with you body and soul."

"Then, madame, we shall succeed—we shall succeed," and in saying so Vibert seized Julia's hands in his own, and shook them warmly.

She let him do so without showing the least astonishment or aversion. Vibert was to her not a man, nor a police agent; he was an accomplice, an avenger.

They seated themselves opposite to one another, and Vibert resumed—"After three days' reflection, you still think that Albert Savari assassinated your husband?"

"Indeed, I do. And you?"

"Yes, I too. I will go further than that—my suspicions

are now almost certainties, but purely moral certainties, and, as you are aware, we must have material proof."

"Have you discovered any method of procuring such proof?"

"Yes, but I need your aid."

"It is yours."

"Do not forget that you will have to display immense energy."

"I have plenty."

"Great patience."

"I will have that, too."

"You will have to conquer your natural repugnance to many things."

"I will do so when the necessity arises."

"The plan which I have conceived, moreover, will appear to you detestable, insane, horrible; you will recoil from it at first."

"What does that matter, if I adopt it in the end, and it succeeds?"

"Then listen."

"I am all attention."

And so that she might not miss a word, she seated herself on the sofa beside Vibert. They might have been a couple of lovers on the eve of an interchange of tender sentiments.

"You must know, first of all, madame," said Vibert, after a moment's reflection, "that I have not lost sight of Albert Savari since his release from prison. At my request notice was sent me of the hour when he would be set at liberty, and I awaited him at the gates of the Conciergerie. No sooner was he outside than he jumped into a cab, and I followed him, and for the last three days, none of his movements have escaped me. Whilst I am here with you one of my myrmidons, dressed as a commissionaire, has taken up his post at the corner of the street, and is watching the house, so you see, he cannot escape us. But, in putting in force this incessant surveillance, I have not neglected other points no less important, and likely to be of the greatest use to us. I have been initiating myself into the life passed by Albert Savari, and have been drawing together all the threads which he imperfectly exposed to the magistrate. The conclusion I have formed is that Savari has never, during the whole of his existence as a young man, been in love with any woman."

"How does that concern us?" said Julia.

"Very deeply," was the reply; "and you will be convinced of that if you listen to me."

"Proceed, then."

"There is indeed one woman at whose house Savari is a constant visitor. The lady in question is one Pélagie d' Ermont, perfectly known to the police. This Pélagie has recourse for her livelihood to a walk of industry very popular with some ladies—she gives tea parties."

"What do you mean by that?" interrupted Julia.

"I do not wonder at your asking, since you cannot be familiar with all our Parisian manners and customs. A lady who gives tea parties invites to her house, once or twice a week, some of her female friends, amongst whom she is careful to select the youngest and prettiest. As soon as these invitations are out she sends others, to all the men of her acquaintance. To one she says, 'You will meet Cora;' to another, 'The lovely Olympe will be here; come and bring your friends, and we will spend a pleasant evening.' Thus allured, her friends and her friends' friends flock to the house. They laugh, they talk, they drink tea, and then one of the ladies casually proposes a game at 'lansquenet'— only a mild game, with a five franc piece as the first stake. 'Come and sit by me,' says Olympe, to some young man, whom she has completely vanquished. 'Come—I'll bring you good luck, and you shall win all night.' The youth takes his seat, his friends follow his example; they pull a louis out of their pockets and lose it, and then another, which goes the same way. At 2 a.m. the stakes, which were not to exceed five francs, have jumped up to fifty, or a hundred, and bank notes have taken the place of louis. At 5 a.m. neither bank notes, nor louis, are to be seen on the table; everybody declares he has lost, and, nevertheless, all the money has disappeared. In its place counters, cheques, and I. O. U.s appear. At 11 a.m., jaded and tired to death, the guests take their departure, with losses amounting to three, five, ten thousand francs. As for the mistress of the house she had gone to bed, about 5 a.m., after having carefully stowed away in her capacious pockets all the louis and bank notes in circulation up to that hour, which help to pay for the tea so generously provided."

"I understand," said Julia, who had been listening attentively.

"But," continued Vibert, "amongst the men gathered together by the lady in question there are some who are on intimate terms in the establishment. They have long been familiar with the manner and customs in vogue, and they know perfectly well what a five franc commencement means. They know that it is prudent to 'pass' when Cora cries *banquo*, and that a drawn game with Olympe is dangerous. They know also to a minute when it is prudent to withdraw the louis and bank notes from circulation, and that moment is not lost. So without having, generally speaking, committed any act of dishonesty, properly so called, they rarely lose, and never refuse the invitations which the mistress of the establishment sends them; for they are skilled in attracting other gamblers, in keeping up the excitement, and in raising the stakes. These last details will sufficiently explain to you, madame, the character of the relations which, according to rumour, exist between Savari and Pélagie d' Ermont; you have divined that it is, as far as they are concerned, a simple question of interest. Savari is certainly not in love with her."

"But what do you wish to convey by all this?" said Julia, impatient on account of her failure to comprehend Vibert's drift.

"I conclude that if he has never loved he ought to be, of all men, susceptible of the tender passions."

"Well! whom do you wish him to love?"

"You, madame."

"I!"

"Yes, you."

"I?" repeated Julia, who imagined she had not heard aright.

"It is the only means we have of arriving at the truth. Savari does not know you, and, consequently, will not suspect you. You will enter into his life; you will be a partaker in his existence; you will gain an insight into his past, and, little by little, you will unmask him. With such an adversary as ours, ordinary means would fail. Something," he added, looking fixedly at Julia, who had not recovered from her surprise, "unforeseen, something out of the way and extraordinary, is necessary. I have sought for such a thing, and I think I have found it. You will be the Delilah of this new Samson, you will shear his locks, and he will deliver himself into the hands of the Philistines."

"But this scheme is altogether a mad one," cried Julia.

"I admit it."

"It cannot be realised."

"As for that I will be responsible, with your assistance."

"I should need superhuman courage."

"And you will have it."

"I should betray myself."

"Never! If you adopt my plan you will have but one sole idea—success. Savari will be the one to betray himself, and your husband will be avenged."

And as Julia, pale and in a fever of excitement, did not reply, he took up his hat and his cane, which he had deposited in a corner of the room, and, going towards the door said—"I will return to-morrow, at the same hour. If you tell me, as I hope you will, that you adopt my scheme, I shall have the honour of unfolding it to you more in detail."

"But—," said Julia, as if she wished to detain her visitor.

"Until to-morrow," said he, and he left the room.

CHAPTER XI.

Towards the end of October the Marquis de X—, one of whose interesting letters we have already made public, wrote to his *protégé*, Vibert, thus :—

"I give you my word, most trusty youth, that the contents of your last letter have roused my curiosity. I was beginning to be terribly bored when you appeared on the scene to cheer me up a bit. It is very good of you, and, with a little more amusement at your hands, I shall end by putting you in my will, to the detriment of my nephew, a great over-grown booby who has so far forgotten himself as to air his Liberal ideas in my presence. Yes, he has even dared to cast in my teeth that I am behind the age.

"Zounds! that is a phrase which might easily cost him two or three millions of francs. Behind the age! And why? Because I said the Jardin du Roi instead of the

Jardin des Plantes, and the Rue d'Artois in place of the Rue Lafitte. What does it matter so long as I walk in the Rue Lafitte, and take part from time to time in the saturnalia that take place there?

"Behind my age—I! I not only belong to the present generation, but to that also which is to come, and in it I predict a few creditable catastrophes.

"Ah, my dear nephew, you will have some news of it to tell me, if God grants you life, which is not probable, seeing that you are fading away and are already developing premature decay. Yes, you belong thoroughly to your generation; nobody would argue that point with you.

"But here I am, talking of family matters to you. Am I in my dotage, or is it that—I stop short here, for if there is a secret between us two you will soon discover it. M. Vibert, you are bloodhound enough for that. And now let us hark back to our text.

"I have reflected deeply on the plan which you have conceived and communicated to me. Between ourselves, it is absurd, impossible, senseless, but—it will succeed, if for that reason only. Ah! if your pretty widow of the Rue de la Paix were a Parisian, I should say to you—devil a bit, my dear friend; she is incapable of carrying such a scheme to a prosperous end, she will take the first opportunity of rounding on you and showing you up as a fool for your pains.

"But she is an Italian, a Northern Italian, a Genoese. Those women are to be trusted; they have not yet degenerated, as many of their countrywomen and all our own have. They are not mere drawing-room dolls, they are women, true women.

"Go on your way with this one; you will arrive at your destination, and it is I who say so. She will deliver this Savari up to you; she will dissect him, and there will not be a bit of him left.

"Your idea of comparing them to Delilah and Samson is very happy. Upon my honour, for a man of your time you are not quite a fool, and you deserve to have lived under the old régime.

"But, tell me, has she accepted the plan you proposed to her? Your last letter stopped at the most interesting point; you might be writing a novel in instalments, another nice invention of modern times! Quick, quick, send me a line putting me in possession of all that passed at your last interview with her. At my age, alas! I cannot live on my own account; help me to live in the life of others. You will not regret it; men of my stamp do not forget services rendered; ingratitude is a recent invention.

"P.S.—This Government of July is going on badly enough, and moreover, it has no money. The life that you are going to lead will put you to a great expense, which, believe me, your secret service allowance will not cover, notwithstanding all the promises made to you. Draw on me; do not let it bother you; I am not going to economise for my ass of a nephew. Behind my age, indeed! The idiot! He might as well have called me a blockhead at once. But, *par la sambleu*, he shall pay for it."

Vibert lost no time in replying—

"I called on Madame Vidal, M. le Marquis, at ten o'clock in the morning of the day before yesterday, as I had arranged with her on the previous evening. This time I had not to wait. She joined me at once, and told me without delay that she had reflected well over my scheme, and, seeing that other means were wanting, accepted it.

"'Very well, madame,' I replied.

"Then, without further loss of time, we sat down, face to face, and discussed an infinity of details. Two hours afterwards I left her and entered forthwith on the campaign. The first thing I had to do was to prepare the ground, and study the position of the enemy so as to join issue with him at once, and attack him with the advantage on our side.

"In our last conversation on paper I had the honour, M. le Marquis, of introducing to you a certain Pélagie d'Ermont. I told you that there was a bond of union between her and Albert Savari, and I explained to you the nature of it. It was this Madame d'Ermont that I proposed to circumvent first of all; in her house, if my projects were successful, Madame Vidal and Savari would meet for the first time. And this is how I set about it.

"Yesterday, at 2 p.m., I knocked at the door of No. 10, Rue Blanche, the residence of Pélagie. If you had met me on the staircase, M. le Marquis, notwithstanding all your shrewdness and all your rare qualities of observation, I can assure you that you would not have recognised me. I had put on an entirely new skin. I was got up as a foreigner, quite *comme il faut*, but a flat, if I may make use of the expression. Any moderately sharp woman would have said, on seeing me—'Here's a nice pigeon to pluck!'

"My toilet may be described in a few words—black frock coat, cravat, and waistcoat, dark trousers, lavender kid gloves, crape on my hat, patent leather boots, a gold watch chain meandering over my waistcoat, a diamond pin in my cravat, another diamond on my right hand, which was left ungloved, and a stick with a gold knob set with turquoises.

"You will see, M. le Marquis, that it is the guise at once of a rich man and a foreigner who is not versed in our customs—one of those sensational costumes, so called because of their effect upon certain of the fair sex. It is unnecessary to add to you that both diamonds and turquoises were excellent shams.

"'Can I see Madame d'Ermont?' I asked.

"'I do not know. Will you be good enough to give me your name?' said a very wide-awake looking soubrette.

"I put on a puzzled air, as if I was a novice in the French language, and then I answered with as strong an Italian accent as my intercourse for the last few days with Madame Vidal had enabled me to catch.

"'My name is not known to your mistress, but I have letters of introduction to her from several of her friends. I have just arrived from Naples, and if you will kindly give her my card—'

"I handed her a card stamped with a crest, which I had been careful to procure on the previous evening, and the soubrette, after showing me into an elegant drawing-room, went to inform her mistress.

"I had now fairly penetrated into the fortress, and Madame d'Ermont was not long in putting in an appearance. She is a fair, plump, little woman, so thoroughly made up that it is impossible to say whether she is pretty or not. Her features are, nevertheless, refined, and at one time she must have been really attractive. She was dressed in a long dressing-gown of blue silk, which clung close to the curves of her well-developed figure.

"'I am delighted, count,' said she, looking at the card which I had sent in and she held still in her hand, 'to make your acquaintance; pray be seated. You are recommended to me, you say, by—'

"'By several of your friends, madame; the Marquis de Santa Vicchini, amongst others.'

"'Ah! the dear marquis. I have not seen him for five or six years. Is he well?'

"'Invariably so, madame, invariably.'

"'You are just from Naples, count?'

"'Direct, madame.'

"'And you have already thought of paying me a visit. That is charming.'

"'I have heard so much of you.'

" 'Ah, you are a flatterer, I see. We are going to quarrel at once,' said she, with a simper.

" 'I should be in despair in that case. Remember that I have neither acquaintance nor friend in Paris.'

" 'Poor young man! But consider my house your own. And what, if may I ask, are you going to do amongst us?'

" 'I am come for amusement, madame. I have experienced much trouble, having in the last few months lost my nearest relatives. You see I am in mourning.'

" 'Indeed! And have you made up your mind to reside permanently amongst us?' she asked with interest.

" 'Possibly; if Paris pleases me.'

" 'You are aware that pleasure in Paris—nay, living well at all—is expensive.'

" 'That is a matter of little importance, provided I enjoy myself.'

" At this reply, uttered with an air of entire simplicity, Madame d'Ermont edged a little closer to me.

" 'And in what direction do your tastes lie?' she inquired. 'I must try to satisfy them, since you are sent to me by my friends.'

" 'Upon my word, madame, I think I like everything that is good and everything that is pretty.'

" 'Ah! say you so? Then you will not be difficult to please. But surely you have preferences of some kind.'

" 'So I have.'

" 'What are they?'

" 'You wish to know them?'

" 'Certainly.'

" 'Well, then, I adore ladies' society.'

" 'I fancied so when I saw you.'

" 'How was that?'

" 'It is natural,' replied Pélagie, doing her best to cast down her eyes, 'that one should be pleased in the midst of those whom we please.　Confess—you ought not to have met many cruel women.'

"I must say, M. le Marquis, that this was the first time I had been paid such a compliment.　I must have been marvellously disguised.　Would you believe that I was fool enough to enter, for a moment, so thoroughly into my assumed character that I blushed?　Do not laugh at me. When the substance is unattainable, we must make the best of the shadow.

"In order not to be behind-hand in politeness with Madame d'Ermont, I took hold of one of her hands, which found its way into mine, and said—

"'Success in Italy goes for nothing—it is in Paris that I long to triumph.'

"'In Paris—nothing easier,' she replied, pretending not to understand me; 'we Parisians are not much more ferocious than your country-women, and if you wish, I can give you an opportunity of meeting some of the most charming of their sex.'

"Pélagie who, encouraged by my stupidity, had no doubt made her plans, resumed quickly—'It so happens that I am giving a tea party this evening to some of my intimate friends, and if you will consent to make one of us—'

"'Alas, madame, all my evenings are taken up; I am not alone in Paris.'

"'Are you married?' she asked, in a tone which did its utmost to appear agitated.'

"'No, thank heaven!' I replied, with a tender glance.

"'Then what hinders you from accepting my invitation?'

"'I came from Naples with a female relative; she does not know a soul in Paris, and I cannot leave her to spend her evenings alone in a hotel.　But—I have it!' cried I, suddenly changing my tone.　'You are so good-natured to me that, perhaps, you would permit me?'

" ' What ? '

" ' To introduce my relative to you.'

" Pélagie was dumbfounded. The blow which I had struck was, indeed, a daring one—to give myself out as a man of the world, and to seek to introduce one of my female relations to Madame d'Ermont, was a dreadful piece of inconsistency. But I was a foreigner, unacquainted with Parisian customs, and I did not appear to be gifted with much *nous*. Pélagie might easily think that I was ignorant of the exact position she occupied in society. With the assistance of her *amour-propre*, she would not, after a little reflection, be very much astonished at my mistake, and it was not at all probable that she would, of her own accord, try to set me right.

" My calculations were exact ; Madame d'Ermont, having recovered her first astonishment, replied—' Very well, my dear count, bring your relation. I shall be flattered by her visit. Only give her warning that it will be a gathering of very intimate friends. In my house there is no dancing, nor does anybody play the piano—we merely chat. But sometimes it happens that the conversation languishes, and then we have a mild game of cards. Are you a gambler ? '

" ' Yes, that I am, I confess.'

" ' You must try not to be one here; I do not like any one to lose more than three or four louis in an evening at my house. We are agreed, then, are we not ? And now good-bye until this evening, my dear count ; I am obliged to leave you, for I must dress to go with one of my friends for a turn in the Bois.'

" I took my leave, and kissed, with as little awkwardness as possible, the hand held out to me.

" There, M. le Marquis, you have a true and particular account of my first interview with Pélagie d'Ermont. I think I acted my part well, and that I deserve your compliments, which I always value highly. To this evening must be left the first skirmish between Savari and Madame Vidal. If she should betray herself, if she should prove to be weaker than she thinks she is ! I tremble at the thought ! "

CHAPTER XII.

VIBERT had played to such perfection his part as a foreigner, a rich man not knowing what to do with his fortune, a pigeon well-disposed to be plucked, that Pélagie d'Ermont took it all for reality. Nothing very extraordinary in that, however. Women of the world, that is of the class to which Pélagie belonged, in their life meet so many men, young, middle-aged, and old, who commit all sorts of absurdities for or around them, that they end by entertaining a sovereign contempt for the whole human race and by placing all men in the same category. In each fresh individual of the species brought before them they see only a lamb destined for the sacrifice after being sufficiently shorn. So, no sooner had Vibert left her than she hastened to summon her circle of friends, from first to last. "At home to-night; tea," she wrote, which meant to say, as we have already explained, that lansquenet or baccarat, in earnest, would be the order of the evening.

At ten o'clock, some of Pélagie's most intimate fair friends were already collected in her drawing-room. Until the hour came for thinking of the serious business of the evening, which consisted of arranging the card tables, the friends of Madame d'Ermont, unfettered by the presence of any stranger, chatted amongst themselves.

"It appears to me," said Adèle X—, a charming gambler, who might have belonged to the sterner sex from the serious·

ness with which she played and the exemplary regularity with which she paid her debts, " it appears to me, my dear Pélagie, that we were not to have met this week."

" That is so, but an opportunity of getting up a really good game presented itself to-day, and I hastened to seize it, knowing that it would suit you all."

" Undoubtedly," was the reply—a perfect chorus.

" Whom do you expect?" asked Ormande, a pretty brunette, then quite the rage.

" I am expecting little Fontelle, you all know him."

" I shall not play with him; there is always a difficulty with men who have not come of age."

" In the first place," replied Pélagie rather coldly, " there is never any unpleasantness at my house, and, in the second, he is no longer a minor—here is the proof."

Pélagie took from the mantel-piece a printed circular, the contents of which she read aloud—

" The Baron Arthur de Fontelle has the honour to inform his friends, his female acquaintances, and his tradesmen, that he attained his majority on the 10th inst.

" His friends may therefore win his money at cards, his tradesmen give him credit, and the remainder ruin him.

" From this day henceforward the Baron Arthur de Fontelle is alone responsible for his acts."

" In the meantime he may receive a little judicious advice, which will not be long in coming," said Ormande with a laugh, " so long as this extraordinary circular passes from hand to hand."

" Well, then, it is all right as regards the baron," replied Adèle ; " who else is coming?"

" Cordier."

" Oh !" said a fair-haired girl called Antonine, " he does not count, he always comes with five louis and runs away when he has either lost or trebled them."

" Well, I have not invited him as a gambler, but as a piece
of furniture ; he helps to set off the table. I also expect
Cravoisier, big Calvet, and the Viscount de Beaune."

" They will do," was the general exclamation, "they play
in earnest."

" I foresee that we shall not get away from here before ten
o'clock to-morrow morning," said Ormande.

" Much I care about that," replied Adèle.   " I took my precautions, and stayed in bed until seven o'clock this evening."

An Italian, a new arrival in Paris, whose transcendent
beauty had already rendered her famous, now observed—
" Pélagie has up to this only told us of people we know ; is
there not a stranger expected ? "

" I kept him till the last," replied Madame d'Ermont,
" he is one of your countrymen, the Count de Rubini."

" I don't know him, but we shall soon make acquaintance.
Is he rich ? "

" Very much so, to all appearance, and I believe him to be
as foolish as he is rich."

" Then he belongs to me," naïvely said the fair Antonine,
" I claim the stranger."

" And Savari ? " asked Ormande suddenly, "shall we not
see him this evening ? "

" Yes, what has become of my little Albert ? Nobody
mentions him now," remarked Adèle.

" I expect him, too," said Madame d'Ermont, " he has
been ill since his misfortune, and he comes out to-day for the
first time."

" He has had enough to make him ill.   Only fancy being
accused of murder ! "

" And being in prison for three days ! "

" And after all there does not appear to have been the least
evidence against him."

"Evidently not, for they set him at liberty after one examination."

"I heard that his arrest was due entirely to a misunderstanding."

"Have you read the opposition papers on this business? They have given the magistrate, judges and all, a pretty good dressing."

"And, on the other hand, have extolled our friend Albert up to the skies ; for a moment he is the hero of the day."

"Well, then, let us give him a regular ovation when he appears."

"Agreed," said Adèle, "and I will give the signal, hip, hip, hurrah ! "

"I think I hear a ring," said Madame d'Ermont.

"I am not sorry for that ; these gentlemen keep us waiting too long. They have adopted a bad habit of paying other visits, or going to the theatre before joining us."

Between eleven and half-past twelve the drawing-room filled to overflowing. Savari was one of the last to arrive, and, as the ladies had decreed, was received with enthusiasm by them, but the men were rather cool in their welcome. In France, whoever is brought in contact with Justice is an object of fear ; everybody who has been engaged in an actual struggle with her is suspected at first sight ; when an honest man is tried at the assizes, and acquitted, not only by the jury, but also by the public and universal consent, every hand should be stretched out to him and testify, by its warmth of grasp, to the interest which he has inspired. Not so does it happen in reality ; every back is turned upon him, everybody is cold, there is a general hesitation as to whether he should be recognised, a common fear of being compromised ; "as far as I am concerned," say one and all, "I believe him to be innocent, but that fellow, over there, who is looking at us now, may possibly believe in his guilt."

Some one has said, "If I were to be accused of having made away with the towers of Notre-Dame, I should begin by running away, and leave my explanation to follow." These words have a foundation of truth; the first whisper of a crime rouses hundreds, a good action only meets with incredulity. So it happens that there are people who still believe in the guilt of Lesurques, simply because he was never officially pronounced innocent. This peculiarity is easily explained. A man is accused of a crime; the whole paraphernalia of justice is at once set in motion; detectives, gendarmes, commissaries, magistrates, all appear on the scene. Domiciliary visits, the judicial seal, arrest, often by main force and within sight and view of all, imprisonment— nothing is omitted. In towns all the district, in the country the whole parish, knows what has happened. Crowds collect before the house of the man who has just been arrested; the public finger is pointed at his family; his crime is in everybody's mouth, and scarcely a friend dares to rise in his defence. It often happens that the suspected person is not guilty. The magistrates discover his innocence and open the prison doors. "Go," they say, "you are free," and he goes. He returns home quietly and without any elation. What has happened has surprised and dismayed him to such an extent that he has no assurance left; he imagines himself still under lock and key, threatened with a criminal trial and with a capital charge hanging over him. He rings at his door, he embraces his weeping children, he blushes before his servants, he withdraws from observation, and for some days perhaps he either cannot or will not show himself. Thus the arrest is noisy and known by all; the return is in silence and often ignored. The arrest is a substantial fact, a cruel certainty, a spectacle at which all the world may assist; the release, on the contrary, is, so to say, a negative circumstance.

The arrival of Vibert and Madame Vidal in Madame d'Ermont's drawing-room did not attract general attention. For an hour previously the card tables had been in full swing, bank followed bank, and every one was too deeply intent on guarding his or her stakes to pay any attention to things foreign to the game. This was just what Vibert had foreseen, and was the reason why he had timed his arrival so late. He mistrusted Julia's strength, and he wished to smooth the first obstacles in her way. But Julia devoted herself to her revenge with all the ardour of her southern nature and the impetuosity of her two-and-twenty years added to an excitable temperament. Everything faded into insignificance before the mandate of her dying husband. When she felt herself giving way she did not appeal to smelling salts to support her, but to the memorandum book of Maurice Vidal, restored to her at her earnest entreaty, in which were written, in the blood of the only man she had loved, the words—" Julia, avenge me."

CHAPTER XIII.

ATTENTIVE and grave, Julia Vidal was seated on a sofa in a corner of the room and could watch at her ease every movement of Albert Savari, who was standing near the card table. She had seen him once previously in the magistrate's office, and through the chinks of the screen had been enabled to become familiar with his features and study his physiognomy.

But he was no longer the same man. Compelled to stand up in defence of his liberty, if not his life, he had then adapted himself to the circumstances in which he was placed; he had put a mask on his countenance and forced on himself the necessary look of impassibility. His very life then hung on a gesture, a look, or a blush. At Pélagie's he was no longer obliged to feign, for he believed that he was unobserved.

All the gamblers were following with greedy eyes the cards as they fell on the table, and were not thinking of him. His features thus had recovered their natural expression, and Julia, deeply interested in their study, drew from them some important conclusions. What struck her most of all was the profound sadness imprinted on his face. He seemed to have gone through some excessive grief, to be a prey to profound melancholy, or to be tortured by some terrible remorse. His eyes, under which formerly dark lines alone were visible, seemed to have sunk, and gave a sombre depth to his expression, interspersed by fitful gleams of light. At the same time his cheeks had fallen away and his face grown pale ; his lips which, under the influence of an all-powerful preoccupation or, possibly, by reason of some nervous contraction, he bit till the blood almost came, alone had preserved their full colour.

Though he appeared interested in the game of baccarat which was going on before his eyes, Savari had not yet taken an active part in it. He held in one of his hands a rouleau of louis, but each time he was on the point of staking them, he hesitated, and his downcast countenance seemed to say— "What is the use? What does winning or losing matter to me? What advantage can I get from a few additional louis?"

Suddenly he felt himself touched on the shoulder. It was Vibert who, after having been observing him quite as attentively as Julia, had made his way by degrees towards him.

"Pardon me," said the police-agent, with the same Italian accent which we have already seen him use, "everybody in the room is playing but yourself, and you hold aloof. Will you kindly do me a service?"

"What service?" said Savari very coldly, after eyeing the speaker all over.

"I am a foreigner, an Italian, as you may easily perceive by my pronunciation, and not at all familiar with the game that is being played. Nevertheless, I want to take a hand in it; first of all, for the sake of distraction, and then, because, between ourselves, I have a decided leaning towards cards. Will you be good-natured enough to devote a moment to initiating me into the mysteries of this famous baccarat, of which I have heard so much over in Italy, but of which I am as yet entirely ignorant?"

"I see no difficulty, if you so wish it," replied Savari, without departing from his coldness of manner.

"Thank you very much. I may, then, take my seat near these ladies, and risk a few bank notes without making a too ridiculous exhibition of myself."

"Oh, as for that, I can assure you a man is never ridiculous with these ladies so long as he has bank notes to lose."

"Indeed! They appreciate them, perhaps," replied Vibert, laughing in the simplest way possible.

"They adore them," said Savari, as he went to the mantelpiece for a pack of cards left there by some of the players. With these he rejoined Vibert, who had remained standing near the table. "If you are anxious, we can commence," said Savari.

"Should we not be more comfortable if we were to sit down for the lesson?"

"That is as you please. Here are chairs."

"But I am not alone."

"Ah!"

"Yes, I have a lady with me, a country-woman, who would not be sorry to profit by this small lesson, and if you have no objection—"

"Where is this lady?"

"There, sitting by herself. She knows nobody, speaks French very imperfectly, and is very timid."

For the first time the glances of Savari and Julia met. The wife of Maurice Vidal bore this first shock bravely, and betrayed not the slightest emotion. Moreover, Vibert, as a prudential measure, quickly made his way to Julia and introduced her to Savari.

"We are very much at sea here in Paris," said he to the latter, "and if it had not been for Madame d'Ermont, who kindly invited us to her charming party, we should not have known what to do with our evening. Ah! Paris is superb; but it seems a vast desert when one, as in our case, knows nobody. But, pardon my Italian chattering," continued Vibert, stopping short suddenly. "You have probably something else to do here than listen to me, and if you are willing to give me my lesson I am at your orders. My dear friend," he added, turning to Julia, "this gentleman is good enough to offer to teach us baccarat. You know baccarat— the game there was so much talk about in Naples last winter. It appears that stupendous sums are lost at it. So much the better, we will lose too."

Savari took his place on the sofa, by the side of Julia and opposite to Vibert, and commenced his promised explanation of the game. Scarcely was this finished when a Spanish lady, who was at the table, said : "Ten louis in the bank— who covers them ?"

"I have a great mind to try my luck," said Vibert, rising.

"You will not, if you take my advice," rejoined Savari.

"Why not? Thanks to you, I know the game now."

"You are not strong enough yet to play against the person now holding the cards."

"Bah! who knows?" replied Vibert, who thought the moment had come for arranging a first *tête-à-tête* between Julia and Savari.

He left them and went to the table, where everybody made room for him, for he had taken care to pull out most opportunely a purse which seemed crammed full of bank notes. In reality, he had arranged this purse most artistically. Two or three bank notes, the fruits of his savings, were wrapt ostentatiously round papers of minor importance, and thus formed bundles on which were very legibly written, 5,000, 10,000, 15,000 francs. This spectacle produced on the male and female gamblers, especially the latter, such an effect that Vibert profited by the sensation to risk only a few louis. He had long known by sight, or common report, a portion of the female element by which he was surrounded, and he had good reason to distrust them.

He played merely to avoid rousing any suspicion, and to carry out, in all its details, his *rôle* as the rich foreigner. In addition to this, baccarat was as familiar to him as it was to his teacher, Savari. Two months prior to the tragedy in the Rue de la Paix, he had been summoned to make a descent on a secret gambling house, and he had been obliged to make himself conversant, for the edification of the police authorities, with the nature of the games played there.

It was, nevertheless, with a certain amount of repugnance and great timidity that he hazarded a louis, saying to himself, " That is enough to lose, and I can include it in my account for expenses." But instead of losing his louis, it so happened that he won another; then two, then ten, and then twenty. Gold and notes seemed to rival each other in accumulating before him. At the same time strange ideas would present themselves to his imagination and bring a smile to his face.

" I wish the Marquis de X——," thought he, " could see me now, how heartily he would laugh. A police-agent playing baccarat with people he is commissioned to watch, and, moreover, winning their money—it is a beautiful idea.

The farce would be complete if the commissary of police of this district were to make a descent on the house and catch me in the act."

Suddenly, just as he had won another large stake, for the luck was following him as it generally does with those who sit down without either the wish or the object of winning, he felt some one lean on the back of his chair. He turned round—it was Savari.

" You are profiting by my lessons," said the latter to him.

" Oh ! very little."

" Very little! Why, you have at least five or six thousand francs in front of you."

" That is nothing," said Vibert, with the careless air of a millionaire.

" Then, since you attach so little importance to your winnings, you will not be angry with the person who sends me to you."

" You have been sent to me. What does anybody want with me ?"

" You are requested to take your departure, and I am sent to tell you so."

" Vibert rose at once, and there was a general outcry— " What, are you going? The evening is scarcely begun. It is not more than three o'clock."

" Ah !" said the Spanish lady, " that is bad, when you are winning so largely."

" He is afraid of losing," said Antonine.

" I had more confidence in you, my dear count," said Pélagie.

Vibert saw that his departure would be taken amiss, and that he would commit an imprudence were he to put his new friends too much out of humour.

" Ladies," said he, " I am compelled to escort home the

companion whom I brought with me, and whom the excitement of the game has caused you to forget. But I shall be
back in a moment, and I leave my money on the table to
keep my place." This last speech settled matters satis-
factorily, and Vibert, rejoining Julia, left the room with
her.

"Well?" he asked, as they went down the stairs.

"I have met him, as you foresaw, but shall I see him
again?"

"Undoubtedly. If you were not to see him again, the
first interview would be useless."

"Where shall I meet him? I do not wish to come here a
second time and mix in a society which is not to my taste."

"You will not return here."

"Then what have you resolved upon?"

"Nothing as yet; but I will hit upon some scheme, trust
me. May I ask you if your convictions with regard to Savari
have been effaced by the interview you have had with him?"

"They have not been effaced, but nothing has transpired
to confirm them." And so saying, they reached the bottom
of the staircase and gained the street.

"I am obliged to go back again," said Vibert.

"Nothing is easier. Call a cab for me, and give my
address to the driver."

"Are you not afraid to go alone at this advanced hour,
madame? I have time enough to see you home."

"No, thanks! If I am to carry out the mission I have
imposed on myself I must make myself familiar with all the
difficulties of my position."

An empty cab appeared. Vibert hailed it, and Julia got
in. "I shall have the honour, madame," said Vibert, shutting the door, "to call on you to-morrow, so that we can
decide upon our future action."

"I shall be at home all day," was the response.

Vibert followed the carriage, which bore away Julia, for an instant with his eyes. Any one who had seen him at that moment would have noticed something peculiar in his look. But he quickly passed his hand over his forehead, as if to chase away some thought which had taken possession of him. He drew his small figure up, his eye assumed another expression, and he wended his way without delay towards the house he had just left.

"The first step is taken," he said to himself, as he went upstairs, "but what about the second? If this very night I do not discover some method of getting hold of Savari, he will escape us. How to create, without awakening his suspicion, an excuse for seeing him again, seeing him often? Will it always so happen that the boldest spirits, whom neither danger nor obstacle, however serious, can daunt, have to meet with little difficulties, and be beaten by them?"

All at once he stopped and cried—"I have it! Eureka! as my protector, the marquis, would say. Why should fortune abandon me now, after having just helped me?"

He rang Madame d'Ermont's bell, and was admitted. It was about 3 a.m. During Vibert's absence the game had taken a fresh lease of life. Savari held the cards, and fortune was declaring for him. He had nearly three thousand francs in the bank. Vibert sat down noiselessly and waited. After a short interval, the deal came round to him, and the cards were shuffled and cut.

"Make your game, gentlemen," said Savari.

"What do you stake?" some one asked Vibert.

"I cry *banquo*," replied he.

"You mean that you cover all that is not covered by the rest?"

"No! I go the whole bank myself. Have not I the right?"

"Certainly," replied the players, withdrawing their stakes.

"Which card do you back?" asked the banker. "Right or left, or would you rather stake on the line?"

"On the line be it. I don't know what you mean," he added, with an air of innocence, "but that's all the more reason why I should win."

Savari, in spite of his great experience in gambling, was disconcerted. Nothing intimidates a gambler so much as finding himself face to face with an opponent who, on the one hand, seems sure of his game, and, on the other, plays for the first time. Vibert was ignorant of none of these details, and he knew how to turn them to his own advantage.

Savari dealt the cards, looked at his own, and said—"I turn up the eight."

"Then I ought to be nine," replied the police-agent, with imperturbable coolness. And so he was, nine on both sides.

Savari, annoyed at having lost at one fell swoop all his hard-earned gains, hoping for another run of good luck and bent on having his revenge on Vibert, whose assurance exasperated him, started a fresh bank with the solitary thousand franc note which remained to him. The first rounds were lucky; in less than ten minutes he had quadrupled his capital at the expense of all the assembled players. Vibert was the only one who had not staked. He had got up from his chair, and was leaning against the mantel-piece, smoking a cigarette with an air of indifference. But after the banker had dealt two rounds, he went to the table again, and, as in the first instance, called banquo.

"Again!" said Savari, dismayed.

"You have a right to give up the bank," remarked somebody.

"Not I," he exclaimed, "I will not give it up."

"As you please," said Vibert, throwing down his purse, in which real bank notes had replaced the sham rolls which he had invented.

This deal was a repetition of the former one. The bank was broken for the second time, and the money amassed by Savari passed into Vibert's hands. This time considerable applause greeted the feat. The Italian was decidedly at a premium amongst the women. Savari, who had come to the end of his tether, gave up the bank and Vibert took it in his turn. But instead of starting it at a thousand francs, he laid down fifteen thousand. With the aid of this stock-in-trade, he was about to back up his luck by a tower of strength— the strength of capital.

In reality, it is not only the zeros of roulette or the drawn games of trente-et-quarante which do such good service to the gaming-tables of Germany, it is the large sum placed at the disposal of the bank. All the small purses eventually flow into the large one, by way of bearing out the proverb that the river always runs to the sea.

There lives in Paris a very well-known individual, whose fortune is said to amount to eight or ten million francs. He owes it, for the most part, to gambling, which, to him, was a species of profession, a commercial speculation. In the exercise of this line of industry he was, relatively speaking, strictly honest, never having had recourse, throughout his long career, to prepared packs, or marked cards, or any of the infamous and petty rogueries so common amongst dishonest gamblers. He contented himself, instead of playing against the bank, with always taking it himself, and having in front of him large sums of money with which to hold his own against bad luck and wait for better times. His rooms, for a long time past the rendezvous of the *élite* of society, had become a kind of offshoot to the German establishments. Instead of leaving for Homburg, it was the custom, after dinner, to drive to the house inhabited by X—, who gave you a charming reception, offered you refreshments and cigars, delighted you with his lively wit, and won your money into the bargain.

Vibert, in his capacity as ex-secretary in the office of a commissary of police, was acquainted with all Parisian eccentricities. He had no doubt heard of X— and his *modus operandi*, and wished to imitate it. His fifteen thousand francs did wonders, for, in a very few minutes, all the money which was lying on the table had helped to swell his pile ; the large capital had absorbed the smaller ones. Then happened what always comes to pass in games of this kind which are not regular, and where there are no rules. After having played for ready money, they played on honour —just what Vibert was waiting for with regard to Savari.

The latter, disheartened by the first successes of his opponent, and knowing, by dint of long experience, the dangers of the fresh lease the game had taken, was at first very cautious in his play. He might possibly have given up playing any longer against his ill-luck if he had commenced by losing. But chance made him a winner of his first five hundred francs staked on honour. He thought his good luck had come back to him, and that he was going to relieve Vibert of all that the latter had raked together. He played, but imprudently, with a sort of feverish excitement, and he began to lose once more. All the skill gained by ten years' practice availed him naught.

This was simply because it was no longer with him, as in the preceding rounds, a question of merely winning or losing money ; he no longer fought against an impersonal being, whoever might hold the bank, or against a material thing, the run of cards—he was fighting against a man, against Vibert, whose unvarying good fortune exasperated him, whose coolness irritated him, and whose cringing manners, mincing tone and exaggerated politeness, acted on his nerves to an indescribable degree.

He felt that this opponent was hostile to him ; he knew not why, and he was very far from even a suspicion of

Vibert's plans. He took him, in all good faith, for a foreigner, but something told him that he was face to face with an enemy, and that he had better be on his guard. And the farther he went, the more obstinately did he determine to conquer this invincible foe. A species of drunkenness, the most dangerous of all—that produced by gambling—had seized on his mind ; the cards spread out on the table were no longer cards to him—they were swords, whose points he was endeavouring to direct against Vibert's breast.

But the latter, equally ready for attack and defence, parried his adversary's blow, and, on every occasion, in- dulged him with a fresh thrust. The battle had, moreover, become general, and the confusion terrible. From the time when all the money of all the players had passed into Vibert's bank, papers of all sorts and sizes, and "kites" of every description flooded the gaming table. One wrote on a scrap of paper, " Good for ten louis," " Good for a thousand francs," another put down a ring, saying that it represented five-and-twenty louis. A third, who had already staked his keys, his watch, and his sleeve-links, rummaged in his pockets for the last time, and finding only a tooth-pick there, handed it to the banker for two thousand francs.

It was a curious thing to see all these people attaching a considerable value to articles intrinsically worthless, and disputing with obstinacy over them as if a fortune was in question. And yet, such is the power of gold that when a real louis appeared by chance on the table, every player at once made innumerable efforts to gain possession of it. The man who was hesitating whether to play or throw up, decided on the former, for the simple reason that in his oppo- nent's pile his eye had suddenly caught the glitter of a solitary louis.

At 8 a.m. Vibert still held the bank. But for some time

past he had been taking the precaution to stuff away, in his purse and in his pockets, all the I.O.U.s. signed by Savari and all the actual coin. He no longer played with any money but what was owing to him, and against tooth-picks he staked other tooth-picks or something having an equally imaginary value. He seemed to attach veritable importance only to the "kites" flown by Savari. On these Vibert looked as on bank notes ; he put them by themselves in a heap, and never on any account made use of them to pay any losses which he sustained. It so happened that he had to hand over five hundred francs to the Spaniard, but he preferred pulling five-and-twenty louis out of his pocket to parting with an I.O.U. signed by Savari, which he had in his hand.

At length, when the Savari heap had assumed respectable proportions, Vibert declared that he was thoroughly done up, and that his bed urgently demanded his presence. There was nothing contrary to custom in this. They had commenced by agreeing to cease playing at eight o'clock, then at nine, and then at ten, but it was now eleven, and even the heaviest winners were at liberty to leave off without being accused of shirking. Nevertheless they prevailed on Vibert to have one deal more. He consented and held this last bank with an air of utter indifference, and a jovial good-nature which conciliated every one's goodwill. He even seemed to wish to make blunders so that everybody might leave off quits. In this way at the end of the deal the women had regained their rings, and all the men their I.O.U.s., their articles of jewellery, and their tooth-picks. Savari alone, when all accounts had been squared, remained in debt on paper to Vibert to the extent of fourteen thousand francs.

The game was over. There was a general move. Everybody stretched his arms and legs, and fatigue in various shapes, forgotten in the excitement of play, came over all when the gambling ceased. At the same time, thanks to the curtains being too suddenly drawn aside, the sun streamed into the room, and his brilliant rays threw into the shade the expiring candles. Every one looked at his neighbour and discovered that he was horribly ugly ; the women especially appeared under a thoroughly disenchanting aspect. The rouge and violet powder with which they had been embellished in the evening, the belladonna which had served to make their eyes look larger, all the trivial things scarcely perceptible by candle-light but which would not bear the light of day, gave them a strange appearance. Cabs were sent for and the jaded revellers made the best of their way home.

Before taking his leave, Savari said to Vibert—" Where shall I send you the amount of my debt?"

" To the Hotel des Princes, in the Rue Richelieu, if you please. I am living there for the time being," replied the police-agent without hesitation, for he was expecting the question.

They parted with a courteous good-bye, and each went his own way.

CHAPTER XIV.

VIBERT walked down the Rue Blanche. He needed exercise and fresh air. His head was heavy, his eyes were hot, and all his joints ached. It had been enough to tire anybody, to sit down at midnight, to remain there till 11 a.m., and during the whole time to do nothing but shuffle the cards, say over and over again the same words, and do over and over again the same things ; not to be able to get up, nor to walk about for fear of changing the luck ; to be hungry, and yet be prevented from eating by the dread of losing a moment ; to be dying of thirst and not to be able to drink, lest your self-possession should be left in the glass ; in short, to live in a pestiferous atmosphere, in the midst of a cloud of tobacco smoke which blinds you !

But the passion for gambling brings about an insensibility to all privations and all sufferings, both moral and physical. A gambler, so long as he has cards, money, and somebody to play against, is never unhappy—nothing can touch him. Shut four gamblers up in the same dungeon, give them full liberty to indulge their passion, and you will not have to accuse them of an attempt to escape. Nay, more, if on the day of their release they are engaged in some tremendously exciting game for high stakes, they will beg another twenty-four hours' imprisonment.

In the midst of his fatigue, Vibert did not suffer from want of sleep—a winner never is sleepy. He counts his money, makes his calculations, and indulges in innumerable dreams. It is the losers who sleep heavily when they lay their heads on the pillow, and thus forget a loss which is bound to be felt, whatever it may be, or however great may be their income. Besides, they must somehow get together strength enough to enable them on the morrow to go in search of money to discharge their debts of honour.

But Vibert cannot be simply set down as a fortunate gambler only. It was not the satisfaction of being a winner, and counting his gains, which kept him awake ; it was his exultation over a first victory, and the favourable opening of his campaign. He did not promise himself all sorts of long-ings gratified with his newly acquired bank-notes ; he hugged to himself the thought that he had Savari at his mercy, that out of his own resources he had enclosed him in a net stronger than the walls of the Conciergerie, that he had him, as it were, in solitary confinement, and that he must speak out. "I am," he reasoned, "a more formidable examining magistrate than M. Gourbet, because I have both time and space before me, besides having a woman at my side with whom I can do what I will, and who is even more devoted to my schemes than I am myself." Then he reflected that, with the money in his pocket which he had won, he could live the same life as Savari did, share his tastes and his pleasures, dine at the Café Anglais, if it was necessary—he, who was accustomed to a shilling restaurant—and hire a job-carriage instead of hesitating over an omnibus. In short, he could surround himself with all the necessary luxury and deceive everybody as to his identity, for nobody with any common sense would suppose that a minor *employé* of the government would chuck his money out of the window. That would be an unheard-of thing. Then, stopping short in these reflections, he exclaimed—

"And to think of my arriving unaided at the desired result, without having recourse to the purse placed at my disposal by the Marquis de X—, and without having to ask the Minister of the Interior to trench upon the secret service fund! Secret service indeed, a correct definition—so secret that we secret service agents never see it, and yet there are people who imagine that we live on fifty thousand francs a year. What a mistake they make!"

Thus talking to himself, Vibert, after going down the Rue Blanche, reached the Boulevards by the Chaussée d'Antin. His head seemed lighter, his limbs had regained their activity, and the pure air had refreshed his eyes; he felt himself in the vein, alert, ready to begin again. At the same time, like a prudent general who is never rendered lazy by success, he had evolved another scheme. There was nothing wanting but to put it in execution, and to that end his energies were at once devoted. He got into the first cab that he came across and drove to the Rue de l'Arbre-Sec, where was his own modest dwelling-place. Having mounted up to the fifth floor, he paid some attention to his toilet, placed the greater part of his money in a place of safety, wrote according to promise to the Marquis de X—, and, getting into the cab which he had kept waiting for him, made his way to the Rue de la Paix, where Julia Vidal was expecting him.

He told her what had happened in the drawing-room of Pélagie d'Ermont after she left, and then unfolded for her ready approval his new ideas. "Once consent to meet Savari as often as possible," he remarked, "and you cannot continue to live in this house. If he were one day to follow you here he would know who you are, and all would be lost."

"Evidently."

"Then you have made up your mind to change your residence?"

"No, I shall retain these rooms, which I cannot give up because of the reminiscences belonging to them. But I can take other apartments whither I can go whenever necessary."

"Will you authorise me to select those apartments?"

"Yes."

"Where do you wish to live?"

"It does not matter to me in the least. You have only to tell me what my new address is."

"You shall have it this evening."

When he left Julia, Vibert, careful of even the minutest details, betook himself to the Temple bazaar, and there bought two travelling trunks, such as might have belonged to some rich foreigner and which actually had on them the labels of the countries they had passed through. He filled them with no end of things, ready to hand in that extensive bazaar—appurtenances for the toilet, notepaper, envelopes, blotting-books, all with a crest on them, gold-headed canes,

ready-made shirts, and fashionable clothes. The look of
these trunks ready to burst with their contents could not
fail to inspire the people of the hotel whither he was going
with unlimited confidence. He had nothing more to do now
but install himself in the hotel he had mentioned to Savari
and await the arrival of that individual, an event which, according to Vibert's calculations, would not long be delayed.

The Hotel des Princes, on the site of which now stands
the Passage des Princes, enjoyed in 1847 a certain renown.
It was the Grand Hotel of that period. The only rooms
vacant for Vibert were fifteen francs per diem, but the Count
de Rubini was indifferent to the expense. Since morning he
had become so lavish that he no longer recognised himself,
and consequently his first act, when he was alone, was to
look in the glass to see whether it was really himself, Vibert,
who was hiring vehicles by the hour and was living in a
front room on the ground floor of the Hotel des Princes.
The glass reflected his veritable image, only it appeared
beautified. Luxury, so it seemed, became him well.

As soon as he had opened and emptied his trunks, arranged the various articles on his chest of drawers, filled the
wardrobes with clothes and linen, as soon, in fact, as he had
arranged his stage according to his fancy, he emerged from
his rooms with considerable pomp of manner, put on grand
airs as he passed a waiter, gave orders at the office that the
hairdresser, bootmaker and hatter attached to the hotel
should be sent to him when he got up next morning; and
then went out on to the Boulevard in search of lodgings for
Julia Vidal. It would have been better for her to have
taken up her abode, as he did, at the Hotel des Princes, and
if he had said to her, "I have taken rooms for you next
mine," she would probably not have made any remark.
Julia had only one thought—revenge. Vibert, as far as she
was concerned, was not a man; he was a means to an end.

And all means were good to this outraged wife, to this Italian, under the influence of the strongest of all passions—hate.

But if he in her eyes was not a man, she was in his, undoubtedly, a woman, and he had a peculiar delicacy regarding her. Unless it should prove impossible to act otherwise he would not compromise her. His one idea was to gain his end without causing Julia Vidal to suffer in her womanly dignity. For this reason he was very fastidious in choosing rooms for her. One set was too near the Hotel des Princes, another too far from it. This one was on the fourth floor, and Madame Vidal could not put up with so many stairs; in that one the chimneys smoked, and in the other there was a troublesome neighbour. One lodging was indeed everything that could be desired, except that it was too expensive, and as Julia had not won at cards nor received any subsidy from the police, but had to pay her own expenses, Vibert, prodigal where he himself was concerned, was economical in her interest. At last, after a long search, he chose apartments in the Rue de Grammont, saying that they were for a relation of the same name as himself, the Countess de Rubini.

The rooms had one great advantage ; they were furnished, yet did not form part of a regular lodging house. The previous tenant, obliged to leave Paris suddenly, was endeavouring to get as much as possible, during his absence, out of his lease and furniture. This furniture, without being new, was still fresh and in good taste, and there was nothing about it to wound the susceptibilities of any woman, however elegant. But what took Vibert's fancy more than anything else was the circumstance that the rooms had two entrances, by two separate staircases. The drawing-room, besides its main communication with the dining-room and the principal entrance, thus also opened, by means of a glazed door, on to a small passage leading to a servants' staircase.

Vibert, ever on the alert, managed to be left alone in the rooms for a moment, and profited by his solitude to put the key of the servants' staircase in his pocket and to scrape away a small portion of the frosted glass of the door, and by this means he secured an opening through which he might see as well as hear what went on in the drawing-room. " One never knows what may happen, and it is just as well to take every precaution," said he. " It is sometimes of no use, but it never does harm."

For more than thirty-six hours the police-agent had not enjoyed a moment's repose, so he went home early and betook himself to bed at once. Nevertheless, he did not sleep as soundly as one might imagine he ought to have done. Accustomed to an uncomfortable bed in the Rue de l'Arbre-Sec, he was possibly ill at ease on the spring mattress, the three hair mattresses, and the feather bed of the Hotel des Princes.

Or was it some fond memory that kept him awake?

CHAPTER XV.

On the following day, Vibert, after having interviewed various tradesmen, breakfasted and then calmly awaited the arrival of Savari. Gambling debts are generally paid within twenty-four hours, and he had, therefore, every right to expect a visit from his creditor of the previous evening. He had only one fear, which was that Savari might have been able to get hold of the fourteen thousand francs he owed him, and that he would bring them. An ordinary creditor would have been only too delighted at such punctuality, but the mere thought of it caused Vibert the greatest uneasiness, for his whole plan depended upon the very probable assumption that Savari would find it impossible to discharge his debt. As for the idea that he would simply not pay and keep away, as may and does happen every day, it would not hold water for a moment. Savari, since his arrest, was in too insecure a position to play such pranks. He was far too prudent, under such circumstances, to give any handle to well-founded suspicions, and so bring his name into prominence, and again draw attention to the sad affair in which he had been mixed up. It was, therefore, palpable to Vibert that his creditor would either pay up, or, what was still more probable, be unable to pay and ask for time.

Up to one o'clock in the afternoon there was no sign of Savari, and Vibert, whose nerves were being affected by the unwonted inaction and solitude, could not help giving way to apprehension. "Suppose," he reasoned within himself, "he were to write to me instead of giving me a verbal explanation. But surely it would be difficult for any one to be indifferent to meeting her again. However *blasé* he may be, she must have produced some impression upon him." Vibert could not realize the possibility of Julia Vidal passing unnoticed, nor that anybody could see her once without wishing to see her a second time.

At three o'clock his nervous irritation was allayed, his doubts were at an end—a waiter announced that somebody wished to see the Count de Rubini.

"Show him in," said Vibert, who managed to recognise himself under that title, notwithstanding the novelty of so aristocratic an appellation.

As soon as Savari made his appearance, the police-agent rushed to meet him. "Ah! is it you, my dear sir?" he exclaimed, resuming his Italian accent with its attendant exaggerated expressions and *empressé* manner; "come in, do. I am delighted to see you. All right after yesterday? I'll lay odds you have been in bed ever since. At all events that is where I have been; I had a bath when I came home yesterday, and a champagne breakfast to follow. And what champagne it is! It is worth while coming to France to drink it. After that I went to bed, and there I stayed until about an hour ago."

"I have not had half as much sleep as you have," said Savari, as soon as he could get a word in edgeways.

"How was that? Surely you were tired out."

"Yes, but I was preoccupied."

"Preoccupied? And suppose you were—does not sleep take precedence of the most absorbing preoccupations? But I see how the land lies. I would bet a trifle that you are in love with one of those charming ladies whom we met at Madame d'Ermont's. They were too delightful. What grace, what wit, what elegance! Ah! these Parisian women! Well may people rave about them. The Italians cannot hold a candle to them."

"But—" began Savari.

"No, no, my dear sir, you are going, out of sheer politeness, to make a pretty speech about my countrywomen. But you will not change my opinion on that score; I tell you that they are not to be compared with yours. For instance, my relative, to whom I introduced you—"

"Your relative?" said Savari, with astonishment, just as Vibert had expected.

"Yes, do you not remember her?"

"Perfectly, but I certainly did not imagine that she was a relation of yours."

"Why not?"

"Because—well, because you brought her to Madame d'Ermont's."

"Was there anything wonderful in that?" rejoined Vibert, with all the simplicity imaginable.

"You were ignorant, then, of the style of society there?" asked Savari, in his turn.

"The society there? They played cards there, as I have been told is the case in every drawing-room in Paris."

"Perhaps. But they do not play in that particular style, and up to 11 a.m., except in certain drawing-rooms, and in a certain world."

"What do you mean? Do you wish me to infer that my cousin's visit to Madame Pélagie was a mistake?"

"Since you put the question to me, I suppose I must reply—yes."

"Good heavens! This comes of being a stranger and not knowing the customs of a place—I, too, who thought--why, one of my friends, when I was leaving Naples, told me to be sure and find out Madame d'Ermont, No. 10, Rue Blanche, because she was a charming woman, with a nice house, where society was always to be found."

"There is, indeed, a good deal of society there," observed Savari, smiling.

"So you see, the first thing I did was to make my call and introduce my cousin. Fortunately, she did not speak to a soul besides yourself; everybody else was too intent on the game to think of her. But, do you know, this Paris of yours does not resemble our Italian towns in the least. I must go to school again here."

"Only for certain branches of learning," replied Savari, politely.

"I wish somebody would take me in hand," continued Vibert. "I shudder at the idea of committing some fresh gaucherie. This Madame d'Ermont, when I saw her in the afternoon, appeared to be so nice."

"As a stranger, you might very easily be mistaken. Madame d'Ermont has very agreeable manners when she pleases, and probably she was agreeable with you."

"So much so that I was taken in. What a lucky escape!
—If my cousin had suspected anything of the kind—and
yet, I took her there with the very best intentions. Poor
girl! She lost her husband only six months ago, and her
grief, I verily believe, would have seriously affected her
health if she had not resolved upon this trip to France with
me. The journey did her a great deal of good, and since
our arrival in Paris I have been endeavouring to find some
distraction for her. My first attempt in that direction does
not appear to have been very happy. I ought to have
asked my friend for further information about Madame
d'Ermont. He was under the impression that I was
travelling alone, and his information was meant for the use
of bachelors."

"I called—" began Savari, changing the conversation.

"You have called," said Vibert, hastily interrupting him,
"to settle that little affair of ours. 'Tis what you were
about to say. Don't mention such a trifle."

"But— "

"Allow me rather to continue under the impression that
you wish to improve an acquaintance which I value highly.
As for the paltry sum I had the misfortune to win from you,
put it on that table and let us talk of other matters."

"The fact is—" said Savari, becoming more and more
ill at ease as he saw his creditor treating the matter so
lightly.

"The fact is?" repeated Vibert unconcernedly—

"That I am compelled to remain in your debt for some
days longer. In consequence of a succession of losses I am
in rather a strait, and—"

"Not really?" said the police-agent with the air of a
man astonished that anybody could be driven into a corner
for so little.

"And I come, count," continued Savari, "to beg of you,

in the first place, not to mention my temporary embarrassment, and, secondly, to give me a little time for the payment
of my debt to you."

"With the greatest pleasure imaginable," replied Vibert.
" I will give you, my dear sir, as long as you require. A
week, a fortnight, if you like. You have, no doubt, to realize some securities. I should find it difficult to refuse you,
more especially as I have to rely upon your courtesy for an
important service."

" You ?"

" Yes, truly. Will you allow me to explain ?"

" Do so, I beg."

"You have already had an opportunity of seeing," replied Vibert, with a clever assumption of carelessness and
good-fellowship, " that I have no experience whatever in
this world of Paris, and that I am liable to go astray at any
moment if I have not a trustworthy guide to lead me aright.
It was this which made me eager to seize upon the opportunity of making the acquaintance of such an one as yourself, and of asking you frankly to aid me by your advice and
superior knowledge."

" Pray, make use of me," eagerly replied Savari.

The proposal thus made to him was too favourable to be
lost sight of. He already saw resulting from it the vague
possibility of getting rid of a debt which had, since the previous evening, for reasons already explained to our readers
and rightly divined by Vibert, caused him the greatest
anxiety.

Gambling debts, indeed, can only be considered really
serious amongst strangers or, at all events, ordinary acquaintances. Intimacy, it is true, cannot annul such obligations,
but at the same time it is scarcely permissible to dun a
friend or post him as a defaulter.

"Thank you very much for your kindness," said Vibert,

when Savari consented to be made use of. "But take care that you are not undertaking an impossibility. I am not alone. I have with me one who is sad and suffering, and whose amusement is my object. Between men these matters are easily arranged. I might possibly make myself a boon companion, because I should share your tastes and should take a liking to your pleasures, which would become mine. But in assuming charge of me you will also be saddling yourself with my cousin, and it is of her that you must think. That will not be quite so easy, I imagine."

"Why not?" replied Savari. "In my short interview with her I thought her a charming woman."

"We thought so in Italy, 'tis true. She had even, I admit, in Neapolitan society, both before and during her married life, a great reputation for wit. But you Parisians are spoiled in this matter and many others. Don't try to persuade me otherwise—in taking charge of us you are rendering us a great service, and nothing less."

"Be it so, if you insist on it."

"Very well, then. I agree, and it will not be long before I put your good nature to the proof, I promise you."

"So much the better."

"I have a mass of information to get from you—addresses, names of the best tradesmen, and above all, advice, and plenty of it. We reckon on remaining in Paris all the winter, and we should like to pass the time as agreeably as possible. What are we to see? Where must we go? All this bothers one, I can tell you, and you can be of the greatest use. When may I have the pleasure of introducing you to my cousin in her own house, and in a more correct fashion than on the first occasion of your meeting?"

"Whenever you please."

"Then, to-morrow. You see I take you at your word."

"To-morrow be it."

They separated a quarter of an hour afterwards. Vibert was in ecstacies. As for Savari, he, too, was perhaps not ill-pleased with the bargain he had just struck.

CHAPTER XVI.

THREE weeks passed away, during which Albert Savari had become the inseparable companion of Vibert. He got up in the morning, went out and betook himself to the Hotel des Princes, where, as a rule, he breakfasted with the police-agent, who was more and more completely disguised and a more and more perfect travesty of the rich foreigner.

In truth, Vibert had so thoroughly lost himself in the Count de Rubini that he no longer looked upon that person-age as imaginary, nor did he remember that he was only acting a part. He was so used to hearing himself called "count" that plain "sir" irritated him. Even in the solitude of his chamber, when communing with himself alone, he would hardly acknowledge that he was the Vibert of old, sprung from no noble stock.

"As soon as I have done with this Rue de la Paix case," he wrote one day to his powerful patron, the Marquis de X——, "I shall be obliged to institute a search after my genealogical tree and ransack the past both as regards my-self and my ancestors ; there must be in my veins a few ounces of right-down aristocratic blood."

"And suppose there is, you idiot," was the reply of tho ever-encouraging marquis, " what then ? "

On the score of expense Vibert refused himself nothing ; he might have been living all his life on an income of five-and-twenty thousand francs. A champagne breakfast was the rule whenever Albert Savari made his appearance, and he did not scruple to tell the famous Privat, mine host of the Hotel des Princes, to reserve for him his choicest wines.

In common justice, however, to the generous and truly hospitable instincts of the Count de Rubini, it must be recorded that he was lavish only to his guest. In his absence, Vibert made the gold seal give way to a thin *vin ordinaire* which he kept in reserve at the bottom of one of his trunks. The same course was observed in every other particular.

For example, if Savari was spending the evening with him, his room was a perfect blaze of light; but as soon as he was alone he came down at once to the economical taper. If he shut himself up in his room to write to the Marquis de X——, or to the Prefecture, he took off his frock coat, built by a fashionable tailor, and put on a garment which he had brought with him from the Rue de l'Arbre-Sec, and for which he appeared to have a special affection, seeing that, to prevent any wear and tear to its sleeves, he always covered them with false ones of alpaca.

Thus Vibert succeeded in establishing a double identity— on the one hand appeared in majestic fashion the Count de Rubini, a nobleman to the tips of his fingers, and on the other hand stood the old insignificant public servant, on twelve hundred francs a year, economical from force of habit and necessity.

Generally speaking, after breakfast the programme for the day was discussed by Vibert and Savari over a cigar.

"Look here, *mio caro*," said the count, as the smoke curled from his lips in graceful whiffs, " you are good-nature itself, assiduous in attention and full of forethought for my cousin, and I thank you with all my heart. But we are not carrying out our famous programme, drawn out with your assistance. Here we are very nearly at the end of the sixth week, and we can scarcely be said to know Paris. Let us reckon up what we have accomplished—do you agree ? "

" I have no objection."

" First of all, then, you took us to dine at the Palais Royal—that day, you know, when you gave us such a stupendous idea of your head ; do you remember it ? "

" Perfectly."

" Yes, Madame de Rubini, in a moment of caprice, wanted to make you tipsy, and I seconded her in the attempt to the best of my ability. But it was all in vain. You drank whatever was put before you and never lost your head for a moment. We had not a chance of getting at one of your secrets."

" Perhaps there were none to get at."

" Everybody has one or two, and especially a man who, like yourself, has lived all the days of his life. Ah ! you are a model of discretion with your friends—nothing slips out from you. Why not take example by me ? I am the impersonation of candour. You know the whole of my life, and I have let you into all my little secrets. But that is not what we were talking about. Since the dinner in question what have we done? Nothing, absolutely nothing. We were to visit all the lions of Paris. I have not seen a single one of them ; yet I cannot go back to Naples and say—I did not see the lions at all."

"That would indeed be dreadful."

" Now you are making fun of me ; but it would certainly be dreadful. It is bad enough to have to keep aloof from the theatre on account of our mourning. The lions remain —let us see the lions. When will you undertake to show us Notre-Dame, the Louvre, the Luxembourg, the Tuileries, the Palais-de-Justice—I am particularly anxious to see the Palais-de-Justice."

" There is nothing wonderful there."

" There speaks the true Parisian. You are all so thoroughly satiated with the marvellous that you have no wonder left in you, literally none. You will hardly even condescend to cast a contemptuous glance at your curiosities. Come, I'll bet you anything you like that you have never asked for a permit to visit your prisons."

"I should think not, indeed; but, all the same, I have paid them a visit without a permit."

"Indeed! And how was that?"

"That would be too long a tale. I had a friend at court."

"You were fortunate, indeed. And could you not do the same for me? It only requires a little stretch of good-nature. Let us go back there together."

"No, thanks; I cannot say I should care for it."

"You do not take any interest in these things?"

"The one view I have had is quite enough for me."

"Then get me a permit, and I will go alone."

"Agreed—I will see after one."

"And then the Musée d'Artillerie, that I long to see, and the Gobelins, &c., &c., for I should never end, when I have once begun."

"That is just the reason why we had better not begin."

"But I say—yes! I want to begin, and as soon as possible. To think of my still being ignorant of your principal streets. It is true that you took us one evening along the Rue Vivienne, the Rue de la Chaussée-d'Antin, and the Rue Lafitte, but we have never so much as set eyes on the Rue de la Paix, a street people are always talking about in Italy. Tell me frankly why have we not gone down the Rue de la Paix?"

"Most likely because it was not in our way," replied Savari simply, Vibert watching him intently all the time.

"Well, when are we to see all these things?"

"Whenever you like."

"To-day, I vote."

"To-day be it."

Such were the daily plans, constantly drawn up and never executed. The comedy once performed, the police-agent, who did not care about showing himself in public with Madame Julia Vidal, never reminded Savari of his promises, and the latter had no good reason to refresh Vibert's memory.

After breakfast, towards three o'clock, they wended their way to Julia's house in the Rue de Grammont and talked over the fire. Sometimes—but very rarely—they went out for a drive in a close carriage. Dinner was also, from time to time, a rendezvous for the two travellers and their guest, and the evening was passed by them together.

Thus, by the sheer force of shrewdness, Vibert had established round Savari a cordon of surveillance as tight and as extraordinary as can well be imagined. It was tight, inasmuch as the watch was not only over the individual himself, but also upon his slightest movement, his every word, his look, and his most hidden intentions. It was extraordinary, because the person watched came every day in search of the police-agent who was watching him, and, as it were, delivered himself up to the enemy. Vibert was executing his mission, with his feet either on his own fender or on that of Julia Vidal, and without putting himself to the slightest inconvenience.

What a mission it was! Ever on the watch to lay a trap for his adversary, profiting by his slightest mistake, scrutinising his words and deeds, and laboriously gathering together links, both moral and material, which he felt sure would sooner or later unite in a chain destined to bind his victim fast.

At the same time, if one may sit in judgment on so clever a detective as Vibert, we should say that for some time past he had been committing a blunder. What had been his object in begging Julia to work with him? What had been the drift of his conversations with her? After having

E

clearly shown that Savari, by reason of his dissipated life, could never have really loved any woman, he wound up by saying to Madame Vidal—" He must love you."

When Julia was bewildered and failed to see the detective's meaning, Vibert added, " It is our only means of arriving at the truth. Savari does not know you, and will not suspect you. You will become a part of his life, you will share in his existence. You will learn his past, and sooner or later you will unmask him. You will act the Delilah to this new Samson. You will shear his locks, and we will deliver him into the hands of the Philistines."

In this scheme Julia, not Vibert, was to play the leading part. He was retained simply in the position of a confidant, stationed as a rule in the wings and only appearing on the scene at rare intervals to listen to some tirade, to wipe away a few tears, and to receive the heroine in his arms. In a word, he was to take merely an indirect part in the action of the play. But Vibert, carried away, no doubt, by the artistic situation he had created, and animated by an excess of zeal, had managed to thrust his part into prominence and convert himself into a leading character. He might now be seen making a precipitate entrance from the wings, without being called, and insinuating himself into scenes meant to be confined to the two principal actors, Julia and Savari.

Was it that Julia had asked his assistance ? Did she dread being brought into too close contact with Savari ? Did she fear that, if she were left to her own resources, she would not be able to play her part with sufficient ability, that she would betray herself, or that she would be powerless to restrain her legitimate indignation in the presence of the man whom she persisted in suspecting ? But Vibert was not indispensable to Madame Vidal, for had she not Marietta, her attendant, her countrywoman, her friend, on whose presence as a third party she could rely in her interviews, and who might be at hand to intervene if a *tête-à-tête* became dangerous? Besides this, Julia might be held to be above such timidity. Her acceptance of the *rôle* which Vibert proposed; her ready consent to face all the exigencies of a situation she herself had helped to create; her voluntary conversion into the accomplice of a police-agent, and her scrupulous compliance with the will of Maurice Vidal —all these betokened a character of exceptional energy and courage beyond suspicion. Such a woman would march straight on to her goal without ever asking aid or crying out for assistance. Again, would it not have been natural for her to have wished to curtail as far as possible her cruel position, to resume her own character, and get rid of Savari, either by recognising his innocence or bringing him to justice?

The blunder we have pointed out must then be laid to the charge of Vibert alone, clever though he undoubtedly was. By his mistake he indefinitely prolonged a false situation, and instead of retiring into the background, as he ought to have done, he hindered Savari from making himself known to Julia under his true aspect and perhaps committing himself in the course of a confidential *tête-à-tête*.

But the ground was well prepared, the hour auspicious, and all the calculations of Vibert were turning out correct. Was not his scheme based on the love which Julia must necessarily inspire in Savari, and would that love be long in springing into life? The police-agent was right in his estimate, and he had at the same time realised that the moment had arrived when this man, still young, *blasé*, but not exhausted, incredulous about many things, but apt to believe in what was novel, a man who had always lived like a bird on a branch, would long to put an end to all these enervating intrigues, the alphabet of which he knew by heart, to invigorate himself by a more wholesome life, to replace perpetual motion by rest, and, in short, to put aside caprice, which he knew too well, in favour of the more stable affection, of which he as yet knew nothing.

And what woman was more fitted than Julia Vidal to inspire such a feeling? Her beauty bore no resemblance to the attractions of those with whom Savari had hitherto been brought in contact. Her look set him all aflame, her smile dared him on. She spoke little, and in monosyllables when forced to reply to a too searching question, and then her voice had in it a sharp, vibrating ring, which made a strange impression on him. She had in her a combination of sadness and assurance, of sweetness and severity, of vivid contrasts which took hold of his imagination, and, by degrees, of his heart also.

Savari could not long be proof against the fatal charm of this beauty. He already saw the species of fascination which she could bring to bear on him, the sway to which he must sooner or later submit, and the danger he was about to incur; but, instead of avoiding and running away from it, he seemed to take a delight in confronting it. Perhaps he had grave, preoccupying thoughts for which he sought distraction, possibly he suffered from some secret ill, and hoped to cure it by another yet more cruel. Did he not know, by hearsay, though not by experience, that a true love, an unhappy love, an all-absorbing passion, brings in its train evils, terrible it is true, but effectual to consign all others to oblivion?

The state of things which we have endeavoured to explain lasted for some time longer—about a month. At the end of that time Savari had but one thought—to be alone with Julia, to contrive a *tête-à-tête*, and to get rid of the unwelcome presence of Vibert.

CHAPTER XVII.

VIBERT, however, seemed less and less disposed to relax his vigilance. The more Savari tried to keep him away the closer he clung to his customary spot in Madame Vidal's drawing-room. What was the motive of his persistence? Did he take seriously his character as relative and protector? A suspicious husband, a jealous lover who has every reason to remain near his beloved one—these absent themselves sometimes; Vibert, on the contrary, though his own good sense and interest should have sufficed to keep him away, persisted in remaining, always remaining. Had he, then, like Savari, succumbed to the magnetic influence of Julia, and did he forget, when near her, that he was simply a police-agent, delegated by the Prefecture to aid the Law in deciding on the guilt or innocence of an accused person?

One day, however, Savari determined to see Julia Vidal without being incommoded by the presence of Vibert. Accordingly, as usual, he made an appointment with the latter, but, instead of going to meet him at the Hotel des Princes, he went direct to the Rue de Grammont. Marietta informed her mistress that Savari was alone and wished to see her.

Julia hesitated for a moment, and then, summoning all her courage to her aid, embraced Marietta and joined Savari. Possibly she thought the time had come to put an end to a state of things which had become intolerable, or she had already arrived at the conclusion that Vibert, far from serving her, was hindering her designs.

When she entered the drawing-room she was, as usual, dressed in mourning. Following the Italian fashion, a cloud of lace, held at the back of her head by jet pins, covered one half of her luxuriant hair and fell over her shoulders. This toilet, entirely black, made her appear still taller, showed off her magnificent bust, fined down her waist, already small by nature, and gave a commanding, sovereign charm to her carriage.

Savari gazed at her, admired her, but had not courage to speak. This man, who up to now had never betrayed any sign of timidity, who was conspicuous for his assurance, and who looked upon it as a first principle that in love the conclusion should be hurried on, and that women are captivated only by the daring—this man quivered like a leaf when Julia approached him, felt his heart beating as if it would break, and forgot all the fine speeches which he had intended to pour into her ear.

She was the first to perceive the embarrassing nature of this silence, and broke it by saying to him—"What have you done with the count?"

"I fully expected to find him here," replied Savari.

"I thought, on the contrary, that I heard you arrange to meet him at his hotel."

"So I did, but I was late, and I imagined that, instead of waiting for me, he would come on here. Do I disturb you?"

"Me? Not the least in the world," said Julia, with an air of nonchalance.

"I am, then, fortunate, madame, in thus finding you alone."

"Have you anything to say to me?" she asked, simply.

"Ah! yes, I have indeed much to say," cried Savari, with considerable warmth of tone.

"I am all attention, M. Savari."

"M. Savari! You will always call me M. Savari."

"And is not that the proper mode of address?" she

observed, pretending not to understand him. "Then tell me what I ought to say. I am not familiar with all the niceties of the French language, and I am never angry when corrected."

"I have no fault to find; the expression is perfectly correct, and has no offence in it."

Then suddenly getting up from his chair, he said— "Pardon me; I am nervous, agitated, restless—pray excuse me."

"I grant you a full pardon," she replied, with a smile, "but will you not let me know the reason of this agitation?"

He approached her with no laggard step, seated himself at her side, and said—"You do not understand me then?"

"What do you mean?"

"You do not understand that one cannot exist at your side for more than two months with impunity; that it is dangerous to a man's reason to see you constantly, to hear you, to breathe the same air with you, in short, to——"

He was about to continue, but he raised his eyes to her, and stopped. There was a strange expression in Julia's smile; her brow was knitted, her cheeks had turned pale, and her look was frigid as ice. With her wonted courage, she had not shrunk from meeting the danger, but she had presumed too much on her strength. At the first declaration, at the first words of love which escaped from Savari, her whole being revolted; her modesty and her delicacy of feeling were both aroused. What! was it really she to whom any one could dare to speak of love! She, whose husband was barely dead! And the man whom she suspected of having caused his death—he to speak so! Ah! she had not foreseen what suffering was in store for her.

They were both silent for some time—he afraid, and she bruised and wounded in spirit. But by degrees, Julia's face recovered its habitual expression; she passed her hand across her forehead, as if to chase away some unwelcome thought. She appeared to come to some resolute determination, and turning towards Savari so as to look him in the face, she said—" Then you love me ?"

He was not prepared for this method of attack. From the anger betrayed by Julia he anticipated an order to change the conversation, or to be silent, or possibly to leave the room. So far from that being the case, she took up the conversation from the point where he had left it. She completed his thought, and came to his assistance; she issued a challenge instead of saying an adieu.

But he, recovered from his first astonishment, was eager to profit by the opportunity she offered him of dilating upon a love which he took so much to heart. If Julia was a woman of great resolution, Savari, on his side, knew how to be energetic. By a sudden movement, which Madame Vidal could not foresee, he seized both her hands, and, looking at her as she had looked at him, he drew her close in order that she might hear him better.

"Yes, I love you," he exclaimed, "as I have never loved, as I thought myself incapable of loving. You are my first, my only love. If you but knew how truthfully I say it, how miserable I am away from you, and what joy it is to be near you! The first time you burst upon my sight, it seemed to me that I had never seen a woman so lovely. Yes, there is no beauty to be compared with yours; in it lies every perfection, every charm, every grace, every splendour! I, who thought myself so strong, so invulnerable, so dead to wonder and admiration alike—I have had suddenly to realize what a sway beauty like yours can exercise over me. I swore to fly from you, never to see you again. Ah! I could not! Your cousin brought me here; he made himself my companion, he told me to live by your side. I obeyed, but I knew the fate which awaited me; I knew that near you I should have done with repose, that my will would be no longer my own, that I should love you ardently, devotedly !"

The grasp of Savari had tightened on her hands, his gaze was becoming too passionate, and she could bear no more. Disengaging herself, she rose, and, stepping back to lean on the marble mantel-piece, she asked—"Have I encouraged your love ?"

"Never," was the reply. "Neither by word nor look, and by that I am lost. Stay, I retract, you have encouraged me, or, rather be it said, never did woman unwittingly act the coquette with me more perfectly than you. You have not realised that your obstinate silence and your coldness were so many provocations. I longed to fight, I yearned to conquer—I still yearn !"

Savari was no longer the man whom we saw in the magistrate's office, defending himself upon a capital charge with so much self-possession and calm. The blood had rushed to his cheeks, his eyes expressed what his lips uttered; animation and movement were on every feature and lent him an unaccustomed charm. For the first time, perhaps, in his life, Albert Savari really lived. His love had metamorphosed him and had changed him from a cold, self-contained, shrewd and scheming man of the world, into an ardent, impulsive, young and healthy being. He was about to continue the laying bare of his heart, when Vibert was announced.

One glance enabled the police-agent to take in the scene and realise the situation. His brow contracted, an almost imperceptible pallor stole over his face, but he approached Julia with a smile, asked after her health, and, turning to Savari, in a good-humoured manner said—"So you have been here, my friend, whilst I have been waiting for you at my hotel—"

Savari repeated what he had already told Madame Vidal, and his explanation appeared to satisfy Vibert. But whilst the latter was bent on talking of indifferent subjects, the weather and the rumours afloat, Savari, still under the influence of the feeling to which he had just been giving vent, and not being equal to sustaining ordinary commonplace conversation, got up and took his leave, on the score of a pressing engagement.

"Don't forget that we dine together," cried Vibert, "seven o'clock sharp at the Café Anglais."

Savari, who was going out, turned back. He was seeking some fresh pretext for refusing this invitation, when by accident his glance fell upon Julia. Still leaning against the mantel-piece, one elbow on the marble, her head resting on her hand, and apparently lost in thought, she seemed to him more lovely than ever, and he had not the strength of mind to deprive himself of soon seeing her again.

"Agreed," said he, "I will not fail."

CHAPTER XVIII.

FOR a moment after his departure, Julia maintained her silence. Vibert, equally silent, was watching her attentively from a corner of the room. He had all the appearance of trying to discover her thoughts and read her inmost soul, whilst at the same time suffering from the effects of his study. This suffering in all probability became too acute, for he suddenly got up, shook himself, as it were, together, and, coming towards her, said abruptly—"Well ?"

She started, looked at him, and answered—"Excuse me, sir, I did not know you were there."

"I thought as much," said Vibert, with an approach to bitterness, which he could not conceal, "I am no longer anything here. My services are no longer in request since business is carried on without me."

Then he stopped short and resumed more calmly. "At all events something has resulted from this long interview."

"No," said she.

"You are no further advanced than before?"

"No."

"Then we must begin again."

"No," was the reply for the second time.

Astonished at this last response, he looked at her with a questioning air, but she all at once left her resting-place at the mantel-piece, and came up to him with the impetuous remark: "Do you know that what we are doing is infamous?"

"Why?"

"Because he loves me and is suffering."

"Really!" said Vibert, no less moved than Julia, "he loves you and has just told you so."

"Yes."

"And you believe him."

"I do."

He crossed his arms over his breast, and going up to her as she had gone up to him, said shortly: "Well! How does that interfere with your plan?"

"I have no right to make him suffer thus."

He looked at her intently and replied severely in a low voice: "Do you really think that you have no right to do so to the man who killed your husband?"

"But suppose he did not kill him?"

"Ah! You are in doubt now."

"Yes, I am," said she, hanging down her head, as if blushing for her weakness, "so long as he is not here, so long as I am alone with my thoughts, he still seems to me to be guilty, and, as before, I am eager to revenge myself on him; but when he is at my side, I no longer believe, but doubt."

Pale, and with compressed lips, he heard her without interruption, but when she had finished, he said, "There must be an end of this state of uncertainty. It cannot last any longer."

" No," she repeated, " it cannot last any longer."

" He must," resumed Vibert, " give us once for all a proof of his innocence, and then my task will be done. I shall return to my usual avocations, and shall have nothing more to do here." He spoke abruptly, almost passionately, but Julia was too much moved to notice anything extraordinary in his agitation or his apparently unjustifiable manner.

" If, on the contrary," he continued, " Savari is guilty, as I still believe—believe, indeed, nay, I am convinced of it— he must betray himself to us, and we must get rid of him."

These last words, " we must get rid of him," were spoken by the detective in a marked tone. He murmured them rather than said them aloud, for Madame Vidal, instead of paying any attention or replying to them, answered only the first part of the speech.

" It is not sufficient to say," she cried, " that he must betray himself to us—what means have we of compelling him to do so ?"

" I bring them," replied Vibert, producing from his pocket a long, straight object wrapped up in paper.

And as she looked at him in astonishment, he asked her in a brusque tone of voice, and without any of the caution which he ought to have made use of under such circumstances, " Are you aware, madame, of the weapon which was employed by the assassin of your husband ?"

She turned pale, as she replied, " A knife or a dagger."

" It was a paper-knife—a dagger-knife, indeed, which you know, since it belonged to M. Vidal. If you failed in finding it in your house, it was because it was seized by the Law as an important piece of evidence in the case."

" And this knife ?" she asked, growing still paler, and looking at the object which Vibert held in his hand.

" The registrar at the Palais-de-Justice was ordered, at my request, to hand it over to me. Here it is."

She drew back, and asked, " What are you going to do with it ?"

" I shall place it in Savari's hands, and, perhaps, at the sight of it he will betray himself. You, no doubt, will be averse from witnessing the experiment ?"

" On the contrary, I will be present, I would rather be present," she replied with energy, " it is my duty."

" I mean to try it this evening."

" This evening be it. But," she continued, " how will you account to him for this weapon being in your possession ? To show it to him will be to betray yourself—both of us."

" No, there you are wrong. I foresaw that objection and I know what to say. But," he added quickly, " what docs it matter now if he does know who you—who we are ? Have you not determined to abandon the position you have taken up ? Have I not declared that this experiment shall be the last ? If he emerges from it victoriously, if his innocence is made plain to you, will you still continue to receive him, and do you wish him to remain your friend ?"

" No, certainly not."

" If, on the other hand, this experiment succeeds in convincing you of his guilt, what does it matter if he does know who we are ? Ah ! if this should happen, I swear to you he is lost."

No words can convey the manner in which the police-agent said this. In his tone were concentrated, anger, hate, and suffering.   Julia was alarmed, and for the first time, perhaps, she thought of looking attentively at Vibert.   They separated after having arranged to meet in the evening at the Café Anglais.

CHAPTER XIX.

VIBERT undoubtedly aimed too high.   Instead of intriguing for the honour of entering the police force he should have simply come out as a dramatic author, and in that modest career he would have gained an unquestioned success.   He would have been especially excellent in the construction of a piece, and in devising what are called "situations," whilst in arranging the *mise en scène* he would have been without a rival.

He wanted Savari, the hero of his drama, to betray and unmask himself, and he imagined that in putting in his hands the instrument which had been employed in the commission of his crime he had found the means to bring about that end.   It was the crowning situation, to be awaited with impatience, and on it would follow the *dénouement.*

How cleverly he had led up to it !   With what art he had arranged it !   This situation might have been brought about at any moment from the opening of the play, but then it would have been wanting in scenic effect.   Savari, on his guard since his arrest—Savari, distrusting everybody and everything, would have taken the dagger in his hand without flinching, would have examined it, poised it, and returned it quietly to its owner.

Vibert had allowed several months to elapse.   By his intelligence and his craftiness he had inspired Savari with complete confidence ; by kind words and acts he had softened his naturally difficult character, and by the serious love in which he had skilfully entangled him, he had succeeded in mollifying and quelling his energetic nature.

See, too, how well he had chosen the site of the scene—the Café Anglais—the very place where Albert Savari had dined an hour before the murder of Maurice Vidal. If he had done the deed, would he not experience some agitation at thus finding himself in the place where he must undoubtedly, in that case, have thought out and arranged his crime ?

How propitious, too, was the moment chosen for this decisive trial ! Savari had seen Julia during the day ; for the first time had spoken to her of love, had opened his heart to her, had pleaded, had wept, had suffered. His over-excited nerves were relaxed, his mental force less active, and he found himself, by a sort of fatality, both morally and physically incapable of initiative and peculiarly accessible to outside influences and impressions.

At half-past six Vibert entered the Café Anglais, and was at once shown into a room engaged by him on the previous evening and known to the fashionable world as "le Grand Seize." Whilst awaiting the arrival of his guests he made some important preparations. By his orders, bouquets of flowers, bought by him on account of their exhaling the most powerful perfumes, were placed on the table. Vibert, who had studied everything, was a thorough believer in the action of flowers on the nervous system. He also was very particular in ordering the wines, asking for heady but not exciting kinds. Finally, he directed that double the usual number of candles should be lighted, and took especial care that the seat to be occupied by Savari should be in the full glare of all this illumination.

At seven o'clock Madame Vidal, Savari, and Vibert met

and sat down to dinner. The conversation languished at first, and it could not well be otherwise, seeing that each of the guests carried a heavy burden of engrossing thoughts. But very soon Vibert, more master of himself than the others were, drove away all ideas which might have endangered the important end he had in view, and brought the conversation into a channel in accordance with his plan. During the first course it was trifling, varied and almost gay, entering later on into a melancholy phase. At dessert it touched on serious topics and relapsed into moral and philosophical arguments.

Vibert, in order to rise to the level of the occasion, had summoned to his assistance his own reminiscences, his early religious studies, the more or less paradoxical theories evolved by his protector, the Marquis de X——, and all the experience he had acquired in the police, where the majority of social evils and moral infirmities had bit by bit unfolded themselves before him. He enunciated certain new ideas, which he was reputed to have brought from Italy, on prison organisation, the solitary system, and penal servitude. From things he passed on to persons, and entertained Savari with accounts of some celebrated criminals, French and foreign, whose trials had interested him. He manifested a wish to be present during the sitting of an assize court, and asked if there was any interesting case likely to come on soon.

"You cannot imagine," he said, turning to his guests with an open-hearted manner, " how curious I have always been on these subjects. I have read the greater part of the cele-brated trials in various countries, and every book regarding the police system I could get hold of." Then, suddenly ad-dressing Savari, he added, "Do you know why I have always been drawn towards you ?"

"I have not the least idea."

" It is fantastic, ridiculous, I admit, and you will not bear me any good-will for it."

" At all events, I promise you I will bear you no ill-will."

" Well, my dear fellow, your name was familiar to me and seemed to come pleasantly to my lips. It differs only in the mode of spelling it from the name of one of the most distinguished Ministers of Police, René Savary, Duke de Rovigo, whose interesting memoirs I recently read with avidity. I am an original, but what of that? People please me by the most trifling good qualities."

" So much the better for me, since I have no good qualities that are not of the most frivolous description."

" Indeed you have, and I discovered them later on ; but in the first instance it was your name that won me over."

" And it never did me a greater service," said Savari graciously.

Vibert bowed, and continued, with his usual volubility— " Ah ! the police, trials, murders—they are my *forte*. Not that I am telling you any news, for ever since I knew you have I not been asking you daily to gain admittance for me to your prisons and your Palais-de-Justice? By-the-by, I must tell you that I have not waited for you, because you did not appear to be greatly interested in the matter. So I went this morning, before breakfast, and paid a round of visits of this description."

" Of what description ? "

" The Conciergerie, Sainte-Chapelle, and the Palais-de-Justice. I could not contain myself any longer, my worthy guide, and I followed my bent without you."

" Well, what did you see ? "

" Everything, absolutely everything. I took a guide, a brave old man about fifty years old, covered with medals, and an excellent one he was. Yes, I alighted from my cab outside the Conciergerie, and was gazing with wonderment at its huge towers, when my guide caught sight of me, and, no doubt, said to himself—'Here is a stranger, a sight-seer, a fool—I'll take charge of him, show him about, and then fleece him.' He came to me and offered his services, which I accepted eagerly, and as he had a friend at court, he was able to show me over pretty nearly everywhere. I saw the hall of the Pas-Perdus, one of the chambers of Correctional Police, the Assize Courts, and the tower in which Marie Antoinette was confined—it was curious—very curious. I was so thoroughly satisfied that I did not wish to dispense with my guide, and I hoped he, on his part, would stick to me. I owe a famous acquisition to him, too!"

"A famous acquisition!" said Savari, who, with Madame Vidal's permission, was lighting a cigarette.

"Yes, a famous acquisition," replied Vibert. "You shall see. Always accompanied by my guide, I went upstairs one minute, down the next, traversed passages, and, in short, I was examining the whole Palais-de-Justice when all at once I came upon a half-open door.

"'Where does this door lead to?' I asked.

"'To a room belonging to the registry.'

"'And what is in it?'

"'Heaps of papers, portfolios of all sorts, and particularly what at the Palais-de-Justice are called *pièces de conviction*, that is to say, all the miscellaneous articles that are produced on the various trials; the weapon used by a criminal, the hat he lost in his flight, the blood-stained handkerchief found upon him; in several instances the clothes of the victim, the watch which was stolen—in a word, all the different objects which have assisted judges and juries in bringing a case home. Whilst the trial is going on, and according to the necessities of the case, these different objects are removed from the registry to the Correctional Tribunal or the Assize Court, as the case may be.'

" ' But,' I asked, still impelled by my desire for knowledge, ' when the case is over and the matter at an end, what becomes of all these things ? '

" ' Some, under the authority of the public prosecutor, are restored to the owners or their friends, others are sold. You can well understand, sir,' added my guide, ' that even the Palais-de-Justice would not be large enough to contain all the objects of this sort, accumulating year by year.'

" ' And when do the sales of which you speak take place?' I asked, with interest.

" ' At certain dates fixed in advance. There is one going on now.'

" ' Where ? '

" ' Close to this place.'

" ' Indeed ! I should like to see that. I shall buy something, perhaps, which has belonged to a great criminal.'

" ' Nothing easier, sir, if you will have the goodness to follow me.'

" I did not say a word more, but followed my guide, and a quarter-of-an-hour later I was the possessor of a most curious relic, I assure you."

" A stolen jewel ? " asked Savari, between the whiffs of his cigarette.

" Oh ! better than that."

" An article of clothing which belonged to some wretched man who has found his way to the hulks, or the scaffold ? "

" Not a bit of it. I worship curiosities, but at the same time I like them to be of some use, or, at all events, to be free from anything repulsive or disgusting. An Englishman is not so particular. But I am not English, not I—I know how to mingle the useful with the agreeable, *utile dulci*, as the poet has it. But, see."

And abruptly, without further preparation he handed to Savari the knife which until then he had kept under the table, and which he had opened, whilst he was speaking, without any one having noticed him. Julia, pale and trembling, leaning half over the table, looked on.

Vibert, in handing the knife, had risen. His two hands rested on the back of a chair, and from behind his blue glasses he looked on, too. But he looked on coolly, ready to seize on the least change of countenance on the part of his adversary. For the moment he forbade his heart to beat, and it stopped.

The waiters had cleared the table, and left the room. No sound was heard but the dull rumbling of the carriages on the Boulevard.

At last, then, the truth would perhaps come out. If Savari were the murderer, it appeared impossible, considering the surroundings of the scene, cleverly prepared as they were, that he could avoid betraying himself by a start, an exclamation, or a shudder, at the sight of the weapon, which would recall his crime to his remembrance in the most vivid and matter-of-fact manner.

Savari, at first, showed a certain unwillingness to touch the knife held out to him, but, after having at length taken and carefully examined it, he replaced it on the table, with the remark—"I should not advise you, if you are ever attacked, to make use of this weapon. It is in a shocking bad state."

Vibert was confounded. All his calculations were upset, his plans destroyed. The expense of the dinner at the Café Anglais and the *mise en scène* was thrown away. For three months he had been wasting his time and working at a dead loss ; he had been hunting on a false scent. Truly it was enough to drive him to despair.

Whilst giving way to these reflections, it occurred to him to discover the impression made upon Julia. He went back to her side, whilst Savari, without troubling himself any

more about the knife on the table, had risen and was lighting
a second cigarette at one of the candles placed on the piano.
Julia had not changed her attitude ; only she was not quite
so pale, and a sad smile passed over her lips.   One would
have said that she was indifferent to the futile result which
had been obtained.

This was too much for the irascible Vibert.   What! whilst
he was in despair, his companion, his accomplice, she who
was even more interested than he in the success of the experiment, did not despair with him !   He was defeated, and,
to look at her, one might believe that instead of lamenting
his failure, she was rejoicing over it.   Such a piece of
injustice revolted him, but far from disheartening him, inspired him with a sudden desire for revenge.

" The game is not lost yet," he said to himself ; "the experiment that I have just tried was incomplete.   It is
possible that in a moment of fury and exasperation, a
murderer would make use of the first weapon he could lay
his hands on, without even looking at it, and that consequently he would have no recollection of it.   I must complete the experiment."

He rejoined Savari, talked to him for a few moments on
indifferent subjects, took his arm, and walked up and down
the room, bringing him nearer and nearer, by degrees, to the
table and the place he had previously left.

" So," he said at length, sitting down at his side, and
pointing to the knife on the table, " this weapon, which I
was fortunate enough to buy, will not, according to you, be
of any use."

" I do not think so ; the point is blunted.   Look at it
yourself."

" So it is," said Vibert, appearing to scrutinise it closely.
" 'Tis easy to understand how that comes about.   The point
must have struck a rib-bone on entering the victim's body."

"What!" asked Savari, quickly.   "Was somebody actually struck by this weapon?"

"Yes, and the blow was mortal."

"Who told you that?"

"My guide, of course.   Do you think I buy things of this sort without collecting every particle of information as to their origin and history?   This knife has a history, and I have it at my finger's end.   It was the property of a young man, who was murdered in the month of October last, in Paris, at No. 6, Rue de la Paix."

Savari started.

Vibert continued—"This young man was called—wait a moment—I shall remember the name directly—he was called—"

"Maurice Vidal," said Savari.

It was Vibert's turn now to start in surprise.   "You know the case?" he asked.

"I was directly mixed up in it," said Savari.

"How?"

"I was charged with Maurice Vidal's murder."

"You!"

"Yes, I!   So when you spoke to me so abruptly of this crime, my emotion was extreme.   The very memory of it distresses me, and I have every reason to turn as pale as death.   Have the kindness to pass me the water bottle."

Vibert complied.   Savari drank a mouthful of water, and resumed—"If you only knew the misery and annoyance I suffered from that affair!   Would you believe that I was arrested, thrown into prison—?"

"Impossible," said Vibert.

"Alas! It is only too true.   I had to appear before a magistrate; I was in solitary confinement.   I even had the handcuffs on, according to the custom of the police in France. Yes, it is of no use being calm and going where you are told; the handcuffs are put on all the same. It is a pre-cautionary measure."

Then turning towards Julia, he continued—"Pardon my emotion. I know it is not quite the thing at the end of a dinner party, and in the presence of a lady, but when I think of all my sufferings I am no longer master of myself."

"If I had suspected for a moment," said Vibert, "believe me, my dear sir—"

He stopped in the full swing of his excuses, and after-wards said with a perfectly natural air—"May we know how you got out of all this difficulty?"

"By proving in the clearest manner possible that I could not have been the culprit."

"But how came the idea of suspecting you into any magistrate's head?"

"Simply because I had been in constant communication with Maurice Vidal up to two days before his death."

"By heaven, this is too dreadful," cried Vibert, "I suppose that if you were to be murdered to-night, I should be sus-pected of the crime because I had spent the evening with you."

"Certainly you would stand a good chance of being arrested if nobody had discovered the real culprit. I advise you to be on your guard," added Savari, whose colour was returning.

"Justice is rather eccentric," remarked the detective.

"Not so much so as you might imagine; after all, she does her duty, and you see that she loses no time in re-leasing those who are innocent. But, all the same, I have suffered terribly, and you have this evening re-opened a wound which was barely healed."

For the last few minutes he had been speaking calmly, without anger, and in a measured tone. A sort of melancholy appeared to be diffused over him, and there were tears in his voice. All at once he reached across the table, took the knife in his hands, and submitted it to a long and silent examination.

"And it was with this that you were killed, poor Maurice Vidal!" he said. "You were no friend of mine, and I had with you some unpleasant discussions in my own interest. Yes, you, the upright man *par excellence*, the man successful by sheer force of toil, energy, and honesty, you would not set yourself to understand the difficulties of my life, the obstacles, both social and innate in myself, which stood in the way of my being what you were. You were ever stern, harsh, unjust perhaps, to me, still I have no grudge against you for that, Maurice Vidal. You had youth, wealth, and strength, and one second of time, one blow with this thing that does not even resemble a weapon, sufficed to rob you of all!"

Savari hesitated for a moment, and then, without looking at Julia or Vibert, resumed—"Ah! if the man who killed you had been aware of certain details of your life, as I knew them after this lamentable event had taken place, if he had known that you loved and were beloved, and that you were expecting on the morrow the companion of your heart, then perhaps his hand would have trembled, and the fatal blow would not have been struck. Poor fellow! Poor woman!"

Savari was silent, and heavy tears coursed down his cheeks. At the same moment Julia, whose courage had up to this time sustained her, but who was shaken by all that she had gone through during the day, broke into a passion of sobs just as the last words fell from the lips of Savari.

Vibert's first impulse was to rush to her, but, remembering that this sudden outburst of grief required explanation, he turned towards Savari, and said with an air of annoyance —"This, too, is all our fault; we have been too dramatic. For the last hour we have done nothing but talk of murder and assassination. You have been growing sentimental over this story, I was stupid enough to be engrossed by it, and she—she has a nervous attack, and I must say with some excuse too !"

Savari did not utter a syllable, but watched Julia's tears without going near her.

"Come," said Vibert, desirous of putting an end to this scene, "what we had better do now is to separate, and come to a mutual understanding to be more lively in future."

He rang, ordered a cab and took Madame Vidal home, Savari meanwhile going his own way. In Julia's present state Vibert was unwilling to come to any explanation with her, so he confided her to Marietta's care, and left.

What explanation, in fact, was there to have ? What fresh proof did he possess of Savari's guilt ? He had anticipated producing a great effect ; that effect had been produced and had exceeded his expectation. Savari did not confine himself to turning pale and trembling. He had given way to tears, and had exhibited every indication of a real, lively emotion. But this emotion admitted of a very easy explanation, and Vibert was caught in his own trap. He had contrived for his own pleasure an admirable *mise en scène*, he had brought about an excess of feeling on the part of his adversary, had softened his heart and disposed him to sentimentality. What more natural than that Savari should break down over the recollection of an affair in which he had found himself so directly concerned, and from which he had suffered so cruelly ? His paleness, his tears, his emotion, were no evidences of guilt ; they merely testified to the fact that the suspicions which were rife against him, his arrest, and the hours he had passed in prison, had inflicted on his heart a wound which still bled. While seeking to confound Savari, Vibert had given him an opportunity of appearing in the most favourable light possible. This man, who had hitherto been credited with being trivial, common-place, and even incapable of high sentiments, had suddenly shown himself serious, impressionable, and reflecting. He was moved at the death of Maurice Vidal, he had eulogised him who at one time had been his enemy, he had paid a tribute to his memory, and had mingled his tears with those of Julia Vidal.

In giving way to these various reflections, all tending to render him downcast, Vibert made his way to his rooms in the Rue de l'Arbre-Sec, which he had not thought of giving up. He was not sorry to resume for a moment his old character, to lay aside the habiliments of the Count de Rubini, which had profited him so little, and to indulge in the reminiscences of a life which, if not merry, had been at least uniform and peaceful, and which was recalled to him by his little room on the fifth floor.

" Ah ! M. Vibert," said the porter, recognising him, "it is a long time since we set eyes on you—"

" I have been in the country. Has anything happened during my absence ? "

" Nothing, except that this letter has been left for you."

Vibert took the letter handed to him. It bore the stamp of the commissary of police of the Tuileries section, and was couched in the following terms—

" My dear Vibert—During the time you were employed in my office, you had under your consideration, in my absence, the case of an escaped convict, called Langlade, and a tall red-haired girl, known by the nick-name of Soleil-Couchant.

" Information, which you alone can give, is required at the Prefecture in connection with these two persons, and I should be obliged if you would come and see me as soon as possible in my office, so that I may be enabled, in concert with you, to draw up the required memorandum.   X."

" I will go to-morrow morning before returning to the Hotel des Princes," said Vibert to himself, as he put the letter in his pocket and went upstairs.

PART II.

CHAPTER I.

AFTER having passed the night following the dinner at the Café Anglais in his little room at the Rue de l'Arbre-Sec, and after having on the morrow given the commissary of police of the Tuileries section the required information with regard to Langlade and Soleil-Couchant, Vibert returned to his rooms at the Hotel des Princes.

He had been debating seriously within himself as to whether he had not better give up the game, write and tell the magistrate that Savari was either innocent or too clever to furnish weapons against himself, pay a last visit to Madame Vidal and express his regret that he was unable to serve her further, and, in short, resign his post as a police agent on extraordinary service.

Restrained by his *amour propre*, or by some feeling of a totally different nature, he did not give effect to these ideas, but resumed, for a time at least, the part of the Count de Rubini, which he had so wonderfully created and made his own. The only difference consisted in his not playing it with the same perfection; he was, so to speak, merely a substitute for the original character. Carelessness in his dress, formerly attended to so scrupulously, might now be noticed; in speaking, he sometimes forgot that he was an Italian, and at times he appeared surprised when the waiters at the hotel addressed him as "count."

Simultaneously with all this, his temper became unequal,

his manner abrupt and hasty, and his mode of life decidedly irregular. He appeared to labour under some fixed idea which occasionally, when he was pacing with long strides his sitting-room in the hotel, would force from him senseless exclamations, fragments of sentences, or soliloquies—

"Fool!" he would say to himself, "you wanted to leave your peaceful office in the Rue Saint-Honoré, to live, forsooth—well, you are living. What have you to complain about? To suffer is to live! To live is to suffer! Ah! you have life enough, for you suffer much."

He would stop for a moment, draw his hand across his forehead, and say, "It is well done—I tell you it is well done. That will teach you; instead of remaining quietly in your hole, you wanted to have passions like the rest of the world; you gave your heart leave to beat—and it has profited by your permission, like the artful creature that it is. It beats, but to make up for not having beaten until to-day it hammers away now with force enough to burst its fragile casing."

He would break out into a laugh, and add, "Well, and if the casing were to burst, what then? No more anger, no more rage, no more envy, and no more suffering! A few feet of earth, a common grave, a wooden cross, perhaps, given by the Marquis de X——, and all is told! No," he cried, savagely, "I will not die, I am not such a fool as to die of such things as these—I, Vibert, die because—Bah! this is too absurd. How the Marquis would laugh, and I, too, first of all, in my tomb underneath my little garden— No, on the contrary, I want to live, to live well, and indulge in every kind of folly. Folly, indeed—I'll have enough of it. I will live in one year sufficiently to make up for all the time during which I have been only existing."

He would stop short once more, and then resume his monologue more calmly but with a sort of bitter sadness, "I boast, but I could not live so. One cannot change one's habits in a day. At thirty-five one cannot burn for pleasures yet untasted. Besides, there are memories which cannot be effaced, thoughts not to be chased away at will, images whose place none others can take—Ah! if I had a son," he continued, still harping on the same idea, "I would launch him at eighteen out into the world's ocean and the whirlpool of passion. 'Go,' I would say to him, 'love, rejoice, suffer, expend your energies, wear your heart on your sleeve, let who will peck at it, drag it through every bramble on your road. So you will make it invulnerable and insensible, and when the strength of your manhood comes upon you, you will laugh instead of weeping, you will make others suffer, but escape suffering yourself.'"

Then he would laugh mockingly again. "Make other people suffer, did I say? Vibert, my friend, you are mad. Your son would, no doubt, be like you, and no one built after your mould would make others suffer. Look at yourself! Here is a glass, take courage and contemplate the handsome image there reflected. With a figure such as that, with a physique such as yours, a man may suffer, but he will not be the cause of suffering in others. Make up your mind, my worthy fellow, and turn away your face quickly, lest you should be frightened at yourself."

Then, passing rapidly to a different train of thought, he said, "Let me reflect; what am I doing here? Why am I not at the office? I am a government servant, after all; I draw my salary, but I am only playing at work—I am scribbling on the margin of my duty—I have a mission to fulfil, and I am not fulfilling it. I have given no end of trouble, I have said I was certain of success. Well, what about this success? I have thrown up my hand in the middle of the game, without finding out whether it is lost. It is not lost —the devil take it, it shall not be lost, and I will pick my cards up again."

Then, if he were in his rooms, he would go out at once ; if he were already out, he would hurry with rapid strides towards the Rue de Grammont. But when he reached a certain door he would stop short suddenly and begin again one of his never-ending soliloquies.

"What is the use of going up? What shall I learn up there? Yes, he is at her side, by heaven, I know it well. What can I do there? I must wait now; wait without showing myself or disturbing them. It is my only method of getting at the truth, my sole plank of safety—and it is but a shaky one—I suffer atrociously at being obliged to trust to it."

One day, however, Vibert did not stop at Julia's door; he hurried past the porter, went up the back staircase, and did not come down for an hour afterwards. Nevertheless, he was not shown in to Madame Vidal; Marietta did not hear him ring; nobody suspected his presence in the house. What became of him during all that time?

He in all probability did not learn anything to his satisfaction. Undoubtedly this mysterious visit was a source of great discouragement to him and made him thoroughly disgusted with life, for on the day after his visit to the Rue de Grammont he committed one of those terrible acts of imprudence which generally serve as a cloak to some unavowed idea of suicide.

Being summoned in the morning to the Prefecture of Police to recount the details of the case entrusted to him, he was shown into the office of the chief of the detective force. Just as he entered, he overheard the following conversation between the chief and one of the *employés*.

"You place entire credit, therefore, in the information given by the woman."

"Yes, sir ; it is certainly her interest to speak the truth."

"According to her, Langlade will sleep to-night in the Rue Croix-des-Petits-Champs?"

" It is more than probable."

"Nothing, then, hinders you from arresting him to-morrow morning ?"

" No, sir; none of my men will hesitate to follow, but I must warn you that their lives will be in great danger. This Langlade has a terrible reputation. Twice he has escaped from the hulks at Toulon and Brest. He is gifted with enormous strength and never lies down without a pair of loaded pistols ready to his hand. The first man who enters his room is sure to be killed."

" Bah ! that is, if he does not know his business," said Vibert, who was standing near the door.

The chief and the inspector turned round in astonishment. " I should like to see you there," said the inspector.

" That is easy enough. You have only to follow me if I am authorised to go to-morrow morning to the Rue Croix-des-Petits-Champs."

" Who are you ?" said the chief, looking at him more attentively.

" I am called simply Vibert, sir, and you have summoned me in connection with the murder in the Rue de la Paix."

" Ah ! very good. I remember you now; we have not heard of you for some time. Well, what have you to tell me ?"

" Nothing new, sir. I am still waiting, and very impatiently, I can assure you."

" Very well ; we know your zeal, and we rely on you. Now, to return to Langlade—you offer to arrest him."

" Certainly."

" But," exclaimed the inspector, " you do not know the man you have to deal with."

" There you are mistaken," replied Vibert. " Langlade has already passed through my hands, when I was secretary to the commissary of police in the Rue St. Honoré. He was bold enough to come one morning, accompanied by a woman, to ask me for a passport for England. His manner seemed to me suspicious, so I had him followed and arrested. After that he escaped a second time from the hulks, whither I was the cause of his retreating."

"Since you know him so well, I wonder he does not frighten you more. You, doubtless, remember his gigantic size?"

"Perfectly. I am a dwarf by the side of very many people, and particularly so by his, but I do not forget the victory of David over Goliath."

"Do you mean to say you think of engaging him in single combat?"

"Why not?"

"You intend to arrest him, alone?"

"And if I do?"

"You want to be killed, I presume!" exclaimed the inspector.

"That does not concern you. It is simply a question of performing a difficult task. Nobody likes to undertake it. I, on the contrary, will take it in hand, and I ask neither reward nor assistance of any kind. Allow me to say, sir," he added, addressing himself this time directly to the chief, "that to refuse so disinterested an offer of service would come with a bad grace from you."

"But nobody does refuse, and I am about at once to put you in communication with those who can give you all the necessary information. One word more. Are you not afraid that, whilst you are engaged with this Langlade, you will be neglecting the other very important affair entrusted to you?"

"Sir," replied Vibert, "two hours will suffice for the arrest of this Colossus of yours. I will take them out of my time for sleep—not a very difficult matter, seeing that I do not sleep."

"Well," said the chief, with a smile, "the description I have had of you is correct; you are indeed a singular policeman." Vibert, by way of reply, bowed gravely.

CHAPTER II.

On the following morning, about half-past five, Vibert climbed, with a determined step, up the staircase of the house in the Rue-Croix-des-Petits-Champs, where Langlade was supposed to be sleeping. After having looked in vain for a bell outside the door pointed out to him, he knocked vigorously.

"Who's there?" shouted somebody inside the room.

"A detective to arrest you," replied Vibert.

"You are joking," said the voice. "If you were a detective, you would not say so. Those gentlemen take more precautions than that before they venture into my society. It's you, is it not, Crampin?"

"Yes, yes, open the door."

"It's hard to get out of a warm bed, but for a friend one may brave the cold. I'll open the door, and jump into bed again."

Hardly had the bolt been shot and the key turned in the lock, than Vibert, who was all ready at the door, pushed it open quickly, burst into the room, made one bound towards the bed, and laid hold of a double-barrelled pistol loaded and at full cock, which was lying on a table close by. Presenting it at Langlade, he exclaimed—"Stir a step, and you are a dead man."

"A thousand devils!" shouted the convict, "it is a detective."

"Did I not tell you so, fool? Come, you are caught. Surrender."

"I surrender—never," exclaimed Langlade, exasperated. "I'd rather eat you, you rascal! You have my pistol, but I have a heavy fist, and teeth that cut like steel."

F

"Pooh!" said Vibert, quietly; "to make any use of them you must catch me, and if you move an inch towards me I'll stretch you on the ground."

And with the pistol in his right hand raised to the level of his eye, just as if he were in a shooting gallery taking aim at a plaster figure, he sat down calmly on the bed which Langlade had just quitted. At four paces from him stood the convict, half-naked, foaming with rage, but not daring to advance. They looked at each other for a moment, the one ready for a spring, the other to fire.

Vibert was the first to speak. "Well," said he, in a bantering tone, "you have given up your idea of eating me. I am sorry for that. I should like an original kind of death."

"You must be a fool-hardy swaggerer to dare to get in here," exclaimed Langlade, suddenly controlling himself and looking round for something to make a weapon of.

"Enough of that," replied Vibert; "report makes you out much more terrible than you are. Come, don't fidget about in that way, or I shall be obliged to shoot you in the leg to keep you quiet. What is it you want? What are you looking for? Your slippers, perhaps; you are cold about the feet. Here they are; take them. I am a good sort of fellow, and I shouldn't like you to catch cold."

And, always on his guard, he picked up with his left hand, a pair of shoes which were at the foot of the bed, and threw them over to the convict.

"Thanks," said Langlade, who had by this time regained all his wonted assurance. "One is firmer on one's feet with shoes on."

"That's just why I gave you yours. Would you like your coat, trousers and waistcoat? Don't worry yourself; I have them here close to my hand."

"Well, if you don't mind, I should like nothing better," replied the convict, wondering at this excess of politeness.

The coat, trousers and waistcoat, thrown across in the same way and with similar precaution, went after the slippers.

"Without wishing to be impertinent, what do you think you are going to do when you are dressed?" asked Vibert, as Langlade hastily put on his clothes.

"I don't exactly know yet; I have thought over it, but I have not quite made up my mind. I think I should throw myself upon you, if you had not that infernal pistol, which annoys me slightly."

"Would you like that, too?"

"That I should, but—"

"But you are afraid that I should like to keep it. There is no knowing. Come, if I give it up, what will you do with it?"

"Kill you with it, of course. That's a nice question to ask," replied the convict, shrugging his shoulders.

"Are you quite sure?" asked Vibert.

"Quite."

"At one shot?"

"With one shot. I'll aim at your heart."

"Aim away, my friend. Here, take your pistol."

Vibert left his place, walked straight up to Langlade, gave him the pistol, turned his back on him, and seated himself again on the bed. Then he crossed his arms, and said—"I am waiting."

"You can't be a detective," said the convict, dumbfounded.

"What an ungrateful fellow you are!" said Vibert. "I have been kind to you, treated you in fact like a son, and you refuse to give me my title."

"What! You are a real detective?"

"Of course I am. What do you want me to be? A peer of France, perhaps. Not such a fool. They bore themselves too much. I know one who does nothing but eat his words all day long. I am a detective, a real one. Look here, I have in my pocket the principal attributes of my profession—a pair of handcuffs. They are, indeed, all I brought with me. I have left my sword-stick at home."

"Well, you are a cool hand!"

"You made that remark before, my dear Langlade," observed Vibert, lying down on the bed on the side near the wall. "You are becoming monotonous."

"And you really think I am going to let you put those handcuffs on me?"

"You are going either to kill me, or to let me put the handcuffs on. Between ourselves, the choice lies with you; it's a matter of indifference to me. All I ask is that you will do one or the other."

"You don't care much about your life, then?"

"Don't be stupid! Should I have come to call you this morning if I had cared for my life?" Then abruptly turning his back on Langlade, and changing his tone, he continued—"It is rather cold here, and you have forgotten to light your fire. Let us go; they are waiting for us."

"Where?"

"At the Conciergerie, an establishment where, I think, you will be suited down to the ground. You will be just in time to be examined to-morrow. Make yourself easy! In your position as a *cheval de retour*, they will pay every attention to you. You won't be herded with the small fry. You'll have a cell to yourself, I undertake to say."

"What! You ——," shouted Langlade.

"Don't make such a noise; you will rouse the neighbours, and it is only just six o'clock."

"The shot that I am going to fire straight at your heart will rouse them better."

"Leave me alone. You are always threatening and never doing. It is becoming wearisome," replied Vibert, stretching himself this time at full length upon the bed.

Langlade made one bound at him and presented the pistol full at his chest. Vibert murmured a name, looked fixedly at Langlade, and waited.

It was impossible for this giant, whose strength was doubled by anger, not to get the better of his puny, wasted, sickly, and unarmed enemy.

Nearly a minute passed away, and then the convict's eyes fell; he let go the pistol, and, stepping back, said—" Ten thousand devils ! I dare not kill him ! "

"Well," said Vibert, getting up, "I ought not to have reckoned on it. I must suffer still."

"You are unhappy, then?" asked Langlade, coming near him.

" As the stones in a prison wall ! So unhappy that I would exchange my place as a detective for yours as a convict on his way back to the hulks. Ah, if you could make that exchange you would be doing me a brave service. But I did not come here to unfold my paltry sorrows. This time nothing hinders us, let us go."

" Go, if you will. I shall not kill you. As for me, I stay here."

" That is impossible, my dear Langlade," replied Vibert, whose good humour was returning by degrees. "I have sworn to bring you with me. Come, don't let us stand on ceremony; you are a good sort of fellow, and so am I. Let us come to an understanding, and as quickly as possible. You are attached to a tall red-haired girl, are you not, called Stéphanie Cornu, nick-named Soleil-Couchant ?"

" How do you know that ? "

" Do not we detectives know everything ? It is our trade to be well informed. Besides, if you insist on details, I do not mind telling you that Soleil-Couchant herself told us where you were to sleep to-night."

" It is false," bellowed Langlade.

" It is true, I tell you. If it were not true I should not amuse myself so uselessly at your expense. I have a great respect for love affairs, and I hold it to be cowardly to tell a man that his sweetheart is betraying him when such is not the case. It would be more merciful to kill him outright."

"Ah, you are right," said the giant, whose expression had entirely changed. "I wish you had struck me with a knife instead of telling me of this deed of treachery."

"You are not exacting, at any rate," said Vibert, with a sigh.

All of a sudden, Langlade confronted the detective, and, presenting the pistol at his breast, said—"You swear that Soleil-Couchant has betrayed me?"

"I swear it," said Vibert, without moving a muscle.

The convict looked long at him, and then drawing back, said—"You can't be lying, you are too brave."

He sank into a chair, his arms hanging helplessly down and whispered to himself—"'Tis the reason I have not seen her these two days past. The wretch! And yet I love her so well! She is all I love on this earth."

Then, turning towards Vibert, he added amidst a passion of tears—"I give myself up; put the handcuffs on me."

"What do you take me for?" said Vibert. "Take advantage of your weakness—never! Now that you are in a calmer frame of mind, we will see what can be done."

After a moment's delay he went up to Langlade, slapped him on the shoulder, and said—"Come with me, and I will take care that you see Soleil-Couchant."

The convict drew himself up—"You know, then, where to find her?" he said.

"Of course. She has been in prison since yesterday. Fear got possession of her; she was compromised in some very serious matters; she thought she was lost, and destined to be imprisoned for the rest of her life, and she betrayed you in order to secure the good graces of the Prefecture."

"The coward! And you offer to bring me to her?"

"At once."

"But I shall kill her."

"That is your affair. I am merely ordered to arrest you, and you will find that you are sufficiently arrested when you reach the prison. If it then pleases you to kill Soleil-Couchant I have nothing to say against it. One woman more or less does not much matter," added Vibert, contemptuously.

"I am ready ; let us go," exclaimed the convict.

"Let us go," said the police-agent.

CHAPTER III.

VIBERT, accompanied by Langlade, went down the stairs. The convict did not seem to know what he was doing. Buried in his thoughts, his head hanging down on his breast he followed the detective mechanically, as a dog follows his master. Soleil-Couchant had betrayed him. What mattered anything else ?

A cab was passing, and Vibert hailed it. Then, pushing Langlade before him, he said—"Get in first, I beg. Don't stand on ceremony."

He told the driver to proceed in the direction of the Palais-de-Justice, and seated himself by the convict. For a moment neither spoke, each giving way to his own reflections without disturbing his companion. Soon, however, Langlade, whose nerves were being shaken by the forced inaction, gave a vigorous kick at the seat in front of him, and exclaimed—

"To betray me thus—me, who have done so much for her ! Have I ever let her want for anything? Never ! She has had from me all she desired. I was the slave of her every whim. If she had said to me, 'I want that shop-ful of jewellery,' I would have stripped the place the next night. One day, as we were walking along the Rue Vivienne, she called out, 'That dress would suit me to perfection.' That same evening it was in her room."

"You bought it ? " asked Vibert ironically.

"No," replied the convict proudly, "I stole it. Did I want

money for myself?" he went on to say. "Nothing of the kind.
A glass of wine, a hunch of bread, and a truss of straw. I asked
for no more. It was for her sake that I was bound to have
money at all risks. It was to meet her expenses that I first
turned thief, and then murderer."

"Forsooth," said the detective sententiously, "take any crime
you like, scratch the surface of it, and you will find a woman
underneath. That idea is none of mine ; it is as old as the hills.
Would Adam have picked the apple if Eve had not hankered
after it ?"

"The last time I was sent to the hulks," continued Langlade, following out his own train of thought, "it was her
doing. Did I ever reproach her? No, and at Brest I still
found means to get hold of money for her to spend. For
that I made those straw boxes and cocoa-nut manikins. But
that was not enough. One day she wrote to me to say that
she wanted a hundred francs. A hundred francs, how was I
to find them on the hulks? I thought of robbing three convict
warders of their savings. For that I was condemned to the
black hole for a month in double irons, but she got her hundred
francs to pay her rent."

"Men are unjust," remarked Vibert, "robbing a warder
merited a reward."

"In short," said Langlade, continuing to soliloquise in his
corner, "it is for her sake that I have committed all my
crimes, those that have come to light, as well as those that
nobody knows of."

Here Vibert started involuntarily. With his head indolently
resting against one of the sides of the cab and his legs stretched
out at full length on the opposite seat, he had contented himself with embellishing the conversation with an occasional
aphorism. The convict soliloquised on one side, and the *employé*
of the Prefecture of Police on the other—a very harmless mode
of passing the time. But the convict's last words, "the crimes

which have come to light, as well as those that nobody knows," aroused Vibert from his listlessness. The detective, devoted to his profession and enamoured of his art, awoke to consciousness. On the previous night these words might have been used in his presence with impunity. He had been in such a state of syncope, in a condition of such mental and bodily prostration, that he would not have thought of paying any attention to them. What did the police, or his duties, or the crimes of a Langlade matter to him then? He waste his time indeed on a convict! It was Savari that he was after, and Savari alone. The world for him began and ended in the Rue de Grammont. When he volunteered to arrest Langlade, it was from no zealous motive, but merely in the hope of finding some distraction from his grief. This distraction he had found. The expedition he had just been engaged in, the danger he had run, his futile attempt to bid adieu to life, his morning drive in Paris cheek by jowl with a notorious criminal—all this had to a certain extent recalled him from his stupor. He took a new lease of life, and the Count de Rubini disappeared to make way for Vibert, the police-agent. There were then in Langlade's career crimes which were hidden from the world. They must be brought to light.

" By-the-way, do you know what time it is?" said Vibert, after a momentary pause of reflection.

" Hem! What does it matter to me what o'clock it is?"

" An idea has just flashed across me."

" What?"

" It is too early yet to see Soleil-Couchant."

" Ah!" shouted the convict in a threatening tone, "you are already on the look-out for an excuse to break faith with me."

" You are a queer customer," said Vibert calmly, "at the slightest provocation you go off for all the world like a squib. What I have had the honour to convey to you is, nevertheless, very simple. I cannot present myself at the depôt of the Pre-

fecture, and say to the jailers, 'Gentlemen, allow me to introduce my friend, M. Langlade, an escaped convict. He is
desirous of a moment's interview with his sweetheart, Mademoiselle Soleil-Couchant, who at the present time is an inmate
of your house ; would you have the kindness, gentlemen, either
to request the young lady's attendance in her drawing-room, or
to conduct M. Langlade to her chamber !' The jailers would
reply, ' This visit of M. Langlade does us much honour, and
gives us even greater pleasure from the hope that we entertain
of his making a long stay with us. But we have no power to
disturb Mademoiselle Soleil-Couchant. To secure an interview
with her, a permit, duly authorised, is necessary, and the individuals who could oblige your friend with such a document
are, at this early hour, still in bed !' That is what would
assuredly happen to you. You are no fool, and you will
acknowledge the difficulty."

"Well, and what then?" asked Langlade curtly, altogether
insensible to the sportive sallies of the police-agent.

"*Mon Dieu !*" replied Vibert as mildly as ever, "I simply
propose to wile away two or three hours, where and as you
please. There is a little delay, that is all. You can rely upon
me, because I promise you I will not leave you. At 9 a.m.,
we will betake ourselves to the Prefecture, I shall interview the
chief of the detective force for an instant, I will tell him that I
have pledged my word to you, and he will assist me in fulfilling my engagement. At 10 a.m., at the latest, you will be
in the presence of Soleil-Couchant. Does that suit you ?"

"It must suit me," said the convict surlily.

"Come, now, you are showing yourself amenable to reason.
I expected as much from you. The question is, what are we to
do with our spare time ? Have you an idea ?"

"No."

"What say you to a good breakfast ?"

"I am not hungry."

"Selfish being! That you may not be hungry is quite possible, but as for me, who had to get up at 5 a.m., to call upon you, you don't think of me. Besides you have been giving me no end of new sensations. You wanted to kill me, and you did not want to kill me. I shut my eyes and I opened them again. I said, 'it's all over'—and, presto! I began to live once more. All this kind of thing tends to create a vacuum, you understand." And leaning out of the door, Vibert called to the driver to put them down at Baratte's, in the Market Place.

" No, not there," cried Langlade.

" Why not? Do they feed you badly there?"

"I have another reason."

" You owe money there?"

" No, I don't owe anything."

" What is it, then?"

" I dined there three days ago with *her*," replied the convict, sighing.

Vibert looked at Langlade without any sign of astonishment; he understood him. A police-agent and a convict, two extremes, meet on some points. Still, Vibert perceived an advantage to be gained by bringing Langlade again to the room where he had dined with Soleil-Couchant.

They got out of the cab, went past the bar and ascended a kind of ladder, mis-called a staircase. On the first floor they were shown into a room, which drew from Langlade the exclamation—" It is the same. I recognise it."

"Just the sort of thing that would happen by accident," replied Vibert, the philosopher.

He then ordered an excellent breakfast, suitable for the occasion, and seating himself opposite to the convict, said to himself—" I am not fit to belong to the police if by the time we have finished breakfast I have not wormed all his secrets out of this fool. I wonder what nice things, in hidden crimes, he has been guilty of?"

CHAPTER IV.

BREAKFAST opened with four dozen oysters, and Vibert, by way of setting a good example, lost no time in doing honour to them. Langlade was not slow in keeping up. with him. Either from the return of his appetite, or from braggadocio, he evidently was not desirous of seeming any longer to regret his faithless fair one.

"Give your orders," said Vibert, when the four dozen had disappeared ; "don't be bashful. The State pays the piper. I have some secret service funds."

"Then I vote for a ' chateaubriand,' " said the convict, who was cheering up under the influence of the first bottle of white wine.

"A 'chateaubriand' be it, then. You are still sweet on this Soleil-Couchant of yours, eh?" asked Vibert abruptly.

"No, I don't care for her any longer," replied the other, bringing his heavy fist down on the table with such force as to smash a couple of wine-glasses. "Ah !" he went on to say, "if you only knew the tricks she has played me."

"I have some idea of them ; women are always the same. And after each prank, you adored her all the more; is it not so?"

"Alas !" He drank off a glass of wine, and added—"But I don't want to talk any more about that. I should, perhaps, say too much—"

"That's worth knowing," muttered Vibert. "Rest easy, old fellow. We shall come back to it before we have finished breakfast."

Then turning towards Langlade, who was sitting, apparently in a dream, with his elbows on the table and his head between his hands, he said—"What! have you finished already?

Think better of it; you won't sit down to such a breakfast again, perhaps, for a long time."

" Why not?" asked the convict, raising his head.

" Why? You ought to know by this time, after your long experience, that the State is not in the habit of indulging her lodgers with ' chateaubriands.' "

" I know that well enough. But, perhaps, I don't intend to take up my abode again with the State," said Langlade, looking the detective full in the face.

" Really ?" replied the latter, without appearing in the least disturbed. " I laboured under the impression that I had had the pleasure of arresting you this very morning."

" You arrested me, I admit; but who is to prevent my going away when I have finished breakfast ?"

" I!"

" You !" said the giant, laughing. " You have not had a good look at me, I suppose ?" He stood up, and his head touched the ceiling of the room.

" Well," said Vibert, looking at him through his glasses, " you are a fine man. I knew that, and I don't think it is very kind of you to make a parade of your physical advantages before me."

" I only wanted to make you understand," said the convict, sitting down again, " that when breakfast is over, it would be the easiest thing in the world for me to take you up in my arms, stuff a table-napkin in your mouth to prevent your crying out, and pitch you under the table whilst I took myself off at my ease to my own affairs."

" Yes," replied Vibert, helping Langlade to half an omelet which the waiter had just placed on the table, " all that you have just said would appear at first sight very easy to carry out, that I admit, only—"

" Only ?"

" You won't carry it out."

" Why ? "

" Two considerations will prevent you."

" What are they ? "

" First of all, you will not be able even to get near me."

" You are joking."

" Not a bit of it, I am quite serious.   Look here."   And as
he said this he placed a double-barrelled pistol before him.

" Do you recognise it ? " he asked.

" It is my pistol."

" Evidently.   Just now, in your despair, you forgot it.   I,
on the contrary, took possession of it.   If, during your
absence, a domiciliary visit had by chance been paid to your
residence, the discovery of this weapon would have compromised
you, and I wanted to save you that unpleasantness.   Oh," he
continued, " it is of no use your casting longing eyes on the
pistol.   I am not going to give it up to you again.   Times
have changed considerably in the last hour.   This morning I
did not care one straw about my life; now, your society and
this white wine have made me quite sprightly once more, and I
wish to live.   Have the goodnoss to remember that.   What
shall we have for dessert ? " he added, resuming his pleasant
manner.   " I propose Roquefort cheese, some almonds and rais-
ins and a cup of capital coffee with a dash of brandy in it.
Does that please you ? "

" As you like," was the surly reply.   " But you spoke to
me of two considerations which would prevent me leaving the
restaurant without you.   You have told me the first—now for
the second."

" Oh, the second is a better one still."

" Let us have it."

" I promised that before lodging you in prison I would
procure you the pleasure of seeing Soleil-Couchant.   You would
not wish to put it out of my power to keep my promise ? "

"Pshaw! I value my liberty more than a woman," replied Langlade carelessly.

"That may be, but still you want to see her to cast in her teeth all the reproaches your heart has been heaping up against her for the last two hours, and which are choking you."

"Yes, yes, that is it," cried the convict, who an instant before had tossed off a whole glass of neat brandy. "And when I have told her all that is in my heart I'll strangle her with these hands."

"There you'll be making a mistake," observed Vibert, taking possession of the brandy bottle. He wanted to make Langlade a little tipsy, but did not wish him to become dead drunk.

"Why should I be making a mistake?" asked the convict.

"Because it is a stupid thing to commit murder so long as other and better methods of revenge are possible."

"What are they?"

"A day in prison has frightened Soleil-Couchant. She was afraid of being shut up for ten years, nay, five perhaps, and she has split upon you. Well, split upon her in your turn. She must have been your accomplice in more than one misdeed. One word from you would send her to the Assizes, and the judges would take care to forward her on at once to some central establishment where she would betray no one."

Langlade reflected for a moment, and then said—"No. I should like to kill her, but I don't want her to suffer."

"It is evident you are not jealous, or you would have her shut up so as to make sure of her during your stay at Brest or Toulon."

"I tell you, I am going to kill her," shouted Langlade, as he went up to Vibert and caught hold of his hands with an iron grasp fit to break them. "I am not jealous," he continued, growing more and more excited every moment, "not I—although I once murdered a man on account of her!"

" Don't tell me that," said Vibert, " or I shall be obliged to denounce you." He knew that a man in love or drunk always speaks out in proportion as his confidence appears to be shunned.

" Then denounce me," cried the convict, by this time roused to a pitch of excitement. " Since Soleil-Couchant has betrayed me I would rather mount the scaffold than go back again to the hulks ! "

He seized hold of the bottle of brandy, Vibert this time not making any difficulty about giving it up. Putting the mouth of the bottle to his lips, he took huge gulps of the fiery spirit, and then, coming as close as possible to the police-agent, he continued in a low voice—

" Yes, I repeat, I murdered a man on her account. It is not so long ago either—it was in October or November last. She lived then in the Rue Neuve-Saint-Augustin, near the Carrefour Gaillon. One evening as I was going to call on her I caught sight of her saying good-night to a man at the foot of her staircase. I slipped aside before she saw me and listened. They were arranging another meeting and at parting she embraced him. I was mad with rage. Determined that he should not escape me I followed him. He went along the Rue Neuve-Saint-Augustin and the Rue de la Paix. Suddenly he stopped at the gate of a court-yard and went in. I did the same. I don't know what happened afterwards. I had lost my head. I only remember the cry—a terrible cry—which escaped my victim. Five minutes afterwards I rejoined Soleil-Couchant and said to her—' I have killed your lover ! ' "

This narrative, interspersed with fresh libations, completely exhausted Langlade, and his head fell heavily forward on the table. All the efforts made by Vibert to extract further details were useless. Besides, what need had he of details ? Was not the tale he had just listened to clear enough?

Whilst the convict slept a leaden sleep the detective philosophised. It was evident, thought he, that Maurice Vidal had not thought it unworthy of him to indulge, during his wife's absence, in a flirtation with Soleil-Couchant.

When, an hour later, the convict awoke, Vibert wished to resume the conversation from where they had left off. But Langlade, half sober again, obstinately refused to say a word more. He had only one fixed idea—to see Soleil-Couchant as soon as possible. The police agent saw that it would be dangerous to delay much longer the performance of his promise, so he paid the bill, cocked his pistol, got into the cab, which had been waiting all this time, and drove off with his companion in the direction of the Prefecture.

CHAPTER V.

THE journey of Vibert and his prisoner was accomplished without further incident. Langlade, still stupefied from the effects of his drunken bout, crouched in one corner of the vehicle and said not a word. The police-agent watched him narrowly, with one hand on the pistol, ready to fire at the first sign of any attempt to escape. He had no wish to lose his prize now that he was in sight of port.

When they came within a few yards of the Prefecture, Vibert told the driver to stop, and, as Langlade was about to get out, he took him by the arm, and said,

" One word, please. You have expressed a wish to see Soleil-Couchant, I have promised that you shall see her, and I will keep my word ; first of all, because I have no interest in not doing so ; secondly, because a police-agent who respects himself and his profession, should never, according to my idea, deceive a prisoner. That would be descending far too low. But be assured that when you set your foot inside the Prefecture, you

are neither more nor less than an escaped convict, an habitual
criminal, a dangerous being engaged in open warfare against
society, against whom too many precautions cannot be taken
You can then no longer count upon me ; my influence ceases at
the door of that grim building you see before you.   I have arrested you, I hand you over to the proper authorities, and come
what may, my task is done.   I return to my other duties."

"You will not leave me without bringing me face to face with
Soleil-Couchant ?" said Langlade, who, ever intent on his one
fixed idea, had paid but little attention to Vibert's harangue. ·

"That is understood," replied he, "but before we say good-
bye, do me the favour of holding out your hands."

"Why ?"

"So that I may put on the handcuffs."

"But I will not harm any one," said the convict, quite tamed
and as gentle as a child, "Soleil-Couchant is the only one I have
any grudge against."

"My friend," replied Vibert with his wonted suavity, "for
four hours we have been living side by side, and I have given
you sufficient proof, I think, that I am not afraid of you.   But
from this time we shall not be alone.   I am going to take you
up the staircase, along corridors and into offices, where you will
meet a crowd of people who know you by sight or reputation,
and in whom you inspire very serious, though, I admit, exaggerated alarm.   It is in the interest of their peace of mind that I
propose this small precautionary measure.   Have the kindness
to agree to it."

"Let there be an end to all this," said Langlade, as he held
out his hands.

Vibert, taking advantage of the permission thus given, put the
handcuffs on his prisoner, and then called out to the driver,
"Drive down the Rue de Jérusalem, enter the court-yard of
the Prefecture, and stop at the principal staircase."

Five minutes afterwards, Vibert, having sent in his name,

entered the office of the chief of the detective force with his prisoner. He went up to the desk and said, " I have kept my promise, and have brought him."

" Who ?" said the chief raising his head.

" Langlade—here he is."

" And you, yourself, arrested him ?"

" I alone. Did I not undertake to do so ?"

" It is well done, sir, I thank you on my own personal account. You have rendered us a signal service. In an hour's time I shall see the Prefect, and I promise I will speak of you."

" As you wish, sir, but I shall decline any kind of reward for this affair, which has interested me deeply and has served as a distraction from other engrossing thoughts. I have only one request to make."

" It is granted in advance."

The chief got up from his chair and retired with Vibert to a recess of one of the windows. " It is understood," he said, after a short conversation. " I am, moreover, entirely of your opinion that promises made to persons of this class should always be kept. They fear us, hate us, kill us, but they are forced to re-spect us. Langlade shall be taken for a few hours to one of the cells in the Conciergerie, and I will give orders regarding this woman."

" I should like," said Vibert, " to see her for a few moments before she meets Langlade. I have an important point to clear up in connection with another case, and she may be able to give me some useful information."

" That is enough. You have only to go to the depôt, and here is a note for the head jailer."

Vibert bowed and withdrew, whilst the officers, summoned by the chief, led Langlade away to the Conciergerie. The news of his arrest spread rapidly through the police offices, to the secretary's department, and to the first division. The younger *employés*, the office messengers, and such strangers as happened

to be in the Prefecture at the time flocked to see him pass
On all this assemblage he turned a look of calm indifference
What was the crowd to him ? He reserved all his anger for
the woman who had betrayed him.

CHAPTER VI.

STÉPHANIE CORNU, nick-named Soleil-Couchant, was really red-
haired. It is indispensable that this point should be clearly
understood in these days, when women's hair changes colour so
easily.

> "Souvent cheveu varie ;
> Bien fol est qui s'y fie,"

would have said a Francis the First of the present day.

Soleil-Couchant had all the beauties and all the charms of her
complexion, as she certainly had some of its drawbacks. She
was a tall handsome girl, admirably set up, with broad shoulders,
and small waist. Her bust was developed to perfection, and her
hand and foot, though large, were well-formed. In her physiognomy there was something strange, at once tender and cold,
impassioned and cruel. Very thin and somewhat pale lips closed
on white, small, and sharp teeth, separated one from the other.
Her chin was fat and sensuous, her nose small, decidedly turned
up, and with nostrils very much dilated and always quivering.
Her eyes, of somewhat Chinese shape, had no distinct colour,
but were green, blue, grey, or yellow, according to the time of
the day and the amount of light, and were surmounted by eye-
brows thick and well-arched, a rare thing with such a complexion.
A few freckles appeared here and there, but they were so artistically, as it were, disposed that, far from detracting from the
personal appearance, they lent it additional originality. As re-

gards her hair, we may possibly be asked to indicate, with greater exactness, its precise shade. To say that a woman has red hair, is not enough. If there are degrees in crime, there are still more in redness. We will answer our supposed question then by saying that the nick-name of Soleil-Couchant or Setting Sun which had been bestowed on Stéphanie Cornu, was amply deserved. Her thick, bushy, wavy hair, which, when let loose, reached down to her knees, had all the golden and crimson tints cast by the sun, as he sinks to rest after a hot autumnal day.

Soleil-Couchant's nature was fantastic to a degree, and ever since her appearance on the stage of life, she had invariably sacrificed her interests to her caprices. A tale is told of her that one evening, during the brief period when she had a certain vogue in the upper circles of Bohemia, she took a sudden fancy to talk to a male dancer at the Variétés. To get to him as quickly as possible, she hurriedly left her stage box, in which were seated the son of a peer of France and two *attachés* of an Embassy. She probably manifested similar precipitation in falling in love with Langlade. His vast size, upright carriage, and enormous shoulders captivated her at first sight and, actuated by her inordinate curiosity, she evidently wished to know how such giants spoke of love—whether they were tender, passionate, or eloquent.

As soon as she had acquired this information, her curiosity, as usual with her, was turned elsewhere. But here she met with a trifling obstacle which, in the end, served to complicate her life in a most unmistakable manner. Langlade, while she had been studying his eloquence, had fallen seriously in love, we might say enormously so, as he was a giant. His heart was in proportion to his size, and in it there was room for an ardent, real love and violent passions. He did not quite see the force of being cast aside just as easily as he had been taken up. He declared that if Soleil-Couchant had had enough of him, he had not had enough of her. He obstinately refused to resign in favour of others; he forced himself on her with violence and brutality, and Soleil-Couchant, who began to tremble in his presence, had to submit.

From that moment the life of the lovely Stéphanie Cornu was turned upside down. To be seen in public twice with Lang-lade was sufficient to place her under the ban of refined Bohemia. Her most intimate acquaintances, her most indulgent friends, could not but shun her. This Langlade, though as yet not having paid a visit to the hulks, had already given evidence of a tendency to them. His loose style of dress, his ribald tongue, and his bullying manner rendered him the most compromising individual in the world. He seized upon Soleil-Couchant as if she were his prey; he took possession of her by right of his might.

But one must live, and in modern society physical force is only really useful to pedlars, commissionaires, and the labouring classes; in Paris being strong means from three to five francs a day. That sum might have sufficed for Langlade, but it was not nearly enough for Soleil-Couchant. It was then that he had recourse to theft to keep up with the expenses of his in-amorata, and one fine day, when Langlade, *vi et armis*, was endeavouring to satisfy one of Stéphanie's wishes in a watch-maker's shop, he was seized by the collar, and sent shortly after-wards to the hulks at Toulon.

Hardly had Soleil-Couchant commenced to breathe again, than her dear tyrant, of whom she thought herself rid for ever, re-joined her and awoke her rudely from her dream of independence. Unable to live away from her, Langlade had made use of his strength and broken his fetters.

Stéphanie Cornu now enjoyed, if anything, less liberty than before. Compelled to avoid the attentions of the police—as a rule rather pressing as regards escaped convicts—Langlade thought it very natural that he should conceal himself in the furnished apartments occupied by Soleil-Couchant. He watched over her with the most touching solicitude; he clung to her more closely than ivy to an old oak. Jealous to a degree, he never let her go out, under the pretext that he could not accompany her for fear of being arrested. One day, Soleil-Couchant expressed a wish for furniture of her own. Langlade, always of knightly generosity, hastened to oblige her. He went out on two successive nights, made excellent preliminary arrangements, and on the third night ransacked from top to bottom a country house in the environs of Paris. He carried out this exploit in a most conscientious manner, as a man of his eminently liberal disposition knew well how to do; he even brought away all the kitchen utensils, so that Stéphanie might not have to purchase any.

The proprietor of the house had the bad taste to complain. The police, who were indelicate enough to listen to him, followed up the traces, and arrested, this time, not only Langlade but Soleil-Couchant with him. The result was that Langlade was condemned, as an escaped convict, to twenty years on the public works, and was sent to Brest, whilst Soleil-Couchant, treated as a receiver of stolen goods, was confined for a year to the tender mercies of Saint-Lazare.

The day she left her prison, just at the expiration of the year, she found a carriage awaiting her at the door of Saint-Lazare, and on the box, disguised as a driver, her faithful Langlade, who had escaped from Brest a week previously for the express purpose of celebrating the deliverance from custody of his beloved one.

We know how he was arrested for the third time, and how Soleil-Couchant had contributed in no small degree to that event. All these minute and private details were unknown, however, to the police. They imagined, naturally, that, frightened by her own arrest, and trembling at the idea of being again compromised by Langlade's misdeeds and this time sent to a convict prison, she had denounced her lover in order to secure the favour of the judges in her behalf.

They did not know Stéphanie Cornu. She was not a woman to allow herself to be frightened for so little. She had denounced Langlade for the purpose of getting rid of him until his next escape, and she had caused her own arrest so that she might be out of the way of his first fits of rage and fury. To plenty of heart, Soleil-Couchant could add a more than ordinary intelligence. Red-haired women are never commonplace.

CHAPTER VII.

AT the moment when Vibert entered her cell Soleil-Couchant was sitting on the bed and was playing, like a child, with her hair, which she had unloosed, and gathered across her chest.

A ray of sunlight, penetrating the thick walls of the Conciergerie through the window bars, shimmered over the luxuriant tresses and imparted to her a dazzling effect. Any other man than the police-agent would have admired the picture, but Vibert reserved his admiration for other objects. He shut the door behind him, as Stéphanie Cornu, taken by surprise, cast her hair behind her and essayed to fasten it up.

"So, my child," said Vibert, with a paternal air and without further preamble, "here you are, caught again?"

"*Mon Dieu*, yes," replied Soleil-Couchant, who, during her stay at Saint-Lazare, had become familiar with prison usages, and was, therefore, dismayed neither by Vibert's abrupt entrance nor by his cavalier manners.

"You will end by making them send you to a convict-prison," replied he.

"Let them send me there. I should like that just as well."

"What is that you say? You are not happy in town then?"

"Happy! I happy?"

No phrase can do justice to the expression she put into these words. Vibert divined in a second the ordeals through which this woman had passed, the sufferings she had endured, the rage which had possessed her, and the hate which was smouldering within her. After a short silence, he remarked, " It is not sufficient then to be a giant in order to render a woman happy."

She confronted Vibert and said—" You know him?"

"Not quite so well as you do, fortunately for me; but I know him."

" Well," she exclaimed, " I hate him."

"That is easily perceived," remarked Vibert, "and no doubt you'll be glad to learn that, thanks to your excellent information, Langlade has just been arrested."

" Really?" she cried, starting back, " really?"

" Nothing more real."

" Ah! I never expected it."

Her face beamed with delight, and she seemed to breathe more easily. " He did not defend himself, then?" she asked, for she did not dare believe in her good fortune.

"Very little," was the reply.

" And who was bold enough to arrest him?"

"I!"

She looked at Vibert, smiled contemptuously, and said—" It is impossible."

"Why?" he replied, with a suspicion of wounded self-love in his voice, " because I am six inches shorter than he is? Height is nothing," he continued, warming to his subject, "intelligence is everything. You are too material to understand this; physical power dazzles you, and you don't pay sufficient attention to the mind. But, nevertheless, an hour was enough to make a regular sheep of this Langlade of yours. He is arrested, and will be sent to the hulks once more. But he has escaped from them twice and will escape a third time, and then your martyrdom will commence afresh."

Soleil-Couchant's face fell. " You will never be easy," continued Vibert, " you will never sleep with both eyes shut, notwithstanding that you know he is on the hulks. He will leave them as he would a country residence. You could make more sure of him than that."

" How ? " she asked, not yet seeing the detective's drift.

" There are other sentences in the Penal Code than that of penal servitude."

" What ? "

" Death, for example."

She turned pale and said—" They could not condemn him to death ; he has not done anything to merit that."

" Are you quite sure ? " asked Vibert, going up to her, and looking straight into her eyes.

She turned paler still, and the police-agent heard her say under her breath—" I will not speak. No, this time I will not speak. I don't want him to be put to death."

" It is extraordinary," observed Vibert, " what a difference of opinion there is between Langlade and you. You say—' I want him to be imprisoned, but I don't want him to die.' He said to me only a moment or two ago—' I don't want her to be imprisoned ; I want her to die.' "

" Ah ! he said so ? "

" I give you my word he did."

" He wishes to see me die ? "

" Not only to see you die, but to kill you himself."

" How could he kill me ? He is in prison."

" Nothing would be easier. I will even confess to you that at this moment you are in very great danger."

" I told you I was afraid of death, and you want to terrify me—"

" Think what you please, but I swear to you that Langlade is now plotting against your life."

" Why should he kill me ?   What have I done to him ? "

" You have betrayed him."

" He does not know it."

" I beg your pardon, I told him."

" What ! you have—"

" It was my only means of quietihg him."

" It is infamous ! " she exclaimed.   " The Commissary of police, to whom I gave the information as to Langlade's whereabouts, promised that my name should not be mentioned."

" The Commissary has kept his promise.   I did not make any, and consequently said what seemed best to me."

" I am lost !   I am lost if he escapes."

" Let us prevent him escaping, and send him to the Assizes. The jury will send him to the scaffold."

" He might be acquitted."

" Impossible, if he has on his conscience a murder, even in a very minor degree.   There is no joking with a twice-escaped galley-slave, with three previous convictions against him and possessing such a terrible reputation as his."

" It is true," she said, " he will be convicted."

" Then, speak, if you wish to live."

" Certainly I wish to live, but how will you preserve my life ? He is arrested and in prison, but still you say yourself that I run the risk of being killed by him."

" You want some pledge ?"

" It would be better so."

" Listen.   After having learnt your betrayal of him, Langlade, as you may well understand, hesitated still to follow me.   Then, to decide him, I gave him my word that I would bring him this very day, this morning, face to face with you."

" Face to face with me ?" she cried in alarm, " when he had told you that he would kill me ?"

" Assuredly.   What did that signify to me ?   I did not even know you by sight."

She reflected for an instant and said, " Would you keep your promise if I were to tell you what you want to know?"

"It is impossible for me to do otherwise. But there is such a thing as keeping one's promise in the letter and not in the spirit. Instead of having Langlade brought, as I had intended, here into your cell, I will have him taken simply to the waiting-room of the Conciergerie. You will go down there from your side. He will say what he pleases to you, he can insult you at his ease, but he will not be able to touch a hair of your head, for there will be an iron grating between him and you."

"But," objected Soleil-Couchant, who forgot nothing so long as her life was in question, "suppose he has fire-arms about him?"

"As for that, make yourself quite easy. Persons who find their way into the Conciergerie are searched from head to foot. However, as an extra precaution, and because of the interest I take in you, I will have him searched afresh. Besides, you can see for yourself that he is already disarmed, if you cast your eyes on this pistol."

Stéphanie looked at the weapon held out to her by Vibert, and said, "Yes, I recognise it. Ah! he has frightened me often enough with that weapon! He never ceased to threaten me with it. As recently as last week he wanted to blow out my brains on the pretence that I had been flirting with a neighbour through the window. So whilst he was asleep, I took the pistol, unscrewed the barrels, and took out all the powder. Pull the trigger yourself, and see. The pistol will not go off."

Vibert let down the two hammers, the caps exploded, but no report was heard. "And," said he laughing, " here have Langlade and I been threatening each other in downright earnest with this pistol. So much for imagination! But sit down, and don't conceal anything from me, or, I swear to you, you are lost. It depends upon you, and upon you alone, whether you see Langlade half an hour hence in the waiting-room behind an iron grating, or are shut up with him for a *tête-à-tête* in this cell.

This last prospect made Soleil-Couchant shudder. She sat down on her sacking bed, and waited for Vibert to question her.

CHAPTER VIII.

VIBERT this time did not beat about the bush, but went straight at his subject. "A young man," said he to Soleil-Couchant, who listened to him with the greatest attention, "was assassinated this winter in the Rue de la Paix, near the top of the Rue Neuve-Saint-Augustin, where you then lived with Langlade. What information can you give me with reference to this still unpunished murder?"

" But," asked she, " how does it happen—?"

" That I come to you for information? Nothing more simple. This morning, Langlade, in a moment of excitement and intoxication, confessed his crime to me."

" Well?" asked Soleil-Couchant.

" That is not enough," replied Vibert, " the law requires details and actual proof. For these I come to you."

"Oh, very well. Put your questions, and I will answer them."

" For how long had you known the man assassinated by Langlade?"

" Two days."

" Where did you first meet him?"

" On the boulevards, at the top of the Rue Vivienne, about three o'clock in the afternoon."

" At the top of the Rue Vivienne, do you say? Was he coming from the Bourse?"

" That was my idea."

" He noticed you at once?"

"Yes, and I noticed him, for I thought he was a good-looking fellow. There was nothing extraordinary in that; I went out alone so rarely, and I was so continually shut up with Langlade, that all men seemed good-looking to me, little ones especially."

" The man we are talking about was undersized, then ? "

" Medium height."

" What happened then ? "

" My unknown followed me. Soon afterwards I left the boulevard, went down the Rue de Choiseul and reached my own door. He came up, bowed politely, told me how pretty I looked, and said a lot of other nonsense. The end of it all was that I gave him permission to call on me the next day. Unfortunately Langlade, whom I believed to be doing something or other out of Paris, returned unexpectedly. You know the rest, as you say he has confessed everything to you."

" At what hour did Langlade return in search of you ? "

" It must have been about nine o'clock," she replied.

"Did he merely say to you as he came in, 'I have killed your lover'? "

" Yes, that was all."

" What answer did you make ? "

" None. He was beside himself, and would have killed me that night as he had killed his other victim; I never saw him so awful."

" Were his hands stained with blood ? "

" No, and I was surprised at it."

" It is not in any way remarkable," said Vibert, " the blood does not always spirt out of a wound instantaneously, and Langlade fled at once after having committed the crime. Did you afterwards ever upbraid him with this murder ? "

" No, I did not dare," answered Soleil-Couchant, " I have already told you, sir, that I trembled like an aspen before that man."

" Did he ever mention the subject again ? "

" Never."

" Do you remember the exact date when this took place ?"

" It was about the end of October or the beginning of November."

" I asked you the exact date."

" I do not know, sir."

" But surely it was an epoch in your life ? "

" Undoubtedly, but I have always lived a careless sort of life, and have never bothered myself about the day of the month.

" Have you any idea at all of this man's name ? "

" No, I never thought of asking it."

" Describe him to me as precisely as you can."

" He was of medium height, as I have already told you, dark complexioned, and had a not very thick moustache."

She stopped, considered for a moment, and then went on— " Upon my word that is all. I don't recollect anything more— just think, it is nearly three months ago ! " she added, in the most natural way.

" Do you think he was married ? " asked Vibert.

" Very likely he was ; but I really cannot say."

" How was he dressed ? "

" Like anybody else. I fancy he had on a dark overcoat."

" Just so," said Vibert. " Whilst he was with you, did you happen to see his pocket-book ? "

" Yes, he took it out for some reason which I forget."

" What was it like ? Think well before you answer."

" I think," said Stéphanie, after a slight pause, " that it was not a regular pocket-book. It was more like a—"

" Memorandum book ? "

" Yes, that was it. One of those with an elastic band round them."

" Do you recollect the colour ? "

" Oh, yes ! it was red."

" There is no longer room for doubt," said the police-agent to himself. Although the information is not quite complete, it is precise as far as it goes." Then, addressing Soleil-Couchant, "Good-bye," said he, "and now prepare yourself to see your dear Langlade once more. Within half-an-hour he will be brought into the waiting room."

This information had an effect like a shower-bath on Stéphanie, and she recoiled as she exclaimed—"Swear to me that a grating shall separate us."

"I swear it. Good-bye," and he opened the door.

"Good-bye," she answered, sadly.

When she was alone in her cell she began to toy with her hair once more, and thus she prepared to see her athlete again.

CHAPTER IX.

Two warders of the Conciergerie conducted Langlade to the waiting-room, which was then tenantless. As had been agreed between Vibert and the convict, the latter was no longer hand-cuffed. In appearance Langlade was as calm as ever. On the way from his cell to the waiting-room he had looked about him with an air of indifference, and had replied quietly to such questions as were put to him.

One of the warders, the younger of the two, said to his companion, pointing to the prisoner—" He has been maligned; he is a lamb."

"We shall see ; there may be some fire among the embers," replied the other, who was an old hand at prison work and accustomed to these sudden fits of tranquillity, often noticed in the most powerful and violent subjects, and followed, as a rule, by a reaction as terrible.

The old warder was not mistaken ; the reaction was coming.

"By which door will she come in ?" suddenly asked Lang

lade, who had seated himself in a corner, on one of the benches with which the room was furnished.

They showed him a door placed on the other side of the grating which divided the waiting-room into two parts. The convict raised his head—his teeth shut and his nostrils dilated. He was beginning to scent something wrong, and had a vague idea of a trap.

"If she comes in on that side," he replied, and his voice had already lost some of its calm, " how will she be able to join me here ? "

" She will not join you," said the young warder.

" Ah ! she will not join me ! "

" You can go as close to the grating as you please, and can talk to her without interruption," remarked the elder warder persuasively, for he saw that Langlade's features were becoming convulsed, and he wished to appease him.

"Then I have been deceived," cried the convict, bursting into a rage.

" The promise was that you should see her, and you are going to see her."

"I have been deceived, I tell you," he replied still more violently. "She ought to be close to me—at my side. No grating should separate us. It is shameful ! My good faith has been abused ! If I had known I would not have given myself up—I would have defended myself. I would have killed him, the wretch ! I would have killed all of you— scum that you are ! "

He went quickly up to the older guardian, who, with his bunch of keys in his hand, awaited him without flinching.

"I want to be by her side," he exclaimed. " I want her either to be brought here, into this part of the room, or I want myself to go over to the other side."

" My orders are precise," replied the warder. " What you ask is impossible."

G

" It is impossible, is it ? " shouted Langlade.   " Ah ! I have
not given myself up yet.   You have not arrested me.   Nothing
has been done yet—we will begin again."

Without any apparent effort he wrenched from the wall a
wooden bench which was fastened against it, seized a couple of
stools, three straw-bottomed chairs and a small table, and threw
them into a corner of the room.   Then, tearing out one of the
legs of the table to use as a club, he planted himself, with his
back against the wall, behind the barrier he had thus made and,
brandishing his club over his head, he roared at them to " come
on ! "

" Look out ! " said the younger warder, making his way
prudently towards the door, whilst his companion, one of those
brave fellows who are selected from the active police, remained
firmly at his post, and contented himself with shrugging his
shoulders and looking calmly at Langlade.   His coolness completely exasperated the convict, and with one bound the latter
leaped over his barricade and marched straight on the foe.

By this time the warder saw that he was exposing himself to
needless danger, so, with his eyes fixed on his adversary, his
bunch of keys held in one hand, so as to ward off the blows of
the club, and stroking his grizzled moustache with the other, he
backed quietly towards the door without a word or any call for
help.   As soon as he got near the door, which had remained
open since his companion's flight, he made one vigorous bound
backwards, Langlade being all but upon him, and shut the door
quickly after him.   Langlade was now alone.

Whilst this was going on the soldiers on duty—for there is
always a guard in each of the prisons—stood to their arms and
were marched towards the waiting-room.

It was evident that a terrible struggle was about to take place.
The convict, in the end, would have to succumb to the force of
numbers, but not until after an obstinate resistance.   In his
stalwart hands every sort of weapon was sure to be a deadly one.

Moreover, there was nothing to hinder him throwing himself upon the first soldier who came in, wresting his musket from him, and keeping his enemies at bay from behind his barricade for a considerable time.

The soldiers, preceded by the two warders, had reached the door of the room and were on the point of entering, when Vibert appeared on the scene. Just as he was leaving the Conciergerie, on his way to the Palais-de-Justice where he wished to speak to the magistrate, M. Gourbet, he heard an unusual disturbance, and, on inquiry, was informed of what had been going on.

"I expected as much," said he to himself. "It is my fault, after all. Langlade has an undoubted right to complain, seeing that I have not kept strictly to my promise. It is my business, perhaps, to repair the wrong I have done, and to prevent any shedding of blood, even at the price of my own."

A brave and resolute man, such as we know him to be, could not hesitate long. He joined the soldiers and, placing himself before the door they were going to open, said—"Don't go in. I will manage this affair myself."

"What are you going to do?" asked the old warder, who had by this time recognised Vibert.

"I don't know. But send away the soldiers, I beg of you. I have cowed this madman once already this morning; perhaps I shall succeed again. There will always be time enough to summon the guard to our assistance."

"Well, as you please. Would you like me to go in with you?"

"No, my friend, it would be useless. Lion tamers never take any one with them into the wild beasts' cages. It does not do to whet their appetite."

"Then I'll stay here and be at hand to render you assistance in case of need."

"Just as you like."

Vibert opened the door and went into the room. Langlade, who had heard the sound of voices and the rattle of the arms, expected to be attacked and had retired behind his barricade. As soon, however, as he saw Vibert his anger turned to down-right mad rage. With a single bound he was upon him. Seizing him in his arms, he threw him with such force that he sent him flying half-a-dozen yards off.

The police-agent fell on his knees, got up, wiped the dust off his trousers with his coat sleeve, for under the most trying cir-cumstances he was neat and precise, and, without waiting for Langlade to make another rush at him, he went towards him, and, folding his arms, said to him—" You are a coward."

"And you are a traitor!" exclaimed the convict.

"Why am I a traitor?" said Vibert, without lowering his voice.

"You promised that I should see her, and I don't."

"She is there, behind that door, and is only waiting for you to grow a little calmer before she comes in."

"But I shall see her behind that grating. That is not what you promised—"

"I gave you no promise at all on that point. You dare to say that I promised you that she should be beside you !"

"We did not talk about it, but—"

"You should have made your conditions when we were talk-ing about it. I cannot tell what you want by inspiration. As for my promises, I have kept them all religiously. You asked me to have your handcuffs taken off, and they have been taken off. I am a victim of my good-nature to you. If you had not had the use of your hands you could not have smashed everything in this room as you have done, nor could you have acted in such a cowardly way towards me."

"Cowardly !" repeated Langlade.

"Yes, cowardly! I am little, you are big; I am weak, you are strong ; I come in here alone and unarmed, so as to prevent a bloody struggle in which you would have got the worst of it, in the end, and you rush on me like a wild beast. You would have been a great deal better off, wouldn't you, if you had killed me and two or three of those poor devils who were only doing their duty ? "

" Will Soleil-Couchant be brought here ?" asked Langlade, ealming down already. " Shall I see her without that grating between us ?"

" No ; you will see her and speak to her through it. It was she herself who begged that it might be so."

" Ah, it was she ! Why ?"

" No doubt, beeause she was afraid of being elose to you, and no wonder."

" If she is afraid, it is beeause she knows that she is guilty towards me."

" That may be, but I would have you know that the governor of the Coneiergerie, owing to your aets of violenee, and to your having eaused the guard to be turned out, will most likely deprive you of a sight of Soleil-Couehant, even behind that grating."

" Listen," said the eonviet, trying to get hold of Vibert's hand, " if you will only obtain the governor's permission for me to see her, I'll promise to put everything here in its place again, to make my exeuses to the warders, and to be as quiet as I have been violent."

" Very well. I will ask the governor ; but, if you do see her, the first arrangements will not be ehanged. You must stay here, and Soleil-Couchant will eome in on that side. That is settled."

" Well, so be it. I don't want her near me now. My anger has passed off."

" *Mon Dieu!* yes ; it passed off on to me," observed Vibert. " My knees feel as if they were on fire, and the skin is peeled right off them. But never mind. You put this plaee into some kind of order whilst I go to the governor, and don't forget that it is your turn to keep your promise to me."

Vibert went out and found the warders waiting at the door, perfeetly astonished at seeing him again safe and sound.

"He is quiet now," said he to them, "and if Soleil-Couchant does not provoke him too much he will continue so during the rest of the day."

A quarter of an hour later Soleil-Couchant, in charge of one of the warders on her side of the prison, entered the waiting-room, and prudently took a seat as far as possible from the grating which separated her from her dear Langlade. He, on the contrary, as soon as he saw her, went up to the grating, and, pressing his huge face against it, stood gazing at the woman who had been the cause of his capture. For a moment his look was menacing and full of hate, but then it softened. The convict uttered an empty boast when he swore to kill Soleil-Couchant. He would never have had the courage to do it. One look from his inamorata would have stayed his hand on the very point of striking the blow. He said not a word, but continued to look at her, whilst she, expecting a storm of insult and reproach, was quite taken aback. There was something touching in the submissive and resigned attitude of this vigorous and energetic man, this indomitable being, this tyrant. The qualities of the heart, however, were not very strongly developed in Soleil-Couchant; one cannot have everything. Besides, as we have already said, she had for five years been nourishing a bitter hate against this man, of whom she had always been trying to rid herself but without success. She had to pay him out for countless sufferings. He had at last given her an opportunity of revenge without exposing herself to terrible reprisals, and she was not the woman to deprive herself of this enjoyment.

She unbosomed herself, displayed all her wounds. She did not spare her lover one cause of complaint, nor a single reproach; she cast in his teeth all her sorrows. In that moment she repaid him with interest all the insults she had received during the whole five years. She overwhelmed him with outrages of all kinds, as he had overwhelmed her. Instead of blows, which she was powerless to strike, she pounded him with vituperation.

It was a real, furious, armed revolt. In her capacity as a vindictive woman, and possibly as a red-haired girl, Soleil-Couchant was implacable. He heard her out, without interruption, and when at length she stopped, he only said—"Then you love me no longer?"

" I never have loved you !" she exclaimed. "I feared you, and that is all."

He lowered his head, and, after a momentary silence, resumed —"If I were to escape from prison, from the hulks, would you come back to me again ?"

"Never !" she said, with intense energy. "Do not hope for it ! Oh ! it is all over, and well over. Nothing on earth would induce me to live again the life I have lived."

"Wretch ! " exclaimed he passionately. "And yet it was for your sake that I committed all my crimes. If it had not been for you, I should never have been sent to the hulks, nor should I go there again."

He seized the grating with both hands and tried to break the bars. Not succeeding, he attempted to force the grating out of its place with his knees, his feet, his head, even his teeth. He uttered the most savage cries, his eyes were blood-shot, and he foamed at the mouth.

Stéphanie's first impulse on this sudden outburst of fury was to recoil to the farthest extremity of the room. But when she saw that Langlade, despite his prodigious strength, was powerless even to bend a single one of the massive bars which separated him from her, she approached the grating again.

"Ah! you would crush me with pleasure, would you not?" she said, with a laugh. "You would kill me without a moment's pity. But I am out of your reach, and sheltered from your blows; you cannot do anything to me. I am no longer your chattel, no longer your dog. Come, giant of my heart, don't fatigue yourself so. You see well enough that you can't succeed ; you are vanquished ! "

This cruel piece of bravado, these biting sarcasms, so far from further exasperating Langlade, made him recover reason for a moment. An instant before he would only have given utterance to inarticulate sounds and furious cries, but now he could speak. He let go his hold of the iron bars, crossed his arms and cast an awful look on his old love.

"What! do you dare to insult me?" he exclaimed. "You who would be grovelling at my feet and asking for mercy, if this grating did not separate us! Take care of yourself! Don't laugh, coward that you are! You think I am lost, and you brave me, but my turn may come yet, and I shall know how to use it. Yes, they may send me to the hulks; I will escape. They may put fetters on my hands and feet; I will break my bonds. They may send me to the scaffold; I will leap from it to come back and kill you!"

"Fool!" said Stéphanie, shrugging her shoulders. "You talk of breaking your fetters, and you cannot even bend a single bar of that grating. You have imposed upon me. I thought you were strong, and you are not even that."

This last insult, this final lash, gave Langlade superhuman strength and vigour. He took hold of one of the bars with both hands, gave it a fearful wrench, and the bar, yielding to this supreme effort, bent and gave way.

Soleil-Couchant uttered an agonising scream. One wrench more and Langlade would have reached her.

But there is a limit to human strength. Langlade had gone through too much since the morning, and had passed through stages of too cruel emotion. His blood, over-excited to a degree, mounted suddenly to his brain, he reeled all at once, his hold of the bar, which he had grasped, relaxed, and he fell heavily to the ground.

CHAPTER X.

WHILST this scene was taking place at the Conciergerie, Vibert had bent his steps towards the Palais-de-Justice and had sent a message to M. Gourbet asking for an interview. Cordier, the dried-up little man whom our readers may possibly remember and who occupied the post of registrar to M. Gourbet, came to see what Vibert wanted.

"I should like," said the police-agent, " to have an interview for a moment with the magistrate on the subject of the murder in the Rue de la Paix."

" Ah! you bring us some news," said Cordier, rubbing his hands.

" It is possible."

" Good news ? "

" You will see."

" Just wait a few minutes. The magistrate is engaged on important business, but as soon as he is free I will tell him of your visit, and 1 have no doubt he will see you."

"I will wait," said Vibert.

The little man withdrew, gliding rather than walking, in the manner we have already described.

Half-an-hour afterwards, Vibert was shown into the magistrate's office. The first words addressed to him by M. Gourbet were—

" Well, you bring the proofs. It is decidedly Savari, eh ? "

" No, sir," said Vibert, with a sigh, "he is not the man."

" What is that you say ? Why, you and Madame Vidal were so sure of your facts ! "

" We made a mistake, sir."

" The last time I saw you here, in my office, you asserted that your conviction became stronger every day."

"It was true, but times have changed."

"You came to me, I believe, for permission to take away with you from the registry office one of the articles produced in evidence—the knife with which the victim was stabbed."

"It was given to me."

"To enable you to make a decisive experiment?"

"Yes, sir, and I made it."

"It did not succeed?"

"It succeeded, but imperfectly."

"Explain yourself, I beg."

"I mean to say that this experiment upset my conviction for a time; but subsequently, after mature reflection, I was surprised to find myself still believing in the guilt of Albert Savari."

"Was he not agitated when you showed him the knife?"

"No, but that did not prove anything. In the height of a violent altercation, in a moment of anger and excitement, he might have laid hold of the first thing that came to his hand, and after stabbing Maurice Vidal might have thrown the weapon away in terror and fled. It was, therefore, quite possible that the sight of the knife did not at first arouse any reminiscences nor make any impression."

"But you are far too clever not to have found an opportunity of mentioning in his hearing the name of the individual who was stabbed with this weapon?"

"Yes, I spoke to him of Maurice Vidal."

"Well?"

"He showed great sympathy for the sad fate of that young man, whom he had known. He shed tears over his death, and was sharp enough to mingle his tears with those of the widow."

"You say he was sharp enough?"

"Yes, sir."

"Then, according to you, Albert Savari was enacting a part?"

"No, sir, I was alluding to something else."

"You admit that these tears might possibly have been natural."

"Perfectly so."

"Do you think, then, that they were caused by remorse?"

"Remorse also might have had something to do with them."

"All this is becoming more and more vague. You will admit we are not a bit nearer the end than we were three months ago."

"I beg your pardon, sir. I bring you the name of the murderer of Maurice Vidal."

"What do you say?"

"I know now the assassin of whom you are in search."

"Really?" exclaimed M. Gourbet.

"Yes, sir."

"And his name?"

"Langlade."

"Langlade—the name sounds familiar to me. Is not there a convict so called?"

"That is the man."

"I have had that fellow's case under my consideration. He escaped on the last occasion from the hulks at Brest. He has been for three months in Paris, and the police cannot discover his hiding-place."

"His abode was discovered yesterday, and I arrested him this morning. He is, at the present time, in the Conciergerie."

"I must compliment you on his capture."

Vibert bowed.

"And," continued M. Gourbet, "it was Langlade who assassinated Maurice Vidal? What makes you think so?"

Vibert gave the magistrate a detailed account of his arrest of the convict, and informed him of the particulars extracted from Soleil-Couchant.

"Yes," said M. Gourbet, when Vibert had finished his account, "we have found the culprit at last, thanks to your sagacity."

"Oh, sir," replied Vibert, "don't talk of my sagacity. On the contrary, it was at fault. Chance alone came to my aid."

"However that may be, you ought to be delighted at the result."

"No, sir, I am not."

"Because you suspected Savari, and were mistaken—a question of *amour-propre.*"

"If it were only a question of my *amour-propre* I should be well out of it," murmured Vibert, so low that M. Gourbet did not hear him, "but it is a more serious case for me," he added with a sigh.

Whilst Vibert was indulging in this short soliloquy, the magistrate went up to the registrar and said—"M. Cordier, will you kindly hand me the minutes of the examination of Albert Savari, in the month of October last. You should have a copy of them."

"Yes, sir," said the little man, gliding towards a collection of green portfolios arranged on shelves. He took hold of one without the least hesitation, opened it and took out a bundle of papers, which he handed to the magistrate. An automaton could not have performed the duty with greater precision.

After looking over the papers attentively, M. Gourbet turned to Vibert and said—"Admitting that Langlade is guilty, only see how easily Justice may go astray. Many of the most conscientious and cautious of my colleagues would have found in these minutes, which I have just read over carefully, a dozen reasons to induce them to commit Savari for trial at the assizes. I will merely give you one. Can you account for the bills given to Maurice Vidal being found in Savari's house?"

"Yes," said Vibert, "if Savari had met them as he maintained he had."

"But it would appear from these minutes that he could not have met them. In the whole of his life he never had fifty thousand francs in his possession."

" Did he not state positively that he won them at various gambling tables in Germany ? "

" And you believe that ? "

" I believe in anything as regards gambling. "

" Then you have no longer any suspicions as far as he is concerned ? " asked M. Gourbet.

" *Mon Dieu !* " replied Vibert, " I have a bad habit of succumbing to evidence. What interest could Langlade possibly have had in asserting that he had murdered a man?"

" But he did not mention the man by name."

" Soleil-Couchant described him accurately enough."

"Neither of them was precise as to the date of the crime?"

" Both of them fixed it tolerably nearly."

M. Gourbet reflected for a moment, and then said—" And these words, written by the victim in his blood, ' The assassin's name—.' How do you account for them if Langlade did the deed ? Maurice Vidal could not have known the convict."

" That, I admit, is one of the most vital objections. I have already put that question to myself, and I think I have found the answer. Before he was sent to the hulks Langlade lived in Paris and was well known to all the young men of a certain set. They did not shake him by the hand, it is true, nor did they recognise him when they met him in the street, nor did they even speak to him, because he was always decidedly vulgar. But they turned round to look at him, and asked who he was when he appeared in public with Soleil-Couchant. How, indeed, could such a couple have helped being noticed ? On the one hand, a species of giant ; on the other, a strikingly handsome girl, with a brazen look and hair of an unusual colour. For the time being, Langlade became thus a sort of celebrity, and I remember that one evening at a first night at a theatre on the boulevards, one of the gods called out to him, ' Halloa, Langlade, where is your girl with the red hair ? ' It is not very astonishing, therefore, sir," concluded Vibert, " that

Maurice Vidal was able to recognise his assassin and sought to put Justice on his track."

"Yes," replied the magistrate, "your explanation is natural."

"Besides all this," added Vibert, "nothing is easier than to sum up the whole of this affair in two words. Was there anybody else murdered in the Rue de la Paix in the month of November last? You know well enough that there was not; all the world knows it. In that case Langlade is guilty, and Savari is innocent. I see no way of getting out of that."

"I will not contradict you," replied M. Gourbet, "but we have been on the wrong track for so long that a little hesitation is allowable."

"You will hesitate no longer, sir, when you have examined Langlade and Soleil-Couchant, the latter especially, because Langlade may possibly refuse to reply to your questions."

"Why?"

"Because he is not always the most manageable man in the world. Of that you will be able to convince yourself. Ah! Savari would have given you less trouble. I wish he was guilty for your sake, for the sake of the public prosecutor and of everybody engaged in the case, and," he added, in a lower tone with a sigh, "for my sake, too."

"So," said the magistrate, getting up from his chair, as an intimation to Vibert that it was time for him to go, "you undoubtedly refuse to be consoled for your mistake with regard to Savari."

"I confess, sir, that I shall never console myself. It will be the misfortune of my whole life."

He bowed and retired.

CHAPTER XI.

WHAT has become, during all this time, of Julia Vidal and Albert Savari, of whom the exigencies of our tale have compelled us to lose sight?

On the day following the dinner at the Café Anglais, Savari called, about three o'clock in the afternoon, at the Rue de Grammont. "My mistress is unwell," Marietta informed him, "and is unable to see you."

After a persistent but ineffectual effort to gain admission, Savari hastened to the Hotel des Princes. He wanted, at all events, to talk about Julia, if he could not see her. But the Count de Rubini, up to this time so agreeable and communicative, and such a thoroughly good fellow, had become, since the previous evening, cold, ceremonious, and impassive. Instead of stringing long sentences together by way of answer to the most trivial question, he spoke only in monosyllables and maintained an unbroken silence on the subject of his cousin's illness.

We know something of Vibert's state of mind about this time, and the abrupt change in his manner will not cause us any astonishment. But Savari, who had not been initiated, as we have been, into the secret sufferings of his late comrade, was surprised and alarmed. At the same time he cast about for the motives by which the count might be actuated, and he imagined he had found them.

"The fifteen days' grace," he said to himself, "which he gave me for the liquidation of my card debt expired long ago. He, no doubt, thinks I take matters too easily, and the coldness with which he treats me is an indirect reproach and an intimation that I have to settle with him."

From the moment that he conceived this idea, Savari devoted

himself to the task of finding means to discharge his debt to
the Count de Rubini, who was in a position to use considerable
influence towards keeping him apart from Madame Vidal. In
the meantime he had not the necessary fourteen thousand
francs, and none of his acquaintances appeared disposed to
lend him that sum. Had it happened two months earlier, he
would not have hesitated, but would have resorted to the gam-
bling-table. Had not play always been a species of career for
him—his only career, indeed? " I want a hundred louis," he
would have said. " I have not got them. Where is there any
play going on to-night?"

But now he hesitated. It was not that he was intimidated
by his last loss; on the contrary, he thought that he was in a
winning vein again. But he was under the influence of a
species of transformation which, without his knowing it, had
been gradually taking place in his life. Since his love for Julia
had sprung into being, life had appeared to him under a new
aspect; he regarded certain subjects from a more serious point
of view; he was a more severe censor of himself, and the words
delicacy and honourable conduct, about which his views up to
this time had been rather vague, began to have some meaning
for him. In a word, he confessed to himself, that it was a
sorry thing to rely upon gambling for that which work alone
should give him.

There is no doubt that if, when he was in this frame of mind,
he had found some recognised and honest means of gaining
fourteen thousand francs in a short time, he would not have
hesitated to make use of them. Unfortunately these means are of
rare occurrence; so Savari, after—to his credit be it said—some
moral hesitation and great repugnance, found himself reduced
one evening to pay a visit to Pélagie d'Ermont.

" She never requires to be asked," he reflected, " to make up a
game. It is quite possible that at this very moment some
bank or other is in full swing at her house. I have five-and-

twenty louis ; I have not played for a long time, and I am un-lucky in love—all excellent reasons for an unexampled run of good fortune at cards."

Reasoning with himself in this way, he rang at Pélagie's door. Madame d'Ermont herself opened it.

" Ah ! it is you," said she, holding out her hand, and ushering him into the drawing-room.   " It is kind of you to come and see me.   You are not like the rest.   You do not desert your friends when they are in misfortune."

" You in misfortune, my fair one ! And how so ? "

"What, you do not know what has happened to me ? " asked Pélagie quickly.

" I have not the slightest idea.   I have not seen any one belonging to our set for some time."

" Don't you read the papers ? "

"The papers !   What would they have taught me about you?"

" That the police made a descent on my house last week."

" Nonsense."

" It is as I say."

" But what for ?   Had you, without our knowing it, a manufactory of base coin ? "

" I allowed gambling."

" The deuce !   So these gentlemen of the police came here ?"

" Just in the very height of a splendid bank at baccarat. There were on the table more than ten thousand francs in gold and notes."

" They were in the nick of time, then.   You hadn't got to counters ?"

" No, worse luck.   They seized the stakes."

"That was rude."

" If they had only contented themselves with laying hands on the money !" replied Madame d'Ermont.   " They compelled everybody in the house to give their names, addresses, and occu-pations in full."

"As regards the occupations," remarked Savari, "that would not be a very long business."

"It is all very well to make merry over it, but you don't know that they seized my furniture, too."

"That accounts for it!" exclaimed Savari, looking round him without any show of sympathy. "I was saying to myself that you had set up a new establishment."

"It is all second-hand furniture, which I was obliged to buy yesterday."

"Well," replied Savari, "but had they any right to seize the furniture?"

"*Mon Dieu!* Yes; the law is precise on that point," said Pélagie, sighing. "My counsel gave me the clause to read—Clause 410 of the Penal Code. I know it almost by heart—'All stakes which shall be found on the gaming-tables, and all furniture and moveable effects with which the rooms may be furnished or ornamented, shall be confiscated.'"

"Verily," said Savari, endeavouring to look concerned, "the law is no respecter even of the most sacred things."

"And even if that were all!" continued Madame d'Ermont.

"The catalogue is not exhausted yet?"

"There is another paragraph yet. I know it even better than the other one." This time a still deeper sigh accompanied the remark. "'Every person who shall have kept a gambling-house shall be liable to imprisonment for a term not less than two and not exceeding six months, and to a fine of from a hundred to six thousand francs.'"

"You did not keep a gambling-house," observed Savari.

"One is held to keep a gambling-house, so my counsel tells me, when it can be proved that play is carried on in a regular fashion even in one's own house."

"When a business is made of it, which was not your case."

"They looked on the purse, which used to be made for me, as giving it a business character."

"That is downright malevolence."

"Say rather that it is flagrant injustice. Was it not natural for each of you to contribute to my expenses?"

"Quite so."

"Candles are dear, and you used plenty of them."

"About five or six francs per evening," said Savari to himself, "and her purse came to three or four hundred francs!" Then addressing Pélagie he exclaimed, "My dear friend, I cannot tell you how deeply I sympathise with you."

"Finally," continued Madame d'Ermont, "I have to tell you that I am to have the pleasure of appearing before the Correctional Tribunal in a week. If I am not in prison now, it is simply because some of my influential friends gave bail for me."

"All this is very distressing, but how came the police to pay you a visit?" asked Savari. "You must have been betrayed."

"Undoubtedly, but I do not know the name of the traitor."

"You never received any but the regular *habitués* of your house and your friends?"

"Lately, more especially, not a single stranger has come here, with the exception of that Italian—you know who I mean?"

"The Count de Rubini?"

"Yes, that is the man."

"He has never had any idea of denouncing you; he won too much money here. Such ideas as these are only entertained by gamblers who have lost considerably and wish for revenge. Besides, I know the Count de Rubini intimately by this time. He is an original certainly, but a thorough gentleman."

"Then," said Pélagie, "I must have been sold by some of my women friends."

"Probably; your purse we were talking about roused some petty female spite, and out of that has come an anonymous communication to the Prefecture. Any other supposition is impossible, unless," he added, smiling, "some police-agents have insinuated themselves amongst us."

After having sympathised for some time longer with Pélagie d'Ermont, Savari took his leave. From the moment that no gambling was to be done under her auspices, she became useless to him. There was no increase to his five-and-twenty louis. He did not know any other house such as Pélagie's, and, besides, as soon as the police make a descent on one of these establishments, all the remainder of the same class are hermetically closed for a season. Every school-boy knows that.

As for paying a visit to Baden or Homburg to try his fortune there, Savari never dreamt of it. He had not the courage to put one or two hundred leagues between himself and Julia, to say nothing of the fact that his five-and-twenty louis would barely cover the cost of his journey. He resigned himself, therefore, seeing that he could not do otherwise, to remain the count's debtor, but he thought it his duty, nevertheless, to mention his debt, and to apologise for the delay which had occurred with regard to it. Vibert, more and more morose, refused to see him.

Savari was completely disheartened; he did not know what to think. The two persons with whom alone he had spent the last two months of his life failed him together, without his knowing anything of the cause which led to his separation from them. Julia had chosen the day following that on which he had declared his love as the time to shut her door against him. Nevertheless, she had heard him in silence, had almost encouraged him to speak. She might even have answered, if it had not been for the inopportune entrance of the count. And now, just as hope was dawning upon him, she abruptly, and without a word of explanation, placed a barrier between herself and him.

Like an uneasy spirit, he wandered about Paris, passing by preference along the Rue de Grammont at every opportunity. One day when, as was his wont, he raised his eyes towards Madame Vidal's windows, he caught sight of her behind the curtains. Thereupon he lost his head completely, and all his former boldness came back to him. He ran rapidly across the street, rushed up the two flights of stairs, pushed aside Marietta, who made a futile attempt to stop him, went into the drawing-room, and found himself face to face with Julia. This happened on the day after the arrest of Langlade and Vibert's visit to the judge.

As soon as she saw Savari, Madame Vidal went quickly to meet him, no doubt to reproach him for having thus forcibly effected an entrance into her house and her presence against her orders. But he did not give her time to speak. Seizing both her hands before Julia could withdraw herself from his grasp, he poured into her ear a tale of love such as only the most violent and unrestrained passion could dictate.

"I no longer live," he exclaimed, "except by and for you. Without you I shall kill myself! Existence has become odious to me. My life has been a failure, I am a useless being, vicious, corrupt—I am horrified at myself. Have pity on me; you can make a new man of me. A look from you would make me better; a kind word, a smile, some encouragement, would give me all those virtues which I have not now. A week passed without seeing you is a century, an age! If you but knew what I have suffered during that time. Even just now, before I saw you at the window, my strength was deserting me, and I had made up my mind to a violent end. Yes, it is so difficult to live when one is unhappy, so easy to kill oneself! I ought to inspire some pity in you! But you are deaf to me, you heed not when I unfold my griefs to you, when I lay bare my every thought. Hear me, for pity's sake, hear me! I suffer, suffer much, and a man who suffers as I do, who weeps as I am doing now, deserves compassion.

He stopped, for tears choked his utterance. Julia was amazed at this language, so entirely new to her. Her husband had spoken to her in the language of love, but words of passion she now heard for the first time.

Savari continued, "If you were determined to estrange yourself from me so quickly, why did you receive me in the first instance ? Why did you make me welcome ? Did you not see that little by little I was becoming enslaved by you? Did you not read in my eyes that I loved you ? Ah ! a woman is never deceived in such things as these. She needs not that a man should go on his knees, and cry, 'I love you,' to feel that she is beloved. You knew that my heart belonged to me no more. I gave it to you, and you by your silence accepted the gift. Nay, do not exclaim that it is not so ; you accepted it, I say, and you have no right, for the sake of a mere caprice, to make a martyr of me. What evil have I ever done you?"

"I admit I have been wrong," she said in her sweet voice.

At that moment she was true and sincere. When convinced of the guilt of Savari, subdued by Vibert's influence, and at the same time believing herself to be accomplishing a sacred duty, she had consented to enact a comedy unworthy of her, and re-pugnant to her loyal, straightforward and honest nature. By degrees she became blind to the danger and the odious side of her undertaking; enthusiastic in all she undertook, she at last came to play her part in very earnest. But for some time her convictions had been shaken, and she began to doubt Savari's guilt. She confessed to herself that if he were not guilty, the part she had been playing was detestable. He had every right to complain, to accuse her of, and reproach her for his sufferings.

Whilst these thoughts coursed rapidly through Julia's brain, Savari was also plunged in reflection. A man really in love is never very intelligent with the woman he loves. His subtlety and habitual presence of mind are of no avail to him. Savari, with all his talent for intrigue, when face to face with Julia, could no longer sustain his old reputation. Not that he was without his lucid moments, when the clouds which obscured his vision suddenly disappeared and he saw clearly and justly. Then he would say to himself, that a blow should be struck here or there, and he would become shrewd again for a moment, until the sky was once more overcast.

"I have been wrong," Julia had said. Then she was melting, she must be touched. The eloquence of Savari had produced an impression on her mind, if not on her heart. It was one step in advance, a small one truly, but with it he had to content himself, and by it he must profit as quickly as possible. It was especially important that Julia, after having advanced, should not have reason to retrace her steps. Savari was bound not to alarm her by excessive precipitation.

So, rendered more calm and self-possessed by the advantage he thought he had gained, he spoke no more in the language of passion, for fear of alarming Julia. He sat down beside her, and tried to persuade her that she could not shut her door against him, and that she ought to see him from time to time, for the purpose of gradually healing the wound from which he suffered.

"Humour me a little," said he, "treat me as an invalid, as a convalescent, and I shall regain my health."

That was the only language to be used to a woman like Julia, and in different circumstances she would certainly have been persuaded by it, only she found herself in an exceptional position. She was no longer sufficiently convinced of Savari's guilt to continue playing the part she had taken on herself. That enterprise she put away from her, she declined all complicity with Vibert and cancelled whatever engagement she had contracted with Justice and the magistrate. But, at the same time, she was not sufficiently convinced of the innocence of Savari to sign the treaty which he laid before her. As long as a shadow of suspicion rested on him, all she had to do was to shut him out from all intimacy with her.

She mustered up her courage, and approaching Savari, said to him—"If you love me, as you assure me you do, if you have any respect for your love and for me, leave me, I beg of you, and do not seek to see me again."

"And," he exclaimed in despair, "is that all you can find to say to me?"

"Believe me—I cannot reply to you in any other terms."

"But you are breaking my heart."

"Alas !" said she tenderly, "it is not my fault."

"At least," he replied with tears in his voice, "tell me the reason of this coldness, this harsh treatment."

"No, that is impossible; I swear to you that it is impossible."

"This is the acme of suffering—this is too much," exclaimed Savari, as he sank on a sofa and covered his face with his hands, as if to repress the grief which was ready to burst out.

At this moment Marietta entered the room, and going up to Madame Vidal, whispered in her ear—"You are wanted."

"By whom ?"

"By a person whom I do not know, but whose business seems important."

Julia rose, and, without looking at Savari, who for his part did not turn his head towards her, followed Marietta into the ante-room. There she found one of the messengers of the Palais-de-Justice.

"Madame," said the man, "M. Gourbet, the magistrate, charged me to deliver this letter into your hands alone."

"Give it me," said she.

She took the letter, and whilst Marietta was showing the messenger out, she re-entered the drawing-room, went to a window and read as follows—

"Madame,—It is my duty to inform you, without delay, that we have at last discovered your husband's murderer. It is a man named Langlade, an escaped convict. We have against him evidence so convincing as to remove any possibility of doubt. Moreover, he has confessed. All the suspicions we have conceived with regard to Albert Savari should therefore disappear. The surveillance to which he is still subjected will cease from to-day.

"I have sympathised with you, madame, in your most natural

sorrow, and I am happy to inform you that at length the death of your husband will be speedily avenged.

"I have the honour to be, madame, with the utmost consideration—Yours very faithfully,

" (Signed)   GOUBERT."

She read this letter over twice, to convince herself that she was not mistaken, and then went to the fireplace, threw the paper in the flames, and approached Savari. He raised his head and looked at her as she came towards him, without comprehending her intention.

When she was close to him, she said in a low, sweet voice—"I have caused you much suffering. Forgive me, and never ask me for an explanation of my past conduct. I have many wrongs towards you to atone for, and I will atone for them."

The words were scarce spoken, when she burst into tears.

CHAPTER XII.

A LARGE chariot, emblazoned with a coat of arms and drawn by two powerful Norman horses, pulled up with a tremendous clatter one morning in front of the entrance to the Hotel des Princes. As soon as it stopped, a footman briskly descended from his lofty seat by the side of the coachman, and ran to receive the orders of the individual who was seated in the vehicle.

"Find out from the waiters," said this personage, "if the Count de Rubini lives here, and if he is in now."

The footman promptly executed this order, and brought back the intelligence that the count resided there, and that nobody had seen him go out.

" Open the door, then, and assist me to alight," said the owner of the carriage. " Did you ascertain the number of his room ?" he added as he crossed the courtyard.

"Yes, my lord. It is No. 4, on the second floor."

"The second floor? The deuce! It is rather high up for me this morning. I think I have another attack of this infernal gout coming on. Ah, thank goodness! here we are, at last."

"This is the door, my lord."

"Open it, then, instead of keeping me standing here, as if you thought I was feeling comfortable after all this climbing. Now, go. I will come down again by myself."

Vibert, seated in front of the fire-place, was poking the fire when the door opened. He turned his head, uttered a cry of surprise, and then rose hurriedly and went to meet his visitor.

"You, M. le Marquis!" he exclaimed, "you here in my rooms?"

"Yes, I myself in your rooms. Is there anything wonderful in that? Do you not call yourself the Count de Rubini? Consequently there is nothing derogatory on my part. Moderate your amazement, and give me a chair. These flights of stairs are no joke!"

The Marquis de X—, whose acquaintance we have up to this time made solely through the medium of his correspondence with Vibert, bore his sixty-five years well. He had a countenance of remarkable intelligence, thin lips, and whiskers trimmed after the English fashion. A reminiscence of his service in the Royal Body-guard lingered in his figure, which was as erect as a slight stoop would allow it to be. He dressed in a style peculiar to himself. His waistcoat was extremely long, and buttoned up close to the chin; his shirt collars were very high, and his black dress coat (he wore a dress coat on all occasions) was of a peculiar cut. His trousers, ample in their dimensions, were tight round the ankle, hussar fashion. From 1835 to 1848, the Marquis de X— was the spoiled child of the Upper Chamber. His sallies and freaks are still remembered and used to be the talk of all Parisian drawing-rooms. He was the only peer of France who had any amount of popularity. The reports of his speeches were fought for and learnt by heart, and the parliamentary debates were only read if the witty marquis had been amongst the orators. He spoke frequently, to the great delight of his colleagues, who listened to him with extreme pleasure, though they occasionally interrupted him as a matter of form. In the most sudden and unexpected manner he would get on his legs, and plunging his hands into the capacious pockets of his waistcoat, would attack the question on the order of the day.

"But, M. de X—, why do you address the Chamber without permission?" the president would ask.

"Sir," would be the reply, "if I had that permission, I should not be obliged to take it," and regardless of all interruptions the marquis would continue speaking in his habitual trenchant style.

When the Marquis de X— was comfortably seated in an easy-chair, he turned towards Vibert, and said to him—"So you thought you could quickly suppress my daily *feuilleton* without my rebelling or coming down upon you for the rest of the series? For a month past, according to our agreement, you sent me my eight columns every morning in time for breakfast; you kept me informed of the minutest details of the Rue de la Paix affair; you posted me up in all the sayings and doings of the fair Julia Vidal, and that prepossessing adventurer called Savari. You announced for the next day a thrilling dagger scene at the Café Anglais. The interest was becoming intense, when presto, no more *feuilleton*, no more tale, no more anything. Your 'sequel in our next' was merely a catch, and you were making fun of your devoted reader—"

"If you only knew, M. le Marquis," said Vibert, sadly.

"Good heavens! If I knew I should not be asking you for anything more. Come, what have you done with all your characters? I love them all! Your Julia does not speak much —it is but just to her to admit that—but she has plenty of nerve. Your Savari is an attractive production of the corrupt society around us; he pleases me, does that blackguard. Give me news of all of them."

"That is out of my power, M. le Marquis, seeing that for the past week I have not set eyes on any of the persons you allude to."

"Now you want to impose upon me," observed the marquis, "and your profession, what of that?"

"My profession consisted of a search after a culprit. I have sought him out, and I have found him."

"Caught is he, the scoundrel? It is just a little too soon."

"You evidently imagine, M. le Marquis, that I am alluding to Savari?"

"Clearly."

"That is a mistake; Savari is not the guilty party."

Then Vibert narrated to the Marquis de X— all that we know with regard to Langlade and Soleil-Couchant. His account, far from interesting that nobleman, appeared to put him in a shocking bad humour.

"Here's a nice wind-up!" said he, when Vibert had ceased speaking. "The murderer is a mere convict—the crime is a vulgar one committed by a low hound—enough to make one shudder—you deserve to be discharged! This was a case which really promised to be somewhat out of the common—a pretty woman, a handsome fellow, love in immediate prospect; a picturesque situation, in fact. And this taking romance is to end in the most ordinary fashion! Savari and Julia will return to their usual avocations, and there will be nothing but one clumsy fellow more on the hulks. It is painfully commonplace! Yes, we are indeed in the reign of the Citizen King!"

Then, addressing Vibert more directly, he resumed—

"But, if all is over and done with, if your murderer is in durance vile and Savari is as white as snow, why do you still appear as the Count de Rubini, live in this fashionable hotel, and wear clothes that put mine in the shade? Have we by chance made a fortune, or have we, at all events, found a real ancestor or two ? "

" *Mon Dieu !* M. le Marquis," said Vibert, slightly put out, " I am wearing out my clothes and finishing up the fortnight I have broken into at the hotel."

" And, my small *protégé*, you really expect me to credit such nonsense ? You wearing your grand clothes without any object ! You had a thousand times rather sell them to an old clothes man ! You stopping to complete a fortnight in a suite of rooms which must in your eyes be the height of extravagance ! Absurd ! In the first place, the rooms here are let by the day ; in the second, the proprietor of the hotel, I would stake my right hand on it, only asks to see your back. I know you ; it would be a hard task to make you spend money. A dozen fogies of your stamp would ruin a place like this. My dear Vibert, you have other motives for remaining here, and I will tell you what they are if you make a point of it."

" But, M. le Marquis—"

" You don't insist on it ? You know full well that, cunning as you are, I have already found them out."

" Oh, I am not cunning with you, M. le Marquis."

" And you are right, my boy," said M. de X—, going close up to Vibert, and taking him by the ear. " Come," he continued, in a semi-fatherlike way, " tell me all your troubles ; that will be some comfort to you. To whom should you tell them, if not to me, for you have neither relation, nor friend ? I will set you the example of being frank. I have not been drawn hither by a feeling of curiosity alone. You know very well that I take a lively interest in you. I like your turn of wit, your courage, your piquant originality. You are not like the rest of the world. Under the old *régime* you might eventually have been a Louvois, a Richelieu, or a Mazarin. In our day, to turn your qualifications to some advantage you enter the police force, and there you are right. It is, perhaps, a more sensible calling than others. I am not a man to have stupid prejudices, I only have convictions. Now then, let me hear what you have to say."

"What am I to say, unless it is that I am deeply moved—"

"Enough, do not let us go into the question of gratitude. You have simply to confess why you remain in this hotel, or, rather, I am going to tell you why it is. You continue to call yourself the Count de Rubini, to dress like a gentleman, and to live here, because it appears to you that, by returning to the Rue l'Arbre-Sec and becoming Vibert once more, you will be placing a still greater gulf between her and you. Have I hit it?"

"Yes," replied Vibert concisely.

"You really love her, then?"

"Ah, yes, I love her!" exclaimed Vibert, suddenly, "I love her with all the warmth of a heart hitherto untouched. No woman I have met with up till now has made my heart beat one whit faster; as they have passed, I have turned my head aside. But she! she appeared before me, and I was transformed. My blood has a warmer flow, my nervous system is developed. Yes, at thirty-five I am just beginning to live, and at last I have all the passions of a man. But these passions I must stifle! She who has caused their birth can neither comprehend nor excuse them. And yet she is a woman as other women are, better and more beautiful than the rest, but made after their likeness; a woman in every acceptation of the word, ready to respond if one only could touch the right chord. She is no statue, no stone, no idol—she is a true woman. But I—I am not a man like other men ; I am cast in that mould which makes others ask when they see me if I was born out of time : I am taken for a higher species of ape."

Vibert found a sort of bitter pleasure in thus exposing all his sores. He exaggerated his infirmities, made himself more diminutive than he was, uglier and more mis-shapen. He took a positive pride in thus lowering and depreciating himself.

The marquis heard him attentively. He felt himself re-juvenated in the presence of this man, more ardent and impassioned than, in these times, one is even at twenty years of age. It was a pleasure to him, living in a world of officialism, stiff, starched, grave, cold by disposition and set purpose, to find himself side by side with a fervent, earnest being. He had too a certain regard for Vibert. Some far off reminiscence, some mysterious bond of union, perhaps, united the grandee, the millionaire, the peer of France, to the diminutive servant of the Prefecture.

" I am not," said the marquis, " a giver of advice, a blockhead and a dotard, as my age would seem to show. I am not going to tell you that you must conquer your passion and forbid your heart to beat ; I know very well that you would ask nothing better. Neither will I indulge you with hopes which might be dangerous, and in which I have no faith. It would in reality be a difficult matter for Madame Vidal to love you, not because of those imperfections which you exaggerate to such an extent, but by reason of your position towards her. She has not been accustomed to look on you as a man; for her you have been a means, an agent, a thing. If there were no other obstacle than your physical formation I should have some hope. Women are better than we are. We have but one idea—to know if they are lovely. They often seek after our moral qualities, and are taken with the hidden nature rather than the outside form.

The marquis, for the time being, forgot his gout. He started up, took Vibert by the arm, and forcing him to walk up and down the room with him, continued in these terms—" You see, I speak frankly to you, harshly, perhaps, as is my duty and my right. But I can afford you some consolation. What is it that causes all the suffering in love ? It is when one has to say to oneself—' This woman whom I long for so ardently belongs to another ; not only can I not make myself loved by her, but she adores him.' Nothing of the sort is the case with Madame Vidal

Entirely devoted to the memory of her husband, her heart is insensible to every seduction."

Vibert stopped short, let fall the arm on which the marquis
was leaning, and said abruptly—"You wish me to speak out, do
you not? Well then I am jealous, M. le Marquis, frantic with
jealousy ! "

"And of whom ? "

"Of Savari."

"Of Savari ! Does she love him ? "

"She will love him."

"Impossible ! What induces you to think so ? "

"Everything. He is tall, he is handsome, he is elegant, he is
distingué. He talks with ease. He is shrewd and cunning. I
know all his accomplishments. I have, as it were, been on the
watch for them, and I assure you that such a man would invariably succeed in pleasing if he set his mind on it."

"But she ought to hate him—was he not in her eyes her
husband's murderer ? "

"He is so no longer."

"The transition from hate to love is not so rapid as all that."

"There, M. le Marquis, I differ from you, and you know
that I am right. It is precisely from hate that people do pass to
love. There is a proverb to that effect, which I will spare you.
As you very justly said, I have no chance, while he has enough and
to spare. Reflect for a moment that she has been fearfully
unjust towards him ; she has suspected him of an awful crime.
Now she will be anxious to repair the wrong, and it is impossible to
say to what lengths a woman will go with that idea in her head."

"Have it so. I give in," replied the Marquis de X——, " but
you forget, my dear Vibert, that Madame Vidal is a good
woman, who loved her husband and will long remain faithful to
his memory."

"Pardon me, that is the mistake you make ; Madame Vidal
never loved her husband."

" What are you talking about? "

" What I have learnt to be true beyond all doubt. Am I not observant by profession as well as by nature? She was living at Genoa in the midst of her family when Maurice Vidal appeared, saw her, and asked her hand in marriage. She consented to marry him, because the match was a good one, because she wanted to live in Paris, the dream of all foreign women, and because, in a word, the first man who makes love to a girl has always a very good chance of being accepted. She took for love what, commencing in a mere feeling of curiosity, grew into a genuine attachment. As for love, in the true sense of the word, her husband never thought of inspiring her with it. Maurice Vidal, as a man of common sense, would, moreover, have thought it dangerous to excite an imagination already too lively. Possibly he never gave it a thought; of a somewhat cold, hard nature, he knew how to love wisely and after a thoroughly respectable fashion, but of the wilder phases of the passion he was in utter ignorance. He only demanded from his wife what he was prepared to render her—thorough devotion, genuine attachment, and tender fondness."

" How, then, do you account," replied the marquis, " for the violent despair exhibited by Madame Vidal on her husband's death, and that fervid elevation of spirit which you noticed so particularly in her? "

"I have never denied that Madame Vidal was as you describe her. I merely say that she has been kept in a state of repression, and when Maurice Vidal died all her depth of feeling, so long kept under, was merged into a desire for vengeance. Now, tired of searching for a murderer she cannot find, she gives up her revenge. But her natural excitement must find a vent, and here Savari steps in."

After a short interval of silence on both sides, the marquis said to Vibert—" What do you think of doing now? "

H

"I have not an idea. I think of suffering—it is an absorbing occupation."

" Do you intend to remain in these rooms ?"

" Yes, so long as I have a little money at command."

" Shall you make an attempt to see Madame Vidal again ?"

"See her again! Oh, yes! Speak to her—no! What is the use ? She needs my services no longer."

" I do not understand you. How can you see her again without speaking to her? Will you throw yourself in her way will you—?"

" No," said Vibert, interrupting the marquis, " I shall go to her house."

" Well ?"

"I can see her without being seen by her, without her having the slightest suspicion of my presence near her. The day I hired a lodging for her I reserved a hiding place for myself. Yes, I have my little cell in the Rue de Grammont just as Esmeralda's lover had his in Notre-Dame."

" You never forget anything."

" I thought then of surprising Savari's confidences. I think now—" He paused.

" Go on," said the marquis, encouragingly.

" Of feeding on their love !" concluded Vibert. " Is not that my destiny ? Can I live on my own account? Am I not compelled always to live in the life of others ?"

" What ! you will have courage— ? "

" Yes, listen. The drawing-room occupied by Madame Vidal communicates directly, on the one hand, with the bedroom and ante-room. But at the end of it, on the right, on the same side as the fire-place and opposite to the sofa on which she generally sits, there is a glazed door, shut both from within and without by means of bolts. I pass by the porter, who, under the impression that I am going to Madame Vidal's rooms, pays no further attention to me. Instead of going up the front staircase,

I hurriedly ascend the back one. I open a door, the key of which I obtained possession of some time ago, I enter a corridor and find myself at the glazed door. There I crouch down in a corner, put one eye to a little opening I have contrived, and I see without being seen, and hear without being heard, for I hold my breath and press my heart with my two hands to prevent it beating."

" But this is sheer folly !"

" It is wisdom ! By dint of suffering I shall possibly succeed in wearing out my sorrow."

" Give up these senseless projects," said the marquis, " the mission entrusted to you has, thanks to your intelligence, been fulfilled—the assassin of Maurice Vidal is discovered. It is no longer any business of yours ; it does not appertain to the police now, but to justice alone. Resume your former occupation, go back again to the Rue de l'Arbre-Sec and the office in the Rue Saint-Honoré, which you ought never to have left."

" I could not take up my office work again ; my thoughts would be elsewhere."

" Would you rather leave Paris, France, and travel all over the world? I do not know what to do with my money, and my income positively embarrasses me. I have no interest in increasing the inheritance of my scamp of a nephew. Set out on your travels, and I will give you an allowance proportionate to your wants."

" Oh ! M. le Marquis, how good you are!" said Vibert.

" Not I, I am not good. I have a liking for you, and that is all, idiot ; come, do you say yes ?"

" No, M. le Marquis, I shall be strong enough to endure, but I should not have the courage to go away from her."

" Go to the devil, then !" exclaimed the marquis, taking up his hat.

" That is good advice, and I will follow it," said Vibert, as he respectfully accompanied his protector as far as the bottom of the staircase.

CHAPTER XIII.

IF it were natural, as the Marquis de X— had said, that Vibert should leave the Hotel des Princes, it would have been still more so that Julia Vidal should return to her apartments in the Rue de la Paix. Had she not taken up her abode in the Rue de Grammont for the sole purpose of receiving Savari's visits and at the same time hiding from him her past life? Why so much mystery now? Why not resume her real name, and once more re-enter a home still all-pervaded with memories dear to her heart?

"You have been arrested," she might have said to Savari, "you have been suspected of a crime. I did not know you, and I, too, suspected you. I assumed a disguise and appeared in a feigned character in order to obtain the proofs of your guilt. Now that your innocence is recognised, I ask your forgiveness for my detestable suspicions, and I become Julia Vidal once more."

She dared not make use of such language, fearing to place Savari in too false and difficult a position as regarded herself. She perhaps also dreaded being put to the blush before him on account of all her past deception. At the same time she could not help saying to herself—"This state of things cannot last; he must be told who I am. I cannot continue to play this perpetual comedy and conduct myself like an adventuress. I have a name, an honourable name, and I ought to resume it. I will, I must speak out." She did not speak out, however, but continued to keep up her assumed character rather than confess.

They had resumed their former mode of life with the solitary exception that Vibert no longer intruded on their interviews. This sudden disappearance struck Savari at first as being odd, and he asked Julia for an explanation, but she appeared uneasy and made no reply. Savari did not feel himself justified in dwelling on the subject, and thought very naturally that the count, in whom he had noticed a tendency to jealousy, was on terms of coldness with his cousin on his account.

Every afternoon, about two o'clock, Savari made his appearance in the Rue de Grammont, and did not leave until dinner time. Seated at Julia's side, on the sofa in the drawing-room, he spoke to her of his early youth, of his entrance into life, of his struggles and his errors. He tried to give her a knowledge of himself, and to induce her to form a more favourable opinion of him than fell to his lot as a rule.

" I have been reproached," he said to her, " with living from hand to mouth, with not having made for myself any position in the world, with having no dividends to draw, with the absence of official employment, and with being useless to everybody, myself in particular. The accusation is just. If I had my life to begin over again, I should take a different view of things. But ought not some allowance to be made for the innumerable obstacles which I have encountered in my path ? I began life without a protector, without family, without friends, and with only a few thousand francs by way of fortune. I ought to have worked ; but had I been brought up to do so ? Destitute of advice, and dependent on myself alone, I lived as I saw everybody living around me, and badly did I live until the day I met you."

" And are you working now ?" asked Julia affectionately.

" Not yet, but I am on the look out for something to do."

" Then how do you live? I have a right to ask now that I am your confidant."

" Oh, at the present time," he replied, " living is not a very expensive business to me. I no longer, as I used to do, require a continuous supply of louis. I have no longer a desire to show myself in the Bois from three to five, at Tortoni's at six, and at the opera in the evening. When I wake, my first thought is to ask myself when I shall see you to-day? Then I dress and breakfast quietly, and fill up the rest of the time before coming here by perambulating the boulevards near this street. I stay with you until you send me off, and I think of you for the remainder of the day."

She tried to speak to him sensibly, as a friend or a sister, telling him that he should think of his future and struggle against a love to which she could not respond.

"You interest me," she confessed, "and I cannot hide it from you. I believe, too, that you are not entirely responsible for your mistakes, and that you have been judged harshly; you are more deserving than your reputation would seem to imply. I thank you for having been frank with me about your past life, of which I should have always been in ignorance but for your candour. I like you the better for it. But liking and friendship only can exist, as far as we are concerned; love must be banished. Let us have a thorough and sincere affection for each other. Like you, I am almost alone in the world; stand to me in place of family and friends, and respect the tears which I still shed."

He promised everything she wished, or rather all that she believed she wished. He vowed to be content with what she offered him and never to mention love again to her, and the instant he had made his vow he broke it.

So their lives ran on until an accident, easy to be foreseen, happened to disturb them. Since her husband's death, Julia Vidal had been in the habit of reading the newspapers, being interested in knowing everything that might be said on the subject of the tragedy in the Rue de la Paix. One morning she let fall the broad-sheet she was glancing over, and suddenly exclaimed, "It is infamous!" and she called Marietta.

"Read," she said to her, in a state of excitement, "read what French journalists have the impertinence to write!"

As she spoke, she pointed out a paragraph on the subject of the now fast approaching trial of Langlade. After giving an account of how the crime was committed, the article went on to say—" Langlade was madly in love with a woman called Soleil-Couchant. He discovered her embracing Maurice Vidal, followed the latter, and killed him in a fit of jealousy."

Julia, pale with indignation, snatched the newspaper out of Marietta's hand, as soon as the latter had glanced over the paragraph, and exclaimed—" In our country there would be dire vengeance on any man who dared to utter such a calumny. What ! let it go forth to the world that my husband had flirted with a girl like that ! That he was seen with her on the day before he expected me ! I will give a startling denial to that article. It wounds me in all that is dearest to me !"

She turned towards Marietta, and said—" Help me to dress. I am going to the office of this newspaper."

The writer of the paragraph, with whom Madame Vidal succeeded in obtaining an interview an hour afterwards, assured her that he had the news in question from a person employed at the Palais, who was too well informed to be likely to make any mistake. Julia, without delay, directed her steps towards the Palais-de-Justice, and sought an interview with M. Gourbet.

" Madame," said he, as soon as she had explained her motive for coming to him, "the paragraph which distresses you, and very naturally so, emanated neither from my colleagues nor myself. We are not in the habit of giving the newspapers any details with regard to cases under consideration ; on the contrary, we deprecate such indiscretion, which frequently is dangerous. But in this case the indiscretion is committed, and I can only pity you and express to you my sincere sympathy."

" I do not understand you, sir. Pity me ! I am not to be pitied. This article does not grieve me, seeing that it is a lie. It simply excites my indignation."

M. Gourbet was silent.

" You do not reply ?" said she. " Do you believe—you, too, by chance—the extraordinary tale this paper tells ?"

" Madame," said the magistrate, after a momentary pause, " if it were possible to hide the truth from you for ever, believe me, I should not, in spite of your persistence, reply to your question. Unfortunately, the trial of this Langlade will shortly take place : you will be directly mixed up in it, and will be, perforce, conversant with every petty detail of it. It is therefore better to be frank with you to-day—the paragraph of which you complain is perfectly correct."

" Do you mean to say," exclaimed Julia, " that in my absence my husband associated with that creature ?"

" He was killed a few minutes after leaving her."

" It is impossible."

" It is only too true."

" You possess evidence of what you state ?"

" Alas ! Yes, madame."

For three days Julia denied herself to Savari, but she did not shut herself up in her house. She went out several times, and first of all to the church of Saint-Roch, where every morning, since the death of her husband, she had been accustomed to burn a taper. Only instead of remaining, as of yore, on her knees in prayer whilst the taper was burning, she ordered that one should be burnt each day, and paid a month in advance so that she might not be obliged to go again. Accompanied by Marietta she subsequently paid a visit to the Rue de la Paix, packed in her trunks various belongings which she had not transferred to the Rue de Grammont, and ordered the porter to sell her furniture and let the rooms. Finally, she paid her daily morning visit to the cemetery of Père-la-Chaise. Usually, before this visit, she would stop at one of the first florists in Paris and buy a bouquet of violets surrounded by a garland of roses. They had been Maurice's favourite flowers, and she had conceived the touching idea of placing on his grave every morning a bouquet like those he had given her in days gone by. This time she confined herself to laying on the tomb of her husband the customary wreath of immortelles.

At the end of three days, Savari, pale and downcast, at length found Julia at home and visible.

"Ah!" he cried, "why have you once more banished me from your presence? Why?"

She interrupted him, by saying, "Do not complain. I assure you that it would be unjust on your part. You have no reason to complain."

CHAPTER XIV.

As Vibert was going along one of the passages in the Prefecture of Police, where he was obliged to report himself in person from time to time, he one day came across the chief of the detective force.

"Halloa!" said the chief accosting him, "you have got us into a pretty mess."

"What do you mean?" asked Vibert.

"We have been within an ace of losing Langlade."

"Trying to escape again, I suppose?"

"No, he has been on the point of death."

"He would have done far better, poor devil, if he had made an end of it."

"As far as he is concerned, no doubt, but not for us. There would have been no lack of people to say that we had either killed him, or let him escape. All the world is looking forward to an exciting trial, and your Parisian is not amiable when his emotions or his pleasures are interfered with. Happily, however, Langlade is now completely cured."

"What was the matter with him?"

"A rush of blood to the head, or a brain fever of some kind. It followed immediately on the interview with Soleil-Couchant, which you thought yourself bound to contrive."

" That is the reason why his trial has been delayed so long ?"

" Exactly so. We only ask to get rid of him as quickly as possible. He is by no means a comfortable kind of prisoner. He requires constant watching."

" Does he still break out into violence ?"

" No ; he is just now very quiet, even depressed, but we have learnt to our cost to mistrust him, so we are continually on our guard."

" Where has he been moved to ?" asked Vibert.

" Nowhere. He is at the Conciergerie. We prefer having him in our own hands. By-the-way, now that you are here you ought to go and see him."

" I ! what for ?"

" You have a certain influence over him, as you have proved to us, and you may possibly contrive to induce him to reply to the questions put to him by the magistrate."

" So he will not answer ? I expected as much."

" It has been impossible from the very commencement of his examination to get a word, much less a confession, out of him."

" He has confessed once, and that is enough."

" It would be better if he would speak now. It will be a pity to see him persist in his absolute silence before a jury."

" Oh," said Vibert, " you need not labour under the least uncertainty on that point. He will persist if he has made up his mind to it. When an idea gets into a head of that calibre it is not easily got out again."

" Will you try ? I believe you would succeed."

" I raise no objection. I merely say that it is useless."

" Come with me ; I will take you to him."

Langlade, when Vibert entered his cell, was stretched at full length on the bed with his face turned to the wall. Not being accustomed to see visitors, he probably thought it was a warder of the prison on some duty or other, and he did not give himself the trouble of turning round.

Vibert walked straight up to the bed, and, touching him on the shoulder, said—"So we have been ill, old fellow, have we?"

Langlade started up, the colour came into his face, still very pale, and his eyes, dim from illness, brightened as he said to Vibert—"It is you! There, I am glad to see you. How are your bruises?"

"Pshaw! don't talk of them. That's past and gone long ago. I have had none of your luck. I have not suffered from brain fever. During your illness, at all events, you could forget."

"Yes," said Langlade, bitterly, "but I am better to-day."

"Do you still harp upon that creature?"

"Yes, always."

"Is it possible that you still care about her?"

"Yes," said Langlade. "Does that astonish you?"

"I," said Vibert, "I—am I astonished at your stupidity? Why, I am a match for you. I even think I could give you points in the game. Am I astonished at your persisting in worrying yourself about one who does not care two straws for you? It's always so, my dear fellow. You adore Soleil-Couchant because she has behaved towards you in the most atrocious way. If she had been very sweet, very good, very submissive; if she had paid you her morning visit regularly with a bunch of violets in her hand, you would have soon wearied of her."

"You have seen her?" asked Langlade, who had been impatiently waiting until Vibert had got rid of his aphorisms to put the question.

"No," replied the police-agent, "I have not set eyes on her."

"Where is she now?"

"I know absolutely nothing about her."

"I have tried," said Langlade, "to question the warders about her, but they will not answer me."

"That is not very wonderful; prison warders are not, as a rule, very communicative. You yourself, moreover, take advantage of this privilege of silence."

" Yes, they want to make me talk, but it is not in my line.
May I ask whether you, by chance, are on the same errand ?"

"I should not be sorry to persuade you to answer the questions
put by the magistrate.   He is a fine fellow, and ought to have
his own way."

" He wearies me."

" That's his business.   You weary him still more, you do, by
refusing to speak to him."

" What do you want me to tell him?   He asks me a whole
heap of things I don't understand.   He insists on a detailed
account of how I killed that fellow in the Rue de la Paix.   As
for me, I prefer not saying anything about that, and I have determined to act the mute."

" Have you conferred with your counsel?"

"My counsel !   I refused to go into the waiting-room when
he came."

" How, in that case, can he defend you ?"

" I don't care about his defending me !" exclaimed Langlade,
hotly.   " Let them leave me in peace.   They will convict me
all the same, whatever I say and whatever I do."

" But," said Vibert, " you have still a loop-hole for escape."

" Come now, it was you who told me that my case was as
clear as could be."

"I may have made a mistake," remarked Vibert.   " Your
case is bad enough, that is certain, by the light of your antecedents, but a clever barrister can make a strong point of there
not having been any premeditation on your part, and your
having acted solely on an impulse of rage and jealousy, which
made you take leave of your senses.   Besides, in France there
are plenty of juries who, being averse to capital punishment, invariably accompany their verdict with a recommendation to
mercy on account of extenuating circumstances."

"But," exclaimed Langlade, "I don't want any such recommendation.   If I cannot live with Soleil-Couchant I would rather die."

"As you please. You have made up your mind to make no defence. Be it so. It is as good a kind of suicide as any other. Good-bye, then. Do you want anything? Would you like some tobacco?"

"No, I do not smoke."

"Ah, you have no small vices!"

And, with this pleasantry, Vibert knocked at the door, to summon the warder.

He next went to give an account of his visit to the chief of the detective force.

"As I anticipated," he said, "I have not been able to prevail upon him to speak. It is quite likely that he will refuse to answer the questions put to him by the president at the assizes." Vibert might have added, "I have, it is true, an infallible means of drawing him out of his obstinate silence. I might tell him that Soleil-Couchant, when I saw her, repented of the way she had treated him, that from the time she was separated from him she felt that she loved him, that she begged him to forgive her and try to defend himself as best he might, so as to be sent merely to the hulks whence he may, according to his wont, escape to rejoin her."

Langlade would certainly have placed implicit confidence in such a tale ; we are all so apt to believe what can make us happy, and, above everything, we are so credulous when we are in love, and, when suffering, so well disposed to suffer no longer. But Vibert was unwilling to make use of such means. He had had time to come to a conclusion about Soleil-Couchant, and knew that she was not a woman to change her opinion. Far from being anxious for Langlade's liberation, she wished him from the bottom of her heart a speedy condemnation to death, so that she might be freed from him for ever.

"Why," he reflected, "make the unhappy wretch cling to life? If he were to be condemned to death, his having confided in me would be a source of still greater suffering for him. If he be sent to the hulks and escape from them, Soleil-Couchant with her hard-heartedness will kill him by inches."

Nevertheless, Vibert asked what news there was about Soleil-Couchant.

"She has been at large for the last fortnight," replied the chief of the detective force.

"You have let her go, then?"

"Of course. She was only arrested for a misdemeanour, we have remitted the penalty as a reward for her betrayal of her sweetheart. As regards the murder business, it is evident that she could not have been an accomplice, so she will appear at the assizes simply as a witness. It would be useless to give her board and lodging until then, at the expense of the State. We have plenty of more interesting boarders as it is."

CHAPTER XV.

A FASHIONABLY dressed man, still young and *distingué* in face and manner alike, after having walked for some time up and down the Boulevard des Italiens, consulted his watch for about the twentieth time and then went into the Passage de l'Opera, where he bought a rose and a sprig of white lilac. This done, he crossed the boulevards, went down the Rue de Grammont, ran hastily up three flights of stairs and made his way into a drawing-room, where one of the most charming women in the world smiled upon him, and held out her hand.

A few moments later, another man, undersized, lean and insignificant, glided, with a downcast air, into the same house and went up a back staircase, halting on each step to see if anybody were coming down to meet him, or up behind him.

When he reached the third floor, he stealthily opened a door which he as noiselessly shut after him. Step by step, and on tiptœ, he made his way along a small dark corridor and came to a standstill before another door, the upper panel of which, made of frosted glass, allowed a dim light only to penetrate through it. Then he crouched down on the ground, and searched for the cleanest spot in the pane, where the frosted glass had been rubbed so that it was transparent. He was not long in finding it, and at once set himself to watch attentively.

A large wood fire, throwing out a cheerful glow, and a lamp placed on a table, lighted up the drawing-room. Savari was seated on the sofa which faced the glazed door, and Julia was by his side. Still in deep mourning, a careful scrutiny of her toilet showed, nevertheless, that it was not so deep as of yore. Her dress, instead of being high to the throat, was cut rather low, and the crape, which formerly covered her shoulders, had given way to black lace. Her magnificent jet hair was coquettishly arranged, and in it, on the left side of her head, a sprig of lilac was effectively placed. In her bosom was a rose. There was a certain alteration, also, both in her face and manner. Her bearing was more yielding, more in harmony, more voluptuous—if we may use the expression—than before. Her glance was less keen and had lost some of its brilliancy, but it was more tender, more melting. A certain animation overspread her countenance, and her cheeks were not so pale. One could almost see the blood circulating beneath her skin.

" Ought I to believe you blindly," said Julia, continuing a conversation already begun with Savari, " can I place implicit faith in your vows? Do not men accept it as a principle that engagements contracted with us go for nothing? Are we not made to be deceived? Do not interrupt me, I know what I am saying, and I have been witness of more than one act of treachery. You marry a young girl, pure, good, and trusting. She asks of you no account of your past life, but she wishes the present to belong to her, and to her alone. She exacts a fidelity equal to hers, a devoted love, absolute as her own. In her innocence,

her goodness, her simple trust, she cannot entertain an idea of
aught else. No doubt, no suspicion clouds her mind. Would
she dream of deceiving him she loves? Never. Does the
thought of flirting with another man ever flit across her mind
for an instant? No, it is impossible. And while she remains
thus faithful and pure, even in thought, the man to whom all
her trust is confided, to whom she has given herself entirely,
and without reserve, meets by chance a creature, more or less
seductive, looks at her, follows her, and thinks no more of his
plighted faith to another—"

" To another whom he did not love," said Savari.

" Then why did he lie? why did he say he loved her?"

" He believed, perhaps, that he did. There are men who live
after a fashion, so calm and quiet, who are happy in so unruffled
a tranquillity, and are by nature and disposition so protected
from the influence of their passions, that they are often under an
illusion as to the state of their heart. Because its pulse beats
a little more quickly, and their thoughts turn with pleasure to her
to whom they have given their preference, they imagine they are
in love, and proclaim it from the house-tops. Fools!" continued
Savari, hotly. "Have they any right to speak thus, to profane
to such a degree a sentiment of which they know nothing? The
rosewater love that they feel, resembles that other, true love, as
the fire that now glows before us resembles the sun. They were
made but to appreciate the child's play, the puerilities, the
prettiness of love. They will never know aught of that happiness without limit, those sorrows without number, that superhuman joy, those sufferings beyond endurance, which give
here on earth a glimpse at once of heaven and hell!"

Savari became animated to a degree as he spoke thus. His
face lighted up, his eyes sparkled, and in his voice there was a
tone of irresistible persuasion. Julia could not help admiring
his manly beauty, to which some altogether womanly trait lent
additional charm. She did not notice that Savari, whilst speaking

and without being aware of it himself, had drawn nearer to her, that he was touching her dress, and that one of his hands rested on hers. The hearth glow shed its fitful gleams of light on this scene. The lamp encircled her with its subdued rays. The rose and the lilac exhaled an intoxicating aroma.

On the other side of the glass door, looking full upon the sofa, Vibert, ever silent, still crouching down, heard, gazed and suffered. He, too, regarded Savari with admiration. He would have dearly liked to have killed him, but he was forced to confess that he was really handsome, and undeniably eloquent.

Savari went on speaking—" Yes ! " he exclaimed, '· the man who deceives the woman whom he says he loves, does not love her. If he loved her he would have no look, no thought but for her. The most lovely beings ever created might whirl around him, might encircle him with their arms, might intoxicate him with their breath—they would not even tempt him. For him the world would begin and end with the one woman. Near her he would forget the past and the future, the petty annoyances of every day, the difficulties of life, the wounds to his self-esteem, and the vexations of each hour. Remorse even—remorse, which is said to be implacable—could not touch him, nor turn him aside from the thought of her he loves. Ah ! " continued Savari, " do not be amazed at hearing me speak thus. My early youth, spent so frivolously, never foreshadowed such speech even to myself. But I am born again since I saw you. I now understand passion in all its exalted, pure, vehement and real phases. I love with all the strength of my being ! I love you to the verge of madness ! Have pity on me ! I die a living death in seeing you and not daring to clasp you to my heart. Near you I have all the timidity of a child, and yet my blood dances through my veins, my head is on fire, a thousand transports possess me. For pity's sake, be tender to me and tell me my fate ! Must I die or hope ? "

" Hope ! " exclaimed Julia, suddenly. And, with that Italian ardour of hers, that *furia* so long restrained, she threw her arms around him. Their lips met in a passionate kiss.

At the same moment a cry resounded from the other side of the glass door. Neither Julia nor Savari even heard it. To the cry succeeded the noise of a door shut with a crash. Vibert fled.

CHAPTER XVI.

THE proceedings in that serious case, for a long time known at the Palais-de-Justice as the "Tragedy in the Rue de la Paix," commenced at last in the Assize Court of the Seine in the latter half of February, 1848. In spite of the species of political fever which for some days past appeared to have seized on the Parisians, in spite of the attention excited by the famous patriotic banquets then in preparation, an enormous crowd had gathered since the morning in the vicinity of the Assize Court.

At half-past nine, the privileged persons, amongst whom were several ladies of the fashionable world, were admitted into the Court, and took their places behind the seats reserved for the witnesses. The general public entered a short time afterwards, and found standing room in the enclosure appropriated to them.

On the table, where the various articles to be put in evidence were generally placed, there were to be seen only a long knife and a red memorandum book, open at the page where Maurice Vidal had written a few words in his blood. About ten witnesses had been summoned by the Crown. There were none for the defence, Langlade having refused to name any to the barrister who appeared for him.

The Court opened at a quarter past ten, the jury having been drawn by lot in the council chamber. Contrary to the generally received rumour amongst the public, neither handcuffs nor a strait waistcoat had been put on Langlade. The president of the Court had considered such a precautionary measure useless, and in fact it is not usual except in extreme cases, because the prisoner, unless under very exceptional circumstances, ought to have full liberty of action before his judges.

Two gendarmes entered with Langlade and took their seats on either side of him. He did not appear to be conscious of what was going on around him. He was very much dejected, and appeared to avoid looking round the room. The public were to a certain extent disappointed. They had anticipated seeing quite another style of man, and had counted from the very first on scenes of violence.

A rumour was quickly put in circulation till it reached the gaping crowd outside that the prisoner was not equal to his reputation, and that he had suddenly become intimidated by the paraphernalia of justice. The gendarmes who had been cautioned not to lose sight of their prisoner for an instant, were asking themselves if their instructions were not unnecessary. A few minutes more of this inaction and their zeal would begin to abate. •

" Prisoner, stand up," said the president.

Langlade did not budge an inch.

" Gendarmes," resumed the president, " assist the prisoner to stand up."

The gendarmes took Langlade, each by an arm, and raised him to his feet. He looked at them with an air of astonishment, and then, comprehending what was wanted of him, turned towards the Court.

" What is your name ?" asked the president.

" Hector Langlade," replied the prisoner.

" Q.—Your age ?"

" A.—Thirty-six."

" Q.—You were born in the Department of Vaucluse ?"

" A.—Yes ; near Avignon."

" Q.—You have been convicted on two previous occasions and

sentenced ; the first time to five years' and the second to twenty years' penal servitude ? "

" A.—Perhaps so."

" Q.—You escaped on two occasions from Toulon and Brest ?"

" A.—Yes."

" Q.—When last arrested, you were residing at No. 22, Rue Croix-Petits-des-Champs ?"

" A.—Yes."

The president now informed Langlade that his indictment would be read, on which the prisoner dropped into his seat without waiting for an invitation, and, turning his head away, half shut his eyes. The registrar read the indictment, which we omit, seeing that our readers are already fully conversant with Langlade's life and the charges brought against him.

When the reading was finished, the witnesses were called upon to answer to their names, and on hearing that of Stéphanie Cornu, otherwise Soleil-Couchant, Langlade opened his eyes and turned pale, but did not move his head. The witnesses withdrew into the room set apart for them, and the president, now ready to proceed with the examination of the prisoner, requested him to stand up again.

"What for ? " asked Langlade.

" To reply to the questions which I am about to put to you."

" In that case it would be useless, as I do not intend to reply," said Langlade.

A murmur, repressed at once by a few words from the president, ran through the Court, the crowd beginning to see that the prisoner was, perhaps, not quite so manageable as he appeared to be.

" Prisoner at the bar," said the president kindly, " I wish to point out to you that by persisting in your silence you will damage your cause in the eyes of the jury."

" I have confessed my crime," said Langlade. " What more is wanted ? "

"The Court wishes to ascertain from your own mouth, without the necessity of relying absolutely on the evidence to be
given by the witnesses in the case, in what manner the crime
was committed. I repeat, you can only secure the indulgence
of the Court and the jury by deference to the customs in force
here."

"I do not ask indulgence from any one," replied Langlade,
without raising his voice. "Send me to the scaffold as soon as
you can—that is all I want."

The counsel appointed by the Court to defend the prisoner
here leaned over to him, and endeavoured to persuade him to
reason, but in vain. The president, after patiently waiting until the conclusion of this colloquy, directed that, as the prisoner
refused to reply, and the Court had no means of compelling him
so to do, the examination of the witnesses should be proceeded
with.

The first witness called was Madame Vidal, and her appearance was watched with eager interest by the assembled crowd.
The president begged the witness to control her very natural
agitation and to reply to the questions which, unfortunately, had
to be put to her.

Julia Vidal gave the details of her arrival in Paris, the difficulty she had experienced in effecting an entrance into her house
and the state in which she found the rooms. She also replied
to various other questions with a greater amount of calmness
than might have been expected. When her examination, which
the president made as short as possible, was over, Madame Vidal
asked if it was necessary for her to remain until the end of the
trial, and the president, after consulting the jury and the counsel for the prisoner, allowed her to leave. She bowed in a
dignified manner, and withdrew.

The second witness was the porter of the Rue de la Paix,
whose evidence need not be repeated, as it was essentially the
same as that to which he had deposed before M. Gourbet.

The prisoner's counsel, at this point, called the attention of the jury to the fact that this witness adhered to the statement that he had not seen anybody go up to Maurice Vidal's rooms on the 19th October, and he maintained that if Langlade had entered the house, he could not have passed unnoticed, as his imposing stature must inevitably have betrayed him. On this point a discussion between the advocate-general and the counsel for the prisoner ensued.

Langlade, who had kept silence up to this, suddenly gave signs of extreme impatience, and exclaimed—" What's the good of all this? I have said that I struck the blow. Let us make an end of it."

"Prisoner at the bar," said the president, in a firm tone of voice, "since you refuse to speak in answer to the questions put to you, the Court will not allow you to interrupt the proceedings. Your counsel will take whatever line of defence he thinks best. His task is by no means an easy one; do not make it an impossibility."

The advocate-general, in his turn, attempted to explain to the prisoner that his confession was not sufficient for the ends of justice, which required all the proofs necessary for the full elucidation of the case. In conclusion, he said—" When a criminal, abhorring his heinous crimes, abandons himself, the law, that universal protectress, still undertakes his defence." This oratorical effort had not the slightest effect upon Langlade, who contented himself with a shrug of his shoulders.

This second witness was succeeded by several tenants of apartments at No. 6, Rue de la Paix. The only thing gathered from their evidence was that they had neither seen nor heard anything remarkable during the evening of the 19th October.

A man named Jacquet, porter of the house in the Rue Neuve-Saint-Augustin, where Stéphanie Cornu lived, deposed to having seen a young man take leave of her near his lodge one evening in the previous October, but he could not fix the exact date.

The description which he gave of this unknown individual appeared to tally pretty correctly with the portrait of Maurice Vidal, but the counsel for the prisoner remarked that, according to this witness, the man in question was under the medium height, whereas those who had known Maurice Vidal all agreed in saying that, although he was not tall, he would never have been called undersized. The further examination of this witness by the Court was as follows :—

" Q.—Had you seen the young man in question with Stéphanie Cornu before ? "

" A.—I had seen him talking to her at the street door on the previous evening."

" Q.—When you saw the prisoner the following evening immediately after the stranger had left, did he speak to you ? "

" A.—He asked me whether the lady was at home. I was afraid of a row between the two, so I said she had gone out. He told me I was a liar and rushed away after the young man."

" Q.—Was the prisoner a quarrelsome man ? "

" A.—He frequently quarrelled with my lodger, and he was generally out of sorts when he left her."

" Q.—Have you personally had reason to complain of his violence ? "

" A.—Very often ; once he wanted to throw me out of the window."

This reply excited considerable merriment amongst the crowd, which was speedily subdued by the president declaring emphatically that he would take means to stop any further interruption, of whatever kind it might be.

The witness went on to say that, although the prisoner was excessively violent, he was not a bad man, and that when his anger had passed over, he would always ask his, the witness' pardon, and give him a couple of francs.

We are giving a summary of the evidence instead of a detailed account, because our readers have for some time been familiar with the details, and we have no wish to be wearisome. We will, therefore, omit certain important evidence, such as that of the commissary of police of the Tuileries section, the doctor, and Vibert, with all of which we are conversant, and pass on to the examination of Soleil-Couchant. The arrival on the scene of this fresh witness will not add anything to our knowledge of the case, but it was destined to effect a very important change in the attitude of the prisoner, and to lead up to the remarkable incident which brought the trial to an unlooked-for conclusion.

As might have been expected from such a person, Soleil-Couchant had got herself up for the occasion in her richest and most striking costume. When she was called, she stepped forward, without hesitation, and smiled on all those who stretched forward to get a look at her.

The prisoner, still preserving the same attitude, did not turn his head. His half-closed eyes did not open a whit wider, and it might have been supposed that he was as indifferent to this witness as to the others. Nevertheless, an acute physiognomist would have detected certain significant indications. Langlade's brow contracted, the blood left his lips, and his fingers beat a devil's tattoo on the bench before him.

"You know the prisoner?" asked the president, after the usual preliminary questions had been put and answered.

"Oh, yes, sir, very well. Very much too well," she added, smiling.

"You will have the goodness to abstain from all comments," replied the president, severely. "Your 'very much too well' was superfluous; 'very well' was sufficient. You will also be good enough to try, at all events, to conduct yourself with more gravity. Do not forget that you are in a court of justice, and that you have already appeared here on your own account. And now tell the Court all you know about the unhappy man whom your coquetry induced to visit you that evening. When you have finished speaking, I shall have certain questions to put to you. You may begin."

Soleil-Couchant, turning now to the Court, now to the jury, now to Langlade, and occasionally attitudinising for the benefit of the audience, repeated what we have already heard her tell Vibert. Her very figurative language, the cynicism of some of her expressions, and the manner in which she abused her former sweetheart, several times drew from the listeners murmurs which the president, whilst evidently sharing in the general indignation, was bound to suppress.

Langlade alone, accustomed, undoubtedly, to the reproaches and amenities of Soleil-Couchant, made no sign nor uttered a word. On the contrary, he seemed to take a pleasure in hearing her speak. In spite of himself he had turned by degrees towards her, and was looking at her. In his look there was neither hate, contempt, nor anger. It was rather a mixture of sadness, regret, and admiration.

After having replied to all the questions put to her by the president, and having received from him a sharp, but just reproof, Soleil-Couchant returned to her seat. She still smiled just as graciously on the Court, the jury, the barristers, and the public; appeared to try to catch all eyes, and did not seem in the least degree conscious of the bad effect she had produced.

The president examined two other witnesses, and then directed an adjournment for a quarter of an hour. The gendarmes withdrew with their prisoner, and the audience broke up into small knots for a little private discussion.

Soleil-Couchant endeavoured to engage her neighbours in conversation, but, actuated by a sense of shame, even the men found an excuse for getting away from her. In vain did she shoot out her most provoking glances at the junior bar. The briefless ones pulled their bar caps over their eyes, wrapped themselves up in their gowns, buried their chins in their bands, and, for the moment, seemed invulnerable. Her isolation was beginning to weigh upon her when she suddenly caught sight of a young Englishman, who had profited by the adjournment to gain, by means of some pecuniary consideration, an entrance into the Court. This Englishman, who was conscientiously doing Paris, being young and foolish, was much flattered at being noticed by her whom he fancied the heroine of the day. He managed to edge up to her, and they were soon engaged in lively conversation.

A bell rang ; an usher announced the entrance of the Court, and the trial was resumed. This time, as he entered the Court, the prisoner's first look was towards Soleil-Couchant. Simultaneously he perceived the young man, with whom she appeared to be conversing with more and more familiarity, and he frowned heavily.

The president called upon the advocate-general to address the jury, and accordingly the latter rose and commenced his speech as follows :—

"Gentlemen of the jury—In rising to address you in support of this terrible indictment, I cannot shake off a feeling of profound sadness, for it is my duty to ask of you a verdict which will carry with it fearful consequences. But I must silence my grief and recall to my mind that I am here not only as the representative of society outraged by the commission of an awful crime and by the murder of a good man, but also as a pleader in the cause of human life. My task, I know, is a difficult one, but I will endeavour to rise to the level of it. Above all, gentlemen, it is necessary that you should know the man who stands in the dock before you, and whom you are called upon to judge."

After this exordium the advocate-general took Langlade from his birth, followed him step by step through his life, and showed, with great elegance of style, that he had always been a prey to the most detestable passions, and that he never respected any law, human or divine. Then, plunging into the heart of the question, he devoted himself to construct out of the links of evidence a chain of argument to establish beyond refutation the guilt of Langlade. He wound up by maintaining that the prisoner was unworthy of any sympathy, and he expressed his hope that the jury, true to their trust, would put aside any scruples they might have, and strike down the murderer in memory of his victim.

During this address, Langlade exhibited signs of extreme impatience and irritation. Those who noticed it attributed it to his resenting the severe handling he was receiving from the advocate-general; but a skilful observer, who should have studied Langlade's glance, would have found other causes for the exasperation he evinced.

It was now the turn of the counsel for the prisoner. Following the example of the advocate-general he went back to the prisoner's youth, but he took care to show that his youth, destitute of advice and thrown upon itself, desolate and sad, was all in favour of his client.

" The advocate-general," he exclaimed, " has been pleased to depict this man as a prey to the most execrable passions, and given up to all kinds of vice. I look for these vices and I do not find them. The man for whom I appear is neither a gambler, nor a drunkard, nor a libertine. No, he is not a libertine, since one single passion has ruled his life, that which he has entertained for the woman who has appeared before you, and for her fatal beauty. If he had not met that woman he might perhaps have been an industrious man, an honest labourer; and if that woman, instead of being a wretch, had shown any good feeling towards the man who loved her, Langlade would not be here. But, gentlemen of the jury, do you not see, in the obstinate persistence of my client in abstaining from any defence, the dreadful suffering he is undergoing, the deep distaste he has for life, the discouragement which has taken hold of his mind ? The advocate-general calls that remorse ; as for me, I

contend that it is love—outraged, hopeless love! And my con·
science, gentlemen, bids me defend this unhappy man, who re-
pels me, and who is unwilling to be defended. He says he is
guilty, and I say that he merely wishes to die. I assert that
to convict him would be to lend a helping hand to suicide.
That you will not do, you have no right to do !"

These passionate words appeared to produce a great effect
upon the audience. As for Langlade, after having listened for
a short time to his counsel, he made a grimace, as much as to
say, " What a good fellow he is to give himself so much trouble!"
Then he turned towards Soleil-Couchant, who, flirting more
vigorously than ever, was showering her bewitching glances on
the young Englishman.

The counsel now entered on the gist of the matter. He
passed in review, with great conciseness and undeniable ability,
various circumstances which, in his opinion, had never been
cleared up. He laid great stress on the point that Maurice
Vidal, whatever the advocate-general might say, could not have
known Langlade, and consequently could not have had any idea
of writing the name of his murderer, that is, if Langlade had
committed the crime. He reminded the jury also, that Langlade's
victim, according to the evidence of Stéphanie Cornu and the
porter of the Rue Neuve-Saint-Augustin, had a high-coloured,
very ruddy complexion, whilst Maurice Vidal was described by
all who knew him as having been pale to a degree.

" There is in all this case," added the speaker, " something
strange and mysterious, which ought, gentlemen, to make you
hesitate before giving your verdict. A crime has been committed, a man has confessed to having committed it, and there
is a certain amount of proof against him ; all this I admit. But,
in spite of this confession, in the face of this evidence, I should
hesitate, gentlemen, I assure you. Or, rather no, I should not
hesitate. I should acquit this man. I would consent to let a
guilty man go unpunished sooner than have to regret all my

life the death of an innocent one. More than all, I should not forget the words of one of our greatest orators—'When God has not revealed a crime fully to men, it is a sign that He wills not that they should judge it, and that He reserves the decision for His supreme tribunal.'"

At the very moment when it was thought that this eloquent address had been brought to a conclusion, and when a subdued murmur of approbation was heard throughout the Court, the counsel for the prisoner, to quote the newspapers of the day, had a moment of oratorical inspiration, as magnificent as can well be imagined. He turned quickly towards the prisoner, seized his hands, clasped them in his own, and adjured him to say that he was not guilty. A shiver of excitement ran through the vast assemblage ; every heart stood still. Langlade alone appeared unmoved by the efforts of his counsel to save him. His eyes were ever fixed on Soleil-Couchant. Deeply enraged at the flirtation she was openly carrying on with the foolish young Englishman seated by her side, thoughts of vengeance flitted through his excited brain, and, grasping eagerly the hands which his counsel stretched out towards him, he exclaimed— "No ! I am not guilty ! "

The excitement amongst the audience was at its height. Two or three persons stood up, but the first words of the president restored the calm which, for a moment, had been disturbed.

" You are rather late," said he to the prisoner, "in telling us of your innocence. After having refused up to now to answer our questions, you may be supposed to have reserved yourself for the creation of a grand effect ; and we have to beg of the gentlemen of the jury that they will be on their guard. If you are innocent, why did you not say so before ? "

" Zounds ! " exclaimed Langlade, " because I thought I was guilty ! "

" You believed yourself guilty ! " said the president, in astonishment.

The prisoner.—" Yes, I killed a man, but I did not kill your Maurice Vidal."

The president.—"Who then was the man you killed?"

The prisoner.—" I don't know who he was, but he wasn't Maurice Vidal."

The president.—" What makes you think so?"

The prisoner.—" Everything which that gentleman (pointing to the advocate-general) has said. He spoke for an hour of the blood which welled out of the victim's wound, of the knife with which he was struck, of a study, of a bedroom, in short, of a whole heap of things which cannot be true, because it was with my fist—yes, with this fist here—that I knocked the man down, and I did it under the gate of a court-yard, and not in a study."

The president.—" We must call the attention of the jury to the improbability of this tale."

The prisoner.—" The improbability! What interest have I in saying that I killed this man rather than that? I shall be convicted none the less!"

The president.—" That is true, but you hope to postpone your conviction."

The prisoner.—" If I had wished to postpone my conviction, I should have spoken at first. I saw very well that you were on the wrong scent."

Without condescending to notice the disrespect contained in the expressions made use of by Langlade, the president asked him why he was so tardy in his defence.

" That's my secret," said Langlade, casting a stealthy look of hate on Soleil-Couchant.

The president.—" Was it in the Rue de la Paix that you killed the man you mention?"

The prisoner.—" Yes, it was in the Rue de la Paix, but I do not know the number."

The president.—"At what o'clock was it?"

The prisoner.—"It must have been about ten at night."

The president.—" And that was in October ?"

The prisoner.—" The end of October."

" Then," said the president, " you have just pronounced your own doom. No other man but Maurice Vidal was murdered in the Rue de la Paix in October, or even in September or November."

At this juncture, a member of the jury rose and asked the president whether he might make an observation.

" Speak, sir," was the reply, " we are all attention."

" It is my duty," said the juryman " to call attention to a circumstance which has just struck me, and of which the Court is in ignorance. In the month of October last, a few days before the murder in the Rue de la Paix, a friend of mine was found dead under the gateway of a court-yard in that street. He bore upon him no trace of any wound which could lead to a suspicion of foul play, and it was supposed that, as he was of an exceptionally sanguine habit of body, he had been seized with a fit of apoplexy. I ought to add that a large black mark was noticed on his left temple. I was the first to entertain and express the idea that my friend, in falling, had come in contact with the pavement. I can now see that the prisoner's formidable fist could, by a blow on the temple, have produced the mark I have alluded to, and so have been the cause of death."

These words, uttered by an apparently respectable man, whose position as a juryman gave him, at the time, considerable weight, produced a great effect upon the audience. Everybody turned to converse with his neighbour. The advocate-general handed a note to the bench. Several jurymen asked for further information from their colleague who had just spoken. Langlade, never losing sight of Soleil-Couchant, conversed with his counsel. The trial, without having been formally adjourned, was interrupted.

By degrees, order was restored, and the advocate-general addressed the Court as follows—

"Messieurs, on account of the new light thrown upon this case, and the opinion to which a member of the jury has unconsciously given utterance with regard to the trial on hand, I beg to apply that it may be postponed to another sitting."

The judges retired to deliberate. On their return, after a very short absence, the president made the following announcement—

"The Court, after mature consideration, and in accordance with the application of the advocate-general, postpones the case until another sitting. Gendarmes, remove the prisoner."

The Court adjourned, and every one went away in a state of the greatest excitement.

CHAPTER XVII.

On the morning following the sitting of the Court, Vibert presented himself at about ten o'clock in the Rue de Grammont. On this occasion, however, instead of taking every precaution to pass unnoticed by the people of the house, he purposely attracted the attention of the porter, and slowly went up the main staircase.

His countenance was careworn and deadly pale, and his whole appearance was that of a man weighed down by some profound grief. In three months he had aged several years. But there were in his face traces of some new feeling. His mouth, as a rule so serious, actually smiled, his look had more animation in it than it was wont to have, and altogether he had somewhat about him which was at once sad, malevolent, and self-satisfied. He appeared to be still suffering, but to be drawing nigh to the end of his pain. His horizon, although still overcast by clouds, gave an earnest of less uncertain weather. He was hurrying.

perhaps, on to an abyss, but an abyss which he saw and was approaching by a smooth and familiar road.

He might be compared to a soldier who after a long course of fighting in ambuscade, at length comes into action in the open and with the clear sky only above him. He sees a lengthy line of enemies drawn up in front of him, he knows he will fall under their fire, but for a moment he will enjoy the fierce pleasure of beholding the foe, of rushing upon him, and striking a mortal blow before he in turn has to succumb.

On reaching the floor where Julia resided, Vibert rang without any hesitation. " I wish to see your mistress," said he to Marietta, who looked at him in astonishment.

" If you will walk into the drawing-room, sir, I will inform my mistress, who is not yet dressed."

When fairly in the room where he had not set foot for so long, and of which he had only caught an occasional glimpse through the glazed door, a feeling of tenderness came over him. Every spot, each object, recalled some reminiscence. In the recess of that window she had one day pressed his hands in her own as she exclaimed—"You will be devoted to me, will you not? You will aid me to avenge him ?"

Near that door, on another occasion, still unheeding that under the garb of a police-agent there stood a man, and that such familiarity might be dangerous, she had, in one of her moments of despair when appearances were set at nought, leaned her head on Vibert's shoulder and wept against his heart. Here she had smiled on him ; there she had thanked him for good advice. Before that fire-place one evening when, completely absorbed in thought, she had not heard him come in, he had caught sight of a shapely foot resting on the fender, and the graceful outline of a rounded ankle. Yes, in this room his love had grown, little by little, and had become an invincible and terrible passion.

If Julia had entered at that moment Vibert, still under the influence of the memories thus called up, might possibly have

I

renounced the plans he had cherished since the previous evening, and which now caused him to smile so bitterly. But his eye fell unwittingly on the sofa where Madame Vidal used to sit with Savari by her side. The last scene he had witnessed, that scene which nearly cost him his reason, recalled him to his purpose. He forgot the good so that he might remember but the evil, and he vowed to be merciless towards others as they had been towards him.

Madame Vidal made her appearance, and, without asking Vibert to take a seat, said to him—"I did not expect to see you again."

This icy reception did not astonish the police-agent; he was too intelligent not to have expected it. He understood perfectly that Julia must hate him for having formerly dared to suspect of a crime the man whom now she loved. She had entertained those suspicions simultaneously with Vibert—had shared them with him. But that was only an additional reason for detesting, still more thoroughly, the accomplice whom she now disowned with a burning blush of shame.

"Madame," replied Vibert drily, " I suddenly ceased to see you because my mission with you was at an end. Chance enabled me to discover the murderer of your husband; I succeeded in capturing him and handing him over to the authorities unaided, and your assistance, which was so valuable and so necessary to me so long as that Savari was concerned, became useless."

Every one of these words, on which Vibert laid intentional emphasis, wounded Julia to the quick, and she replied tartly— " Well, then, if my assistance is no longer of use, why—"

"Why," said he, completing the sentence, "have I the temerity to present myself here to-day ? The answer is simple, and you may learn it if you will still permit me, madame, to sit down for a moment."

She made no reply, but, appreciating the lesson thus given her, she took a seat, so that Vibert might follow her example.

"You were present at the trial yesterday ?" asked Vibert brusquely, and determined to open the engagement.

"A portion of it," replied Julia. "The president gave me permission to return home at the conclusion of my examination."

"Then, madame, you are not acquainted with the closing scene."

"I am ignorant of it ; and if you are here to describe it you may spare yourself the trouble. I shall know the *dénouement* soon enough, more especially as it might easily be foreseen. As long as there was any question of discovering the murderer of my husband you found me strong and brave. Now that the guilty man is in custody and is about to be punished for his crime, he belongs to justice, and there can no longer exist in my heart any feeling of hatred against him."

"Very well, madame, I will not tell you what the end was since you think you know it. I will merely ask your permission to relate certain circumstances which came to light during the trial after you left the Court. For instance," continued Vibert, speaking still more slowly, "it was proved beyond a doubt that your husband had never spoken to the woman called Soleil-Couchant."

"Ah !" said Julia, turning white as a ghost.

This first blow struck by Vibert was a terrible one. If, a few weeks previously, any one had said to Madame Vidal : "Your husband has been the victim of an odious calumny ; he was always faithful to you," she would have experienced a feeling of unmixed joy. But now, faithlessness on the part of her husband was the sole excuse she could make to her own conscience for having given way so soon to another love, and this excuse was slipping from under her.

For a moment the thoughts which we have expressed so briefly assailed her in full force ; her mind was a prey to remorse. Soon, however, she regained somewhat of her calmness, and, turning towards Vibert, asked—"How did this further information come to light? What other motive than jealousy induced Langlade to kill my husband ?"

"It was not he who killed him !" replied Vibert.

"Not he! What do you mean? Did he not confess his crime?"

"Yes; but it was a case of mistaken identity. He had killed a man whose name he did not know, and he imagined it was your husband. Here, madame, have the kindness to read the *Gazette des Tribunaux*. You will there see the end of this remarkable trial, at which you did not think proper to be present."

With trembling hands Julia took the paper which Vibert held out to her. She was far from divining the end which the detective had in view, but she felt instinctively that she was menaced by a serious danger. After having finished the perusal, she gave herself up to reflection, and the paper slipped from her hands.

Vibert picked it up, folded it with care, put it in his pocket, and said—"So you see we have to begin again."

Julia raised her head quickly. "To begin what again?" she asked.

"The murderer is not yet discovered, and still a murderer there must be. We must recommence the search."

"That is a matter for the law to deal with," said she curtly. "I have nothing whatever to do with it."

"You are soon discouraged, madame," remarked Vibert.

She looked at him haughtily, and, letting her feelings get the better of her, replied—"Spare me your remarks, sir, I beg."

"*Mon Dieu!* Madame," he continued, "if I deplore the discouragement which seems to have taken possession of you, it is because I see our interests endangered by it."

"What do you mean by that?"

"I expected undoubtedly that you would assist me, as formerly, in my search. I was clumsy enough, I admit, to be led astray on a false scent; but I come back to my first idea, which, assuredly, was a good one."

"Your first!" and as she said it the colour fled from her cheeks, for his meaning began to dawn upon her.

" Yes, madame, my first; seeing that Langlade is not the culprit, I have every reason to suspect Savari, as I did from the first."

" Sir !"

" Madame ! "

" Your suspicions can never reach him of whom you speak."

" They reached him tolerably well formerly," was the cruel reply. "In what respect, may I ask, has the situation changed?"

" It is changed," she exclaimed indignantly, " he is an honourable man, I have learned to know him, to esteem him. Pollute him no longer with your suspicions !"

" Madame," said Vibert, by this time thoroughly exasperated at seeing her defend Savari with so much energy, and casting aside all reserve, " since I entered this room you have been pleased to recall to my mind that I am not a man, but simply a police-agent. Very well ! a police-agent only recognises his duty; he is told to seek after a criminal, and he sets about his task without paying any attention to the interest which a woman takes in that criminal, or to the love which she bears him."

She bounded from her seat, stretched out her arms, and gave utterance to but one word—"Go ! "

Not a whit less pale than she was, and wounded equally to the quick, Vibert cast down his eyes and obeyed.

When he reached the door, she thought herself rid of him, and sinking in an arm-chair, she exclaimed—" Whither have I been brought? What country is this where even at home a man can be murdered and a woman insulted ? "

She was sublime in her indignation. Her luxuriant black hair which, in her haste to see the detective, she had scarcely given herself time to coil round her shapely head, came undone, and fell over her quivering shoulders. Her bosom heaved under the lace which scarce covered it. Anger lent warmth to her cheeks and colour to her lips, and her open mouth, from which a sigh escaped, revealed her perfect teeth.

Vibert, who had stopped, lost in contemplation of her, had never seen her so lovely. He could no longer restrain his imagination ; wrought up to a pitch of excitement and yet unsatiated, in a moment he lost his head, sprang towards Julia, took her face between his hands to prevent her avoiding him, and imprinted a burning kiss on her lips.

It was perhaps the first kiss he had ever given a woman. She shuddered at the odious touch, and then wrenching herself free from his embrace by a sudden struggle, she struck Vibert in the face, and rushed from the room in a state of distraction.

CHAPTER XVIII.

OF all the numerous documents which were placed in our hands and enabled us to recount this history, there now remain but a few short notes, destitute of all details. We have reached the fifth act of our drama. The time of delay has gone by, the action of the piece carries us forward, and the facts are hurrying onward to their *dénouement*.

This affair of the Rue de la Paix may be said to have gone hand in hand with the events of which since the 22nd February, 1848, Paris was the scene. It was, so to speak, drawn into the vortex of political agitation. In the Rue de Grammont, incident followed on incident, just as ministers succeeded ministers in the Tuileries.

In the former, a scene of unheard of violence gave place to another still more dramatic ; in the latter, Molé replaced Guizot, who in turn made way for Thiers and Odilon Barrot. The first concession brought a second in its train ; to reform succeeded the Regency, and to the Regency the Republic. This correlation of events furnishes no cause for astonishment. The great invariably draws after it the small. The agitation of the masses communicates itself to individuals, and the fever which spreads through the streets penetrates the houses also.

As soon, after Vibert's departure, as Julia had recovered from her indignation, she, on a moment's reflection, came to an energetic determination and sat down at her desk.

" Do not come and see me during the day," she wrote to Savari, " but be here at seven o'clock precisely. I have a great project to unfold to you."

She sealed the note, and summoned Marietta. "Send this letter at once to its address," said she, " and then come to me again."

When Marietta had executed this commission, Madame Vidal said to her—" We leave for Italy to-morrow. Pack up and help me to dress. I am going out."

Immediately afterwards she drove to her notary's office and arranged several little matters with him, went to the church of Saint-Roch, where she remained for a long time engaged in prayer, and then went on to the cemetery of Père-la-Chaise. She knelt down on a grave, burst into tears, and seemed to be imploring pardon.

It was with considerable difficulty that she accomplished these various peregrinations. It was Wednesday, the 23rd of February, and Paris was in the full swing of open insurrection. Whole regiments, in battle array, were drawn up on the boulevards; strong guards patrolled the streets; the artillery, brought in hot haste from Vincennes, were posted on the quays and in the environs of Portes Saint-Denis and Saint-Martin. In one place a regiment of the line fraternised with the people; in another, the National Guards endeavoured to interpose between the police and the populace. Street-arabs paraded the thoroughfares to the cry of "*Vive la Reforme!*" workmen were planting flags on the barricades, and students sang the "Marseillaise." Cries of " death " to various unpopular personages were heard from the direction of Saint-Merri, and the rattle of musketry sounded in the barracks of Saint-Martin, at the Arts-et-Metiers, and in the Rue Bourg-l'Abbé. And above the din of these shouts, these cries, this fusillade, came the doleful call of the tocsin.

No accident happened to Julia who traversed a great portion of Paris without inconvenience. But, unnoticed by her, a man dogged her footsteps the whole time, and kept unflagging watch over her. He even glided into her house, and made his way to the back staircase as she ascended the main one. It was nearly seven o'clock when she re-entered her home. Marietta, uneasy, ran to meet her, and Savari made his appearance shortly afterwards.

" Well, what have you to tell me?" said he, "what is the great project you mentioned in your letter? Has the insurrection frightened you, and do you mean to fly from Paris?"

" Just so," she replied, " I do not wish to remain any longer exposed to the dangers to which one is liable here. I leave to-morrow."

" Let us go," said Savari.

" You will follow me?"

" Can you ask me such a question?" he exclaimed, kissing her hand.

She looked earnestly at him, read in his eyes all the love he felt for her, and said to him—" Sit down there. I have something serious to say to you."

" I am all attention, dearest," said Savari, sitting down by her side on the sofa.

" I have," said she, " committed a grave fault, one still greater than I imagined it to be. I have just wept bitterly over it, but I do not wish to throw the responsibility of it upon you, and it shall no longer come between us. I trust myself entirely to your love, and I am convinced that it will undertake the task of making me forget the past."

" Yes," exclaimed Savari, " my very life belongs to you."

" I do not doubt it. What would become of me without

you ? I have even lost," she added with a sigh, "all right to remember my former self."

"Do not look back, trust and hope. You speak of leaving for Italy; so much the better, it is what I wished. There, in that lovely country, under that bright sun, near you, resting on your heart, my real nature will be developed, I shall acquire those qualities in which I am now deficient, and I shall succeed in completely blotting out from my life the years I have lost, my errors and my faults."

"And I shall be proud of you !" she said with enthusiasm, for Savari by degrees had imbued her with his ardour and had made her forget the emotion of the day.

"Where shall we go?" he resumed. "To Genoa, to your family ?"

"Yes, I shall indeed be happy in making you love my mother."

"And how will you introduce me ? As a friend ?"

"No, to all who belong to me you will be the man whose name I shall bear as soon as I have completed my term of mourning."

"You consent !" he cried.

"Certainly," she replied simply. "You may marry me in full security," she added with a charming smile, "my family is honourable, and in my past life there is nothing with which I have to reproach myself."

"Ah !" said Savari, "would that I could say as much ! "

At this moment the drawing-room was suddenly lighted up; a band of men carrying torches, passed along the Rue de Grammont, on their way to the Boulevards. They were preceded and followed by an immense crowd, singing the "Marseillaise." Drums and trumpets furnished an accompaniment to the voices. Every man vied with his neighbour in celebrating the victory gained that day by the people over royalty. The reforms asked for had been granted, and a new Ministry had taken office. The barricades were being deserted, the troops were returning to barracks, circulation was gradually being re-established, mutual

congratulations were exchanged, and a general illumination was
being carried into effect without an idea that an hour afterwards
men would be slaughtering each other on the Boulevard des
Capucines.   Independently of the particular opinion to which
each one may incline, there is nothing so generally electrifying
as such songs, illuminations, and enthusiasm as reigned throughout Paris.   They infuse unwonted excitement into the most
tranquil natures ; they give courage to the timid, and work
upon the nerves of the least nervous.

Savari, already deeply moved by the conversation which had
just taken place, was roused to a great pitch of excitement when,
after having watched the animated scene being enacted in the
street, he resumed his place by Julia's side.   He was in one of
those moments when the wisest of men forget their prudence,
are content to obey their passing impulses, and see life from a
new standpoint.   What would a second before have seemed impossible and monstrous to him, now appeared simple and natural.
Strange fancies took possession of him, and he was endued with
unusual hardihood ; nothing was impracticable.

For a considerable time past, Savari had been meditating an
important revelation to Julia.   An unendurable burden was
weighing him down, he was tortured by a constantly recurring
thought, and his greatest enjoyments were poisoned by a
piercing sorrow.   It seemed to him that if he could confide his
secret to somebody, if he could pour himself out, as it were, on
the heart of a friend, if he could make a clean breast of it and
weep, his suffering would be lessened.   Above all, if Julia, in
whom he had implicit confidence, would listen to his tale, and,
after having heard it, could give him absolution, he would be
saved.   But though always on the eve of speaking, he had as
yet held his tongue.   This time he made up his mind to confession.   She had been speaking to him of her life ; he ought to
tell her of his.   There could not be any secrets between them ;
they loved each other too well.   Before letting her bear his

name, honour bade him reveal to her every taint there might be upon it. Who would be indulgent if Julia were not? Who, better than she, could assuage his sorrow, console and comfort him with sweet words?

The shouts and songs still resounded from the street, as he drew near her again, and said—"A seeret oppresses me. Would you like me to confide it to you?"

"Certainly," she replied simply.

"It is a terrible remorse, a remorse which rends my heart."

"A remorse!" repeated Julia, looking up.

"Listen," he replied in an excited tone, "if any one were to tell you suddenly that the man whom you love—he to whom you have given your life—whose name you have consented to bear—had committed an evil deed, nay a crime?—"

"I would not believe it," she exclaimed.

"If it were true, however; if in a moment of anger and madness he had stabbed a man?"

She turned pale and shrank back.

"And if," added Savari, "by an unheard of fatality, the man died from the effects of that blow?"

"Be silent, be silent," she cried instinctively.

"No," he replied, "I have begun and I must finish. This seeret stifles me. You must either condemn or absolve me."

Again she attempted to stop him, but he no longer listened to her. He had risen and was pacing the room with feverish and impatient strides.

"Hear me, and learn to know me. As a rule ealm and self-possessed, I have moments when I am carried away by passion, and have no longer any eontrol over myself. Sometimes certain wines make me lose my head. I had been dining at a restaurant on the boulevards. I was worried and anxious, and to drown my care, I allowed myself to be persuaded to drink more than my custom was. After dinner I went to see a young man with whom I had already had some serious disputes on money matters. I owed him a large sum; I was not in a position to pay him and I wished to let him know it. I found him alone in his rooms; he had just come home and was going to bed. He received me with coldness. I explained to him my embarrassment and the difficulties I was in, and I begged him not to take proceedings. I said to him, 'You will only ruin me and deprive me of the small amount of credit remaining to me on the Bourse, on which I am dependent for a living!' He replied 'that that was no business of his.' I implored him, yes, I condescended to implore him to have mercy. He was deaf to all my entreaties. Then, driven to desperation, I exclaimed, 'You shall have something to answer for. Sooner than be humiliated and hunted down in this way, I'll kill myself!' 'You?' he replied in a bantering tone, 'you kill yourself! Nonsense. See here's a charming weapon; I offer it to you, firmly persuaded that you will not make bad use of it.' I took the knife mechanically, but the blood rushed to my brain, and the heavy wines which I had been drinking deprived me of my reason. I no longer implored my creditor, I complained of his harshness and severity. 'My harshness!' he exclaimed, 'here, take your bills, I don't want to have anything more to do with you. But I shall have the right to proclaim you on all sides as a thief!' I to be called a thief! I sprang upon him, and he struck me a blow in the face. Then, mad with rage, I struck him in my turn with the knife he had put into my hands. He uttered a cry, and fell! I hurled the weapon away from me, and fled in a state of distraction. Yes, all this happened as I have told you. I swear it!"

He stopped to take breath, and then, continuing to pace the room without looking at Julia, he went on—"I thought I had only wounded him slightly—I had killed him! A few days afterwards I was arrested. First of all I wanted to confess everything. No jury would have convicted me of murder. I was an unfortunate, but not a guilty man. I had been the

cause of death, but an unwitting one. Suddenly the recollection flashed across my mind of the bills which he had restored
to me, which I had not wanted to take, and which he had
forcibly thrust into the pocket of my overcoat. They must be
there, and somebody must have found them—if I confessed I
was lost!—I should be nothing but a common assassin—a
murderer, for the sake of the money I owed. It was then that
I determined to defend myself, and to devote all my intelligence
towards saving my own head and putting justice off the scent.

"I said to myself—'If my life is a burden to me, if the remembrance of my crime becomes hateful to me and renders my
existence unendurable, there will always be time enough for me
to kill myself; I can choose my own mode of death, and execute
justice on myself without the necessity of laying my head on
the block.'

"My innocence was believed in, my liberty restored to me,
and at the very moment when in desperation I should probably
have put an end to my existence, I suddenly found myself clinging
to life with all my might—for I had just met you, and I loved
you! Speak now," he added, going close to Julia, but without
daring to look at her, "speak; you know my crime, will you
absolve me from it?"

With her head buried in her hands, she was silent. This
silence terrified him. He put his hand on Julia's head and tried
to make her look at him. As she did so he recoiled with horror
—her face was livid. Two huge tears coursed down her cheeks.

"Oh!" he exclaimed, "I am, then, more guilty than I
thought myself. You will not pardon me!"

She rose, as if with difficulty, and said in a voice which
sounded hollow and strangely muffled, "I am Maurice Vidal's
widow!"

CHAPTER XIX.

SAVARI, pale, overwhelmed, and incapable of any definite idea, mechanically made his way out of the drawing-room, where Julia had left him alone. He opened the door and went down the staircase, holding on by the balusters, his legs seeming to give way beneath him. Having gained the street, he took the road leading to the boulevards. He supported himself against the walls like a drunken man, and reeled at every step.

Those terrible words, "I am Maurice Vidal's widow!" were buzzing in his ears, and he saw them before his eyes, written as if in letters of blood. Each letter seemed to him to be of enormous size and to bar his onward path. One of them underwent a sudden transformation into a human form, and planted itself in front of him. He thought he saw Maurice Vidal distinctly holding out his arms and motioning him to stand aloof. At the corner of the boulevard and the Rue de Grammont he was suddenly dazzled. A line of lights gleamed from house to house, and an immense crowd was circulating in all directions. Flags were waved, allegorical transparencies were displayed, and the people laughed and sang. Universal joy was painted on every face. He understood nothing of what was going on. Leaning against the shutters of a closed shop, he looked with a stupefied air at the surging mob around him. He was jostled and knocked about, but he never perceived it.

Suddenly a spare man, insignificant-looking and pale, seized him by the arm and said—"Albert Savari, I arrest you, in the name of the law!"

Savari, without moving or making any sign, without even trying to shake off the hold on his arm, looked down on the speaker, recognised him, and replied sadly—"I am in no humour now for joking."

"I am not joking," said the little pale man. "I arrest you for the murder of Maurice Vidal."

Nothing could astonish Savari; he did not even wince, but merely said—"Who are you, then, sir?"

"I am a police-agent, and am called Vibert."

"Ah! I understand," said Savari, who was by degrees recovering the use of his reason, "you are no more the Count de Rubini than she was your cousin."

"Just so. Will you come with me quietly, or shall I be obliged to use force?"

"One moment," said Savari, still unmoved. "Why do you accuse me of being the assassin of Maurice Vidal?"

"Because you have just confessed it."

"To whom?"

"To his widow."

"Ah!" he exclaimed, "she has denounced me already."

No words can give any idea of the tone in which he said this. There was no accent of reproach in it, nor even of complaint. It was the cry of a broken heart. An ordinary detective would have been affected by it. An unfortunate rival could not be so, and Vibert did not try to undeceive Savari.

"Let us go," said Vibert.

"Let us go," repeated Savari, with an air of resignation. What were the prison and the scaffold to him now!

At this moment a lengthy column of men was moving down the boulevards. Far more numerous than all the former crowds which had been flocking through Paris during the day, it was composed of students, National Guards, men in blouses, women and children. It came from the direction of the Faubourg Saint-Antoine and made its tumultuous way towards the Madeleine, to the accompaniment of torches and patriotic songs, tricolour lanterns and red flags. Vibert and Savari, too much excited to pay any attention to what was going on around them, had not noticed the approach of this column, and they found themselves suddenly hustled, separated, and then drawn into the vortex.

Vibert, who was bent on struggling and fighting against the stream, was soon jostled to the edge of it, and found himself amongst the rearmost ranks of the mob. Savari, on the contrary, made no resistance, but remained in front and allowed himself to be impelled by the surging flood. It was not long before this mass of the populace, reinforced by all the bands which it met on its way, arrived close to the guard stationed at the Ministry for Foreign Affairs. The commandant of this post ordered the guard, two hundred strong, to form square. The column, impelled from behind and from both sides, was unable to stop, and continued its advance. The soldiers fixed bayonets. "This is infamous," was the universal shout, "we are betrayed."

A pistol shot, fired from some unknown quarter, was heard. The soldiers, thinking they were attacked, came to the present, and the crowd received the volley almost at the muzzles of the guns. About sixty men fell, of whom half were killed outright. The blood ran in streams. When the momentary stupefaction which ensued had passed away, there was a general rush to help the wounded, who were taken to the neighbouring houses and chemists' shops. At the same time, a waggon, drawn by a white horse, appeared, into which the dead bodies were cast, and this funeral *cortége*, lighted up by torches, proceeded through Paris to the oft-repeated cry—" Vengeance ! vengeance ! The people are being murdered !"

Savari, who was in the foremost rank of the column, was hit and wounded mortally. He was carried under a gateway in the boulevard, and, when there, he made signs to those around him that he wished to speak. They leaned over him and caught the words—"Carry me to the Rue de Grammont. I want to see somebody again before I die."

Two men of the people, two of those men who are ever ready with a helping hand for the unfortunate and lend a willing ear to every supplication, improvised a stretcher, laid the wounded man upon it, and set out on their journey. A boy followed them with a torch in his hand, which shed its rays on the bleeding chest of Savari, and lighted up his handsome face, where Death had already set his icy seal. Every one took off his hat as the litter went by; the women wept, the men shouted, " To arms!"

It was nearly midnight ; the assembly by trumpet call and beat of drum was heard in the distance, and the bells were ringing from all the churches. The men who were carrying Savari, and the boy who followed them with the torch, made their way slowly amidst all this tumult. When they reached a certain house in the Rue de Grammont, the wounded man rallied and signed to them to stop. They knocked at the street door, mounted the stairs up to the third story, and rang the bell loudly. There was no response. The rooms were deserted. Julia, driven to distraction by the revelation she had heard, had fled with Marietta half-an-hour previously.

Savari was unwilling to be taken home, and, after an interval of agony, which was mercifully short, he breathed his last at his mistress' door, with her name on his lips.

CHAPTER XX.

WHILST the powerful voice of revolt was thus making itself heard in Paris, the excitement which reigned in the streets climbed the highest walls and penetrated even into the prisons. The watchfulness of the warders relaxed ; they were all ears for news from without, and they feared for their own safety. The soldiers, who could have lent them aid in case of need, were recalled from their outlying posts and concentrated in barracks.

K

The prisoners were excited, violent, ready to profit by every opportunity, to make a rush at the doors, scale the walls, and to massacre all who should attempt to keep them under lock and key. Without, the people were fighting for freedom generally; within, the prisoner was ready to strike a blow for his own liberty.

On Thursday, the 24th of February, at the height of the insurrection, Langlade threw himself on a warder who was imprudent enough to enter his cell alone, stifled his cries by means of a gag, took off his own clothes and put on the warder's uniform, coat and képi, possessed himself of his bunch of keys, and walked quietly out of the main door. Fighting was still going on in the streets, and the superintendents, warders, and assistants of all grades were too much preoccupied to take notice of this bold escape.

Langlade went headlong into the thick of the insurrection, fighting against the people and the troops by turns. It mattered little to him; he had no political opinions. He entered the Tuileries, ransacked the throne, drank the Royal wines, and, smothered with mire and blood, half drunk, a pistol in his hand and a sword dangling at his side by a thick red cord, he betook himself to Soleil-Couchant to finish the evening.

Without losing time by ringing, he burst open the door with a kick, and unceremoniously entered her bedroom, where he found her just gone to bed.

"What do you want with me?" said Soleil-Couchant, half dead already with fright.

"You'll soon know," said Langlade.

"You want to kill me," she exclaimed.

"Of course, I mean to keep my oath and kill you."

"Mercy, mercy!" she wailed, trying to throw her arms round him.

Langlade shook her off, and said—"There is no mercy for you."

"But you are a free man now. We can fly and live together."

" No, I wish it no longer. You do not love me."

" Oh, yes. I love you."

" Silence ! You lie."

" I love you, I tell you. I swear it."

" A woman does not betray the man she loves, she does not accuse him in a court of law nor give him up to justice. Come, prepare to die."

" No—no—mercy !"

" If you believe in God, say your prayers."

She leaped out of bed, threw herself at Langlade's feet, kissed his hands, wept and entreated. He was inflexible, and merely said—" Remember the scene in the prison."

The clock struck. He threw the window wide open, and advanced towards Soleil-Couchant. With one hand he laid hold of both her arms to prevent her from clinging to him, with the other he lifted her from the ground, carried her to the window, and hurled her into space. Then he leaned out, looked at the place on the pavement where she had fallen, got on to the window-sill, and threw himself headlong after her.

When he reached the ground, he was still alive, and there the spectators of this terrible scene saw him crawl along on his bloody hands and knees to the corpse. When he breathed his last sigh, he held Soleil-Couchant fast locked in his shattered arms.

There exists at Genoa, a charitable institution bearing the charming title, " Albergo dei Poveri," the Inn of the Poor. Mark well that it is called an inn, and not an hospital, which means that to gain admission it is not indispensably necessary to be either hurt or ill. To be too old, or too young, or too weak to work, suffices as a claim to find refuge in this hospitable house.

The aged are there tended until death, the young until maturity, the weak until skilful treatment has restored to them their lost strength. The " Albergo dei Poveri " musters more than two hundred inmates, of whom a great number are looked after by women. The Sister of Charity is not French alone; she belongs to every nation. At the side of suffering a woman is ever to be found.

Julia Vidal has retired into the institution of which we have been speaking, and she still resides there, remarkable for her zeal, her devotion, and her sweet disposition, to which all bear witness. Marietta is with her, and aids her in her noble task.

Five years have passed away since a certain lunatic breathed his last in the asylum presided over by Doctor Blanche. He was the richest inmate of the establishment, having inherited from the Marquis de X——, a peer of France, a legacy of a hundred thousand francs per annum.

As a rule, he was quiet and inoffensive, and his madness only showed itself in one form, that of listening unceasingly at doors. He would be seen to glide along the corridors, crouch in a corner near a door, and either look through the key-hole or place his ear against it. In this harmless position he would remain for whole days, and the attendants grew accustomed to leave him alone.

There were, however, certain seasons in the year when his insanity assumed a more dangerous character, and then the strait waistcoat had to be brought into requisition. But this crisis was always preceded by an extraordinary symptom; the lunatic would complain that his lips were burning, and would shriek aloud for water to cool them, rubbing his fingers incessantly from one side to the other of his mouth, as if to efface the traces of a kiss.

THE END.

www.ingramcontent.com/pod-product-compliance
Lightning Source LLC
Chambersburg PA
CBHW020339030726
47496CB00007B/1950